SISTERHOOD OF THE INSTITUTE

'Something happened to me last night,' Jaki whispered.

'Tell me all about it,' Nurse said softly, coaxing while at the same time touching Jaki's excited body.

'At night I was taken from here and . . . and forced to serve others.'

'Did you enjoy it?' Nurse asked, smiling softly, her full lips pursed slightly.

Jaki looked up into Nurse's eyes and felt herself teetering on the edge of complete submission. She would have done anything then, no matter how terrible or degrading, she would have sunk to any depths to prove her devotion. 'Yes,' she croaked, 'I enjoyed it.'

By the same author:

THE INSTITUTE
OBSESSION
HEART OF DESIRE
PARADISE BAY
DARK DESIRES
UNDERWORLD
EDEN UNVEILED
DARK DELIGHTS

Other Nexus Classics:

THE IMAGE
CHOOSING LOVERS FOR JUSTINE
AGONY AUNT
THE INSTITUTE
OBSESSION
THE HANDMAIDENS
HIS MISTRESS'S VOICE
BOUND TO SERVE
BOUND TO SUBMIT
A MATTER OF POSSESSION *January*

A NEXUS CLASSIC

SISTERHOOD OF THE INSTITUTE

Maria del Rey

To wayward people everywhere

This book is a work of fiction.
In real life, make sure you practise safe sex.

First published in 1994 by
Nexus
Thames Wharf Studios
Rainville Road
London W6 9HA

This Nexus Classic edition 1999

Typeset by TW Typesetting, Plymouth, Devon

Printed and bound by
Cox & Wyman Ltd, Reading, Berks

ISBN 0 352 33456 8

To wayward people everywhere

Chapter One

The buzzer startled Jaki. She picked up the phone automatically and pressed the button for the entry-phone.

'Courier,' a male voice reported breathlessly.

'At the top of the stairs,' Jaki said softly and buzzed the front door open.

Not for the first time she wished that there was a mirror close by, a big square Art Deco mirror just by the entrance to the office, opposite the reception desk where she was sitting. She heard the courier struggling up the narrow stairs, heavy footsteps and the faint swish of his motorbike gear. He saw her and smiled, broad face opening sideways to reveal straight white teeth that had been obscured by the wispy black beard he was attempting to grow. She waited a while and smiled back, not too friendly but enough to keep him happy.

'Package for Harriet Greene,' he said, pulling a thick envelope from the padded interior of his crash helmet. He had a faded leather jacket on, the patches and badges hanging on grimly, and his jeans were in no better state. He handed Jaki the package and she saw the dark blue of a home-made tattoo scrawled on his hairy knuckles.

'She's in a meeting,' Jaki said, taking the package. 'Can I sign for this?'

He nodded, blue eyes fixed on her glossy red lips. 'Sure thing, love, you can sign for anything.'

'Thank you,' Jaki said softly, scribbling an illegible signature on the tatty piece of computer print-out he gave her.

'Janice?' he ventured, studying the signature at different

angles. He was smiling still, hovering hopefully by the side of the desk.

She laughed softly, swinging round in her seat to face him. 'Jaki. My writing's not that bad, is it?'

His eyes were fixed on the hem of her pleated blue skirt, several inches above the knee, enough to reveal the silky smoothness of her thighs. 'Oh, it's writing, is it? I thought you were testing the pen.'

'Next time I'll do it in crayon, shall I?' Jaki giggled, looking up through thickly made-up eyes to see him laughing too.

'Don't suppose you'd fancy coming out for a drink tonight, would you?'

She shook her head, long blonde curls cascading over her shoulders. 'Sorry, but I don't think my friend would like that,' she said, her voice poised perfectly so that it didn't sound like a complete brush-off.

'Another time then,' he accepted, eyes back on her skirt, as though somehow he could will it to rise higher just by staring at it.

'Sure, another time,' she agreed politely. She swung back under the desk, the swift twist of her chair making her seem cool and business-like again. He nodded curtly, donned the shining black crash helmet and strode heavily across the reception and down the stairs.

Jaki breathed a sigh of relief. It was still such a thrill to flirt and play little games when she could. Harriet didn't always like it, sometimes she'd be very strict, but then Jaki was certain that Harriet just liked playing at being the boss. She glanced quickly at her watch, remembering that Harriet had ordered coffee for three o'clock, then saw that the courier had forgotten his receipt sheet on the edge of the desk. The door hadn't clicked downstairs and so Jaki grabbed the loose sheet of paper, fraying at the edges and looking more like scrap than anything else, and hurried to the top of the stairs.

'Yeah, I was just coming back for that,' the courier lied, grinning broadly at the bottom of the stairs.

'I believe you,' Jaki said, standing at the top of the stairs, hands on hips and grinning broadly. She knew that from the bottom of the stairs he could get a good long look at her legs, from the black high heels to the loose hem that swirled and twirled as she moved. She held out the paper patiently, her legs were parted and she felt a delicious thrill knowing that he was enjoying the view.

He was taking his time climbing the narrow stairs, making no attempt to hide the fact he was ogling her long slim thighs. He was smirking, a wicked schoolboy grin, his eyes eating her up whole.

'Do you guys talk about this in the pub or something?' Jaki asked, pretending indignation.

'I don't know what you mean,' he replied innocently.

'You're about the third courier in the last couple of weeks that's forgotten something and made me stand here,' she complained, a playful pout of her lips making him lick his.

'Why don't you come down to the pub with us and find out what we really talk about?' he suggested hopefully, stopping several steps below Jaki and reaching out for the paper.

'Shit! I've forgotten the bloody coffee!' Jaki cried, her phone buzzing from Harriet's office. She handed the paper back to the courier and spun round, her skirt spinning up to give him a quick glimpse of white panties.

'See you soon, then,' the courier called after her, but she had no time for him.

She hurried across to the filter-coffee machine and fished two cups from the cupboard. The clock on the wall said it was three fifteen. She knew that voices carried through the thin partition walls of the office, there could be no excuse, Harriet would have heard the gruff voice of the courier. She placed the cups on a small tray and filled them with dark brown coffee, the aroma filling her lungs. Milk and sugar. She poured milk from the carton into a small jug and spooned some brown sugar into a paper cup. She had forgotten how the client, Mr Vaughan, a keen looking thirty-five year old, took his coffee, even though Harriet had told her earlier.

'Sorry, I had a problem with a courier,' Jaki explained urgently, pushing the door to Harriet's office open. Her harried look brought a faint smile to the man's face, dark eyes registering interest. She returned his smile shyly, looking at him through lowered eyelids.

'Yes, we heard,' Harriet said coolly, her grey-green eyes flashing a look of anger for a moment.

'Sorry,' Jaki whispered. She swallowed hard and crossed the office, her heels sinking into the carpet. Harriet's office was smart and elegant, dominated by the antique desk that sat under the window. The pale light that fell across the desk was filtered by thin Venetian blinds, slicing the light into a zebra pattern that was reflected in the polished oak. Vaughan sat opposite Harriet, briefcase at his heel, arms resting on the desk, a pad beside him.

Jaki walked over to the desk, next to Vaughan, and placed the tray on the edge and straightened up. Harriet was angry and that always made Jaki nervous. 'How do you take it, Mr Vaughan?' she asked brightly, hoping to deflect Harriet's silent anger by being extra nice to her client.

'White, one sugar please,' he said, leaning back in his seat and flashing another smile. He seemed very relaxed, brown eyes and wry smile fixed on Jaki. She smiled back, fluttering eyelashes and slightly flushed look making her seem like a silly adolescent girl. Her long hair rippled over her shoulders, wave upon wave of golden curls caught in the mirror opposite Harriet's desk. The mirror: it brought back a sudden image of being punished by Harriet, and the memory made Jaki's cheeks flush pink.

'You'll have to excuse Jaki,' Harriet told him, 'she's usually so efficient.'

Jaki felt a touch under her knee, she looked down and saw that Harriet was touching her, sliding fingers up and down slowly. She could feel Vaughan watching, could sense his eyes tracking the motion of Harriet's fingers up and down. Her face coloured even more, her heart was racing and her hands were shaking a little. The feel of Harriet's fingers was always exciting, especially when Harriet was angry.

'I'm sure she's fine,' Vaughan remarked, amusement in his voice.

Jaki tried to concentrate on the coffee but it was difficult. Harriet's fingers were pressing hard, moving up under the skirt and stroking the inside of the thigh. She jerked up suddenly, spilt a thin stream of milk down the side of the cup. Her skirt was being lifted slowly by the action of Harriet's hand, as though by accident. Harriet's fingers were now moving firmly over the inside of the thigh, caressing, exciting, touching so possessively and so openly.

'I'm sorry,' Jaki apologised again, unable to lift her eyes to meet Vaughan's. Her face was blazing red, she felt shame and excitement in equal measure, as though the excitement could not exist without the shame.

'Be careful,' Harriet warned, 'we don't want any accidents.'

'No, no accidents,' Mr Vaughan agreed, taking his cup from Jaki's shaking fingers.

'I hope that's how you like it,' Jaki asked, her voice barely a whisper now. She turned slightly and saw herself reflected in the mirror, tall and blonde, fair complexion with full red lips, eyes darkened with mascara, loose blouse and short skirt. She could see the steady play of Harriet's hand, now squeezing gently, lifting the back of the skirt and revealing even more of Jaki's long legs. Also framed in the reflection was Harriet's icy demeanour and the fascination on Vaughan's face. Did Vaughan understand the significance of the full length mirror in an otherwise functional office? It was Harriet's punishment glass – her way of adding spice to a punishment session by having it reflected in the mirror, the image of reddened thighs, buttocks or breasts fuelling whatever forbidden pleasure she received in doling out pain.

'Yes, that's fine thank you,' Mr Vaughan said, taking a sip of coffee.

'You can go now,' Harriet said dismissively, slowly removing her hand from under Jaki's skirt.

'If there's anything else . . .' Jaki said, finding the courage at last to meet Vaughan's brown eyes, sparkling with excitement, that smile still on his lips.

'That will be all!' Harriet snapped angrily, making Jaki jump.

Back at her desk Jaki searched her handbag for a mirror. She felt excited still, her heart was racing and her breathing had become unsteady. It was often the way with Harriet's special clients, it would always mean something different. Sometimes she knew in advance what sort of client was going to come in, and sometimes it was a surprise. Vaughan had been one such surprise. Harriet had said nothing about him.

Jaki looked at herself in the little mirror, searching her face for imperfection, looking to see if her other self was hiding there. It was strange, but sometimes she felt that switching identities made a physical difference, as if the psychic transformation led to a physical one. J.K. looked so very different, face more angular, eyes harder and more inquisitive, lips less expressive. Jaki was more feminine, her lips fuller, eyes warmer. The time when Jaki had pondered on her odd lifestyle had long since passed – now she accepted that she had two lives, as Jaki, feminine and sexy, and as J.K., masculine and dull.

It was Mistress Shirer that had shown the way, taking Jaki out of her shell and transforming her for ever. For a time Jaki had been her abject slave, but then things changed and Mistress Shirer had explained that the time had come to move on. It could have been heartbreak, the end of the duality that made Jaki's life possible, but with typical foresight Mistress Shirer had thought of everything. Jaki was introduced to Harriet, who ran a kind of agency that employed many of the ex-Institute women. Harriet needed someone to look after the computers in her agency and she took on J.K. for that task. And with J.K. she took on Jaki, to be employed on occasion as a receptionist and secretary. It was the perfect solution of course, but then Jaki knew that Mistress Shirer could do no less.

The phone buzzed fifteen minutes later and Jaki ran to fetch the coffee pot. She steadied her breathing and walked back across the office, eyes lowered even though she knew for certain that Harriet was eyeing her with renewed interest.

'More coffee, Mr Vaughan?' she asked, her voice a husky whisper that gave the lie to her apparent calm.

'Yes, if I may,' he agreed, tapping the edge of the saucer. His cup was beside his elbow, right across the other side of the table, and he was making no move to bring it closer to her.

'So you think it's worth the solicitor's fee to get the contract assessed?' Harriet asked, ignoring Jaki's presence completely.

Jaki had no choice, she leaned across the desk unsteadily, bending her body at the waist while keeping her legs very straight. There was a slight breeze in the office and Jaki could feel it on the back of her thighs, her short skirt had risen up high at the back. The coffee pot was heavy in her hand, heavy and unsteady as she started to pour slowly. She gasped but held her tongue, Vaughan's hand was on her thigh. His hand was warm, resting just above her right knee. He was talking to Harriet, both of them intent on ignoring Jaki's presence completely.

The coffee pot was shaking, thin rivulets of coffee dripping down into the empty cup. His hand was sliding up very slowly, moving one way with deliberate intent, his fingers travelling over her smooth glassy flesh. Her excitement was making her ache, her breath was short and sharp and the back of her legs were stretched taut. His hand was under her skirt and sliding round to the inside of her thigh. He stopped at the top of her thigh, his fingers kneading the softest skin as though he were revelling in the sensation of skin on skin.

'Is there anything else, Mr Vaughan?' Jaki gasped, straightening up quickly.

'No thank you, my dear,' he said pleasantly, looking into her eyes intently. She backed slowly out of the room, catching a sharp glance from Harriet on the way.

Was Harriet pleased or angry? Jaki didn't know, she never knew in these situations. Harriet was always so arbitrary, sometimes she rewarded Jaki with a pat on the bottom and sometimes she punished with a cane across the thighs. The cane . . . Was Mr Vaughan waiting for an excuse to punish her? The thought made Jaki feel dizzy with excitement. Under her flared skirt her cock was swathed in lacy white panties, her hardness clothed in the finest, most feminine lingerie available. She loved the contrast, loved the sensuous feel of masculine sex and feminine finery.

Jaki sat behind her desk and touched herself surreptitiously, a thin jewel of fluid seeping from the slit in her hard prick.

Simone looked up from her papers, spread neatly across the desk, and stared at Kasia who had barged into the office unannounced and with a characteristic look of anger on her face. Her blue eyes were narrow slits that blazed fire, her thin lips clamped tight as though keeping in the anger threatening to explode inside her.

'Yes, Kasia, what can I do for you?' Simone asked crisply. Kasia, with typical East European brusqueness, ignored the intended reprimand and continued across the office. Her face was flushed, a faint pink tinge on her pale cheeks. She wore white as usual, as though she still worked in a hospital.

'Look . . . look . . .' Kasia spluttered. She stopped in front of Simone's desk and turned over the polythene carrier bag she had been clutching in her hand. She showered the desk with bottles and compacts, brightly coloured lipsticks, blusher, half a dozen bottles of nail polish. They spilled across the desk like shards of broken glass, brightly coloured jewels that settled in oddly geometric patterns on the matt black surface of the desk.

Simone looked at the array of make-up on her desk, shades that clashed and matched in glorious abandon. She knew what it meant, but had to ask Kasia anyway. 'From the male dorm?'

'Where else?' Kasia seethed. Her fury was always so transparent, like a storm that signalled itself from a great distance.

'Today?'

'I had the girls search the rooms this morning. This is

the result,' she said, her sharp accent making each word sound like an accusation.

'And?' Simone asked, waiting patiently for the full story to emerge from Kasia's unpainted lips.

'I selected some of the worst offenders and threatened them with punishment. I threatened to have them caned in front of the entire dorm. It made no difference, Miss Shirer, none at all.'

'And the girls? Did you question them?'

Kasia exhaled heavily. 'I questioned them, of course. To no result also. They all say they do not know how these cosmetics get into the male dorm.'

'Well, Kasia, what do you suggest we do next?' Simone asked, leaning back in her seat and regarding Kasia with interest. She was a relatively new arrival to the Institute and, though she was keen and had many interesting ideas, she had yet to fully adapt to the unique environment of the place. Simone imagined that to Kasia the Institute was one giant laboratory to test theories of sexual motivation and erotic punishment, but it was more, much more, than that. For Simone the Institute was a hot house, a place where the rarest blooms of suppressed desire were encouraged to flower in all their perverse glories.

'You know what I suggest,' Kasia said bluntly. 'Disband the male dorm, it has no place here. Build it elsewhere, somewhere secure, somewhere like this but not here.'

'You know Kasia,' Simone sighed, 'for someone with your background you show remarkably little pragmatism. You know we can't fund another Institute, you know that our very existence is precariously balanced. Unfortunately, the politics of this situation are not in our hands.'

'Then disband it,' Kasia stated decisively, not a flicker of doubt in her icy features.

'That is out of the question,' Simone's anger rose to the surface instantly. 'The success of the male dorm is intimately linked with the success of our whole project. It all succeeds or it all fails, there is no middle way.'

'As you wish, Miss Shirer,' Kasia nodded curtly. Her posture was one of dissatisfaction: an insolent look in the eyes, an exaggerated bow of the head, hands clenched tightly.

'Send Tina in to clear this mess,' Simone said, waving an arm over the cosmetics spread like entrails on her desk, as though the pattern could be discerned and a solution sought in the random spread of bottles and jars.

Another curt nod and Kasia turned on her heels and marched sharply to the door. Her crisp white uniform, starched to perfection, was like an armour holding in her plump thighs and swelling breasts, her neck emerging from stiff collars that matched the stiffness of her face. Simone heard her issue a blunt order to Tina and then the outer door slammed.

'You wanted me, Mistress?' Tina asked nervously, poking her head round the door.

'Clear this mess, please,' Simone ordered, her voice softer.

Tina smiled and came in at once, eager to help and ready to please her brown-skinned Mistress. She wore the simple white top and blue-skirted uniform of the Institute, the skirt well above the knee and the white top tight against her chest. Her eyes were lowered respectfully, but she kept sneaking nervous glances at Simone. Rapidly she began to pick up the abandoned cosmetics, scooping them into her skirt which she lifted with one hand.

'Do you know where these came from?' Simone asked her, casting a glance at Tina's white thighs and realising that the girl had deliberately lifted her skirt high to show herself off.

'No, Mistress,' Tina replied quickly, reaching out across the length of the desk to retrieve a bright pink shade of lipstick.

'From the male dorm,' Simone informed her. 'Do you know how they got there?'

'No, Mistress. I don't know anything about the men's section,' she lied unconvincingly, hitching up her skirt even higher as though to expose her body would distract attention from her deceit.

'When was the last time you were punished?' Simone

asked suddenly, relishing the sudden look of fear that crossed Tina's face.

'Ten days ago,' Tina gulped. She had finished collecting the cosmetics and held them balanced in her skirt, holding the hem with both hands and seemingly unaware that her white panties were fully exposed.

'For what reason?'

'For smoking in my room, Mistress,' the girl flinched at the memory.

'And who punished you?'

'Mistress Latimer. Six strokes of the slipper across the backside, Mistress,' her face coloured slightly as she reported her punishment.

'What do you know about the male dorm?' Simone asked pointedly, leaning forward across the desk, fixing her dark oval eyes directly at Tina.

'Only that it exists, Mistress.' Her lies were transparent, her eyes avoided the Mistress's guiltily.

'If I were to use the cane across that pretty little bottom of yours would it jog your memory?'

Tina swallowed hard. She had been caned just the once by Simone; the experience had not required a repeat performance. 'No, Mistress,' she whispered. Her hands were shaking and, without warning, the cosmetics cascaded to the floor, forming a litter around her feet like the guilty haul of a juvenile shoplifter caught red-handed.

'Pick them up,' Simone sighed, her voice lacking conviction. 'Count them for me and then put them in the drawer with the other lot.'

'Yes, Mistress.' Tina heaved a sigh of relief. She knelt down and began softly to count the items back into the belly of her skirt.

Simone stood and walked to the window, hardly paying any attention to the girl counting the confiscated items. From the window Simone could look out across the distance, to the far walls of the Institute and beyond. The rolling fields in the distance were a world away from the enclosed environment she and Fiona Schafer had created from nothing. It had been a shared vision of how things might be, and for a while it had worked, worked very well indeed. Fiona had gone on from the Institute to work in America, aiming to create a similar regime to the one that had worked so well. Now Simone was the Director of the Institute, and she alone had the responsibility to ensure its continued success.

Kasia was right, the male dorm was not a good idea, but it had been forced upon them. Paradoxically, it was the success of the Institute that was the cause. The politicians had decided that if the Institute could work so well with maladjusted young women it should also work for young men. Simone had been eager to take up the challenge, naïvely she had hoped for similar resources to build a second Institute. In fact she had even found a site, an old public school with a similar secluded location to the first Institute. But her high hopes were dashed against the low rocks of hard-headed political pragmatism.

Against her wishes, and the wishes of her staff, it had been decreed that a male dormitory would be opened in the existing, all female, Institute. The plan was to build an enclosed world inside another enclosed world. One wing of the building was converted for the purpose, and access was tightly controlled with communications kept to a minimum. Additional staff were recruited, and the whole infrastructure expanded to cater for the new arrivals. However, it was an idea doomed to failure from the start. It had been conceived by civil servants who had no idea of the nature of the Institute's work. How else could one explain putting twenty-five young men in the same building as the young women of the Institute? How could they be expected to share the same atmosphere of intense eroticism without problems occurring?

'Mistress? I'm finished,' Tina said softly.

'How many?' Simone asked, turning to face the nervous-looking young woman.

'Twenty items,' Tina reported, lifting her skirt higher.

'Put them away, girl,' Simone sighed, turning once more to look from the window.

Tina withdrew from the room and left Simone alone

with her musings. Things were difficult, the inevitable had happened, some of the women were obviously getting into the male dorm. It wasn't the sex that bothered her, it was the interruptions to the carefully prepared programme of erotic exploration. The Institute was founded on a hierarchy of pleasure and pain, creating a society in miniature where power relations were expressed directly through a complex sexuality. It made explicit the stratification of society as a whole, laying bare the sexual roots hidden by the culture of money and class. It was a radical approach to society, a new way of looking at the world, but it depended on the special atmosphere the Institute induced. If that atmosphere were punctured, if the programme was disturbed in any way, then the path to total exploitation lay completely open.

Something had gone fundamentally wrong, and Simone had to find it and fix it. So much depended on it.

It was after six by the time Vaughan and Harriet were finished. He paused briefly on his way out to thank Jaki for the coffee, but if he wanted to flirt Harriet's presence seemed to put him off. It was getting late, the telephones had stopped ringing and the flow of visitors to the office had ceased. Harriet was back at her desk, going through the batch of documents that the courier had delivered earlier.

Harriet always worked hard, her business was so important to her that it sometimes seemed to blot out everything else in her life. In a sense it was admirable. Jaki liked women that were strong and powerful, and Harriet was certainly both of those. In her mind, Jaki always regarded Harriet as a *Mistress*, a symbolic figure that she could worship selflessly. It was one of the principles of the agency that the strictest rules of the Institute were relaxed, so addressing Harriet as 'Mistress' was out of the question. Harriet was not Mistress Shirer, and the agency operated in the real world not in the perfect unreality of the Institute. Still, Jaki smiled to herself, not all the rules were relaxed – she could still be punished whenever Harriet felt it was necessary.

Jaki made a fresh pot of coffee and took a cup into Harriet, who was still poring over the papers spread out neatly on her desk.

'Busy?' Jaki asked, putting the cup down by Harriet's arm.

'Yes, it's going to be a long night for me I'm afraid,' Harriet sighed, looking up from the report and giving Jaki a quick smile.

'Successful meeting with Mr Vaughan?' Jaki asked, sitting on the very edge of the desk, crossing her legs so that the skirt was forced tight around her thighs.

'He liked you,' Harriet said, smiling. She sat up straight, brushing her hair back from her face. She looked tired, brittle lines webbed around her eyes.

'That was your fault!' Jaki laughed, throwing her head back so that her curls bubbled around her shoulders. She reached out and brushed away a stray lock of hair from Harriet's face, touching her fingertips under Harriet's tired eyes.

'I'm sure you enjoyed every second of his attentions,' Harriet affirmed, gently touching her lips to Jaki's fingers.

'I can't help it.'

'I know you can't, darling,' Harriet said, patting Jaki's thigh with her hand. 'Now, I've got a lot to do. Don't forget to switch on the answer-phone on the way out.'

Jaki jumped off the desk and edged round behind Harriet's chair. She bent down and kissed her on the back of the neck, her lips caressing the soft skin and edging round towards Harriet's ear. She squeezed Harriet's shoulders with her fingers, kneading and massaging firmly, feeling the tightness and the knots of tension in her body. Harriet sighed, moved her head back and closed her eyes. She was breathing deeply, losing the tension that had stacked up during the long day.

'Is that good?' Jaki whispered, kissing Harriet again. She was massaging firmly, pressing the tips of her fingers hard into the tight muscle along the shoulder.

'Very good,' Harriet sighed dreamily. She inhaled deeply, held it and exhaled slowly. Her eyes were still closed, head back, chin high and lips slightly parted.

Jaki kissed again, moving slowly round Harriet's face, travelling from the ear round the cheek and finding the lips at last, traversing the contours of Harriet's face with the soft petals of her mouth. Their lips met, touched and seared together in a single passionate embrace. Jaki's fingers continued the soothing massage for a moment and then moved across Harriet's body, crossing over the chest so that she could caress each breast with the opposite hand.

It was dreamy, Jaki felt herself growing more and more excited, the fire rising up from her belly in a sudden eruption. Her own eyes were closed, the taste of Harriet's lips and mouth mingled with her own. She found the breasts, could feel the lacy cups of Harriet's bra crushing the nipples which were growing harder under Jaki's fingers. Harriet sighed deeply and Jaki swallowed the breath, held it and breathed it back to her again.

Harriet seemed to wake up suddenly, struggling momentarily as though waking up from a delicious dream that threatened to drown her. She pulled Harriet's hands away and her head round, escaping Jaki's open-mouthed kiss.

'What's wrong?' Jaki asked, her injured tone and sad eyes attesting to the confusion she felt.

'Hey, I've got work to do,' Harriet reminded her.

'You need to relax a bit,' Jaki retorted, fixing her hair by the mirror across the room.

'Look at yourself, always staring at your own reflection,' Harriet snapped irritably. 'I've never met anyone so self-absorbed.'

'Don't change the subject!'

'And don't snap,' Harriet warned. 'Don't forget yourself, young lady.'

Jaki thrilled silently, a nerve deep in her head pulsed deliciously whenever she was called 'young lady', its affect was an aphrodisiac that could never lose its potency. 'I'm not forgetting myself,' she retorted huskily. 'Why don't you forget about all of this,' she motioned dismissively at the paperwork on the desk, 'and think about something other than work.'

'Don't talk to me like that!' Harriet cried angrily. She turned and seized Jaki by the wrist, twisting her round sharply.

'I can talk how I like,' Jaki retorted insolently, her face only inches from Harriet's angry lips.

'No you can't,' Harriet whispered slowly, the cold menace in her voice contrasting with the fire in her eyes. Impulsively she leaned forward and forced her mouth over Jaki's.

They kissed hard and long, tongues dancing, faces crushed together in a violent embrace. Jaki's wrist was still twisted round, held tightly, Harriet's nails biting deep into flesh. It was a painful position, she slipped down to her knees in front of Harriet, her face distorted by the pain. She tried to cry out, but her quivering was forced away by Harriet's searching tongue.

'Apologise now, girl,' Harriet ordered, her eyes wide with anger and excitement.

'Let go of me!' Jaki demanded, trying ineffectually to free herself.

Harriet turned to one side, pulled open the desk drawer and took out a thick leather strap. She eased her chair round and pulled Jaki forward, almost pulling her over completely. In moments, Jaki was being positioned over Harriet's lap, arm now twisted up behind her back so that resistance was painful and futile.

Jaki was breathing hard, her heart pounding wildly in her chest. Her face was flushed red with shame and humiliation. She looked round and saw her skirt being lifted high over her waist, revealing lithe thighs and her panties pulled tightly into the cleft of her backside. She struggled harder but that only intensified her excitement and the thrill of pain that seared through her.

'Perhaps in future you'll think before you open your mouth,' Harriet said coldly.

Jaki muffled the cry that rose naturally to her lips. The leather strap tore at her backside, a red heat of pain that cut across both her bottom cheeks. She turned away from Harriet, afraid of the determined look in her eye, and caught the reflection in the mirror. The strap was raised high, a stiff tongue of black leather slavering to take a bite at her soft flesh. Harriet held it high for an instant and then swung it down hard. This time there could be no holding back the cry, it tore from Jaki's lips in a long wail that trailed to silence as the heat bore into her.

Again and again the strap came down, turning her backside a bright pink and then a blazing red. Each stroke was a dagger of sensation, sending spasms and ripples of pure feeling through her body. It stung deep and yet there was a quality to the pain that made it burn brighter, the red heat merging with the perceptions in Jaki's mind to take it over the edge of pain and into the realm of unbounded pleasure.

Being spanked like a recalcitrant child, to be chastised by a beautiful woman whilst dressed as a sexy young woman herself, nothing could equal that feeling for Jaki. In her struggles, as exciting as they were pointless, her male hardness pressed against Harriet's thigh. Her prick was caught in the tightness of her lacy panties, the tendrils of soft sensuous feeling in contrast to the smarting heat of her punished backside. As the strap came down rhythmically, Jaki reached a point where she could hold back no longer. Her lips murmured wordlessly and then she froze, a fresh imprint of the strap still touching her on the backside. She climaxed violently, spurting thick wads of come into her lacy panties, the humiliation burning her face as surely as the strap burned her bottom.

Harriet pushed Jaki to the floor. For a moment Jaki was lost in the dizziness, but then she looked up and saw Harriet's intense eyes staring at her.

'I've made a mess in my knickers,' Jaki thrilled, her voice a fey childish whisper of fascination.

'Always such a naughty girl,' Harriet sighed, an indulgent smile transforming her features. The weariness had seeped away, and so too had the anger that had been inside her. She reached out and stroked Jaki's burning face, a fingertip tracking the outline of Jaki's pouting lips.

There was silence for a moment. Jaki could feel her

backside burning and the slow ooze of her come sliding down through her thin panties. Her face was still red with shame, the guilt like an unextinguished flame inside her. Harriet smiled, her eyes were still glowing with excitement. Jaki smiled back, the gratitude welling up inside her. She loved Harriet, loved her more than anything.

'My turn now,' Harriet whispered. She parted her thighs and pulled back her skirt. Jaki stared at her, at the whiteness of her crotch, the panties already wet with honey. She crawled forward, moving on hands and knees between the passage formed by Harriet's white thighs.

They loved to play games with each other. Harriet's anger, part real and part pretend, and the ritual of punishment, were a natural part of their lovemaking. Now Jaki longed to tease her pink tongue between the groove in Harriet's sex, seeking out the wetness before plying a thousand silky caresses to the throbbing bud. She knew that Harriet's orgasm would be a flood of honey on her tongue, and that only when that had been enjoyed would they drive home together for the night.

Chapter Two

Tiffany caught sight of herself, her reflection captured unexpectedly in the small rectangle of a bedside mirror. The image transfixed her. She experienced a fleeting feeling of disorientation and then she smiled. Of course it was her, dark curls of hair cascading over her shoulders, soft brown skin, dark eyes. It was her all right, but for a moment her heart skipped a beat as she imagined it was Chantel, her twin sister. She didn't want to think about Chantel, but time and again her thoughts went out to her, to her sister who had graduated from the Institute and made it into the big wide world. Departing had been painful, more painful than Tiffany was willing to admit, though Chantel had wept bitterly, even as Tiffany had spanked and fucked her on the night before they were split up.

She sighed, closed her eyes and tried to block out the thoughts, trying to keep up the front she had assumed from the moment that Mistress Shirer had decreed that the twins were to be parted. Chantel had been horrified, and she showed it, the way she did with every emotion. That had been part of the trouble. Poor Chantel had been too honest, too trusting, too emotional. Tiffany had never been like that, she and her sister were physically identical only; in every other respect they were opposites. Where was she now? She felt a twinge of apprehension and worry, afraid, despite herself, that Chantel would be unable to cope on her own. Tiffany had always been the strong one of the pair. How would Chantel be able to survive without her stronger sister to guide her through life?

The thoughts were too dark, too depressing and Tiffany

willed them away with a shake of the head. She reached out and turned the mirror over, no longer willing to be caught out by tricks of the light. Besides, she had better things to do, much better. The clock by the upturned mirror ticked the dying minutes of the day, the second hand sweeping its luminescent green in sharp and precise movements. In the night-time silence the ticks sounded as sharp and as precise as the movements of the second hand.

At last, Tiffany heard footsteps at the door, she switched off her bedside light quickly and closed her eyes, hoping that they were going to be the welcome footsteps of a friend and not the unwelcome footsteps of a nocturnal inspection. The door creaked open a fraction, even with her eyes shut tight she was aware that the room was momentarily flooded with light, and then the door was closed again.

'Tiff, you awake?' a nervous voice asked softly.

'Who is it?' Tiffany replied dreamily, opening her eyes and peering into the darkness of her room. She yawned sleepily, and then sat up in bed.

'I'm sorry . . . I didn't mean to wake you.'

'Who is it?'

'I'm really sorry . . . I thought you'd be awake . . . It's Nicola.'

'You've woken me up,' Tiffany complained, leaning across to switch the bedside lamp back on. The light was weak, as though the bulb was about to give up the ghost, but it provided enough illumination without causing any suspicions outside. Nicola hadn't changed out of her uniform, the short skirt and white top made her seem much younger than the age of eighteen, which was the minimum age for entry to the Institute.

'I'm sorry,' Nicola repeated anxiously. She was regarding Tiffany nervously, her blue eyes darting round the room but always returning to the dark-skinned young woman sitting up in bed with her arms folded across her chest.

'Did anyone see you?'

Nicola shook her head emphatically. 'Nobody, I made

sure that the Bride of Frankenstein never set eyes on me.' She smiled hopefully, as though the disparaging remark about Kasia would win her some favour from Tiffany. It was a vain hope.

'Waking me up was bad enough,' she warned, 'but if you get me into trouble with Kasia you've had it.'

'I promise you I haven't,' Nicola assured her apprehensively. 'And I'm sorry about waking you up, I've been waiting ages for the coast to clear. You know what it's like since this male dorm's opened.'

'I don't know anything about that,' Tiffany said, 'all I know is that Kasia would love to catch the two of us here, and you know what that means.'

Nicola nodded. She understood perfectly; she had been on the receiving end of Kasia's leather strap just once, but her backside had carried the marks for days. All the girls feared Kasia, who had the reputation for being the strictest disciplinarian in the Institute, even more strict than Mistress Shirer. 'Yes, I know,' she finally responded, 'it was Kasia that spoilt my nineteenth birthday.'

Tiffany broke into a smile. 'Yes, I heard about that, you'd only just arrived, hadn't you?'

'To be honest I'd rather not talk about it,' Nicola sighed, shivering at the painful memory.

'In that case you can tell me why you've woken me up in the middle of the night,' Tiffany ordered, her smile broadening.

'You know that already,' Nicola complained, and even in the poor light it was clear to see that her face had flared red with embarrassment.

'I don't know. Tell me,' Tiffany insisted, drawing the quilt higher, making sure that her body was covered completely.

Nicola looked at the floor, turning away from Tiffany's piercing brown eyes. 'You know why I'm here,' she mumbled.

Tiffany felt a thrill of pleasure, relishing the other girl's shame as though it were something to be cherished. 'Tell me, tell me why you're here in the middle of the night. Tell me why you've risked a caning on the bare backside to sneak into my room.'

'Please . . .'

'Tell me!' Tiffany snapped, raising her voice suddenly and enjoying the look of fear that Nicola expressed.

'Because I want to be with you,' Nicola whispered, her face still fixed on the ground. Her hands were held tightly behind her back, her feet crossed in front of her, her bearing that of a silly adolescent brought before an unforgiving adult.

'What makes you think that *I* want to be with *you*?' Tiffany sneered.

Nicola looked lost, her face was burning furiously, a deep red blush of shame and humiliation. 'Shall I go?' she asked, not daring to look directly at Tiffany.

'Go?' Tiffany repeated, sounding thoroughly appalled by the suggestion. 'Go after you've woken me up in the middle of the night? Just like that?'

'Please Tiff . . .'

'And who the fuck said you can call me Tiff?'

Nicola shrank back, battered by Tiffany's harsh tone and cruel words. It wasn't the welcome she had been expecting, not by any means. 'What shall I do?' she asked meekly, trying hard to fight back the tears that filled her eyes.

'What would one of the prefects do if they caught you here?'

Nicola's eyes widened. She looked up and gazed nervously at Tiffany, who was sitting up confidently, fully in control of the situation. 'I'd be spanked,' she said softly.

'And if the head girl caught you?'

'I'd be spanked or caned. And a Mistress,' she added miserably, anticipating Tiffany's next question, 'can beat me with a strap or a cane, or do what she likes with me.'

Tiffany smiled. 'It's a neat system, isn't it?' she remarked approvingly. 'I like the way that the punishment sort of escalates. It's one of the first things a girl learns here. Does it still seem weird to you?'

'Sort of,' Nicola replied, starting to relax a little once more.

'Good, because now you're going to learn one more little rule.'

What's that?' Nicola asked, swallowing hard.

'The penalty for waking me up in the middle of the night,' Tiffany said, her eyes sparkling with excitement.

'Please . . . Tiffany . . .'

'Shut up! I hate girls who snivel and moan, understand? The more you complain the more you're going to get. Now, come here like a good little slut.'

Nicola hesitated, for a moment it seemed that she was going to turn and run away back to her own rom, but then she stepped forward and Tiffany knew that Nicola was hers. She moved towards the bed slowly, managing to keep her eyes averted all the time. As she drew closer, Tiffany could see the deep red of her shame, and the eyes that were sparkling with tears that still threatened to pour.

'Please,' she whispered as she stopped by the foot of the bed.

'Don't go on,' Tiffany sighed impatiently. 'Lift your skirt up, I want to look at you.'

Nicola obeyed reluctantly, taking the hem of her skirt and lifting it slowly, revealing the very top of her thighs and then the white cotton panties that she wore. Her hands gripped the hem of her skirt so tightly that her knuckles turned white, and were held so close to her face that the contrast with her red face was impossible to ignore in the weak light.

'How long have you been here?'

'Not long.'

'Why won't you tell me about your birthday?'

Nicola sniffed, forcing back the tears. 'Because it was so embarrassing,' she said, her voice trembling. Her hands began to weaken, slowly lowering as she stood before Tiffany, who was sitting upright in bed and smiling.

'Isn't this embarrassing too?'

'Yes . . . Please . . .'

'Keep your skirt up,' Tiffany ordered abruptly. 'I want every detail, understand? If I like the story you'll get off lightly, I promise.'

'Do you really?' Nicola asked, sounding hopeful, clutching at the hope in the same way that she clutched at the hem of her skirt that was raised high again.

'Sure I do,' Tiffany assured, smiling broadly, her dark eyes filled with a sincerity that was hard to doubt.

'It was on my second day here,' Nicola began, 'my birthday that is. I hadn't really settled in at all, the place was still very alien to me. I hadn't realised that normal rules didn't apply at the Institute. So I acted like I would have acted anywhere else on my birthday, I tried to have a little party.'

'And you didn't invite me?' Tiffany interrupted.

'Sorry, Tiffany,' Nicola said seriously, not recognising Tiffany's sarcastic tone for what it was. 'If I'd known you I would have invited you, honestly I would.'

'Forget it,' she was told impatiently. 'What happened?'

'Well, I was sharing with another new girl, Amanda, and I persuaded her to join me in a midnight raid on the kitchens. We were after something to drink, and we agreed that there was bound to be a bottle of cooking sherry in there. Besides, we were both new and neither of us took this punishment thing very seriously. I mean, who ever heard of grown women being spanked on the backside like naughty children?'

'Were you and Amanda fucking each other?'

'No!' Nicola cried vehemently.

'I only asked,' Tiffany exclaimed. Nicola had responded with such intensity that Tiffany had to believe her.

'Both of us were used to being locked up so it was easy sneaking out of our rooms and dodging the landing prefects. It was even easier breaking into the larder, as easy as falling off a log, which should have made us suspicious I suppose. Amanda reckoned that if the kitchens were anything to go by then we'd have no trouble running riot here, no matter what Shirer or any of the other bitches said. Well, to cut a long story short we didn't find any booze, not even a sniff of alcohol in the place, though we looked all over the place. So we had to make do with something else.'

'Such as?'

'Orange juice,' Nicola reported glumly. 'There was gallons of the stuff, and as there was nothing else to do we decided to drink the place dry. You know what it's like when you're all keyed up, we just decided that drinking gallons of juice was really clever. I suppose we wanted to take something just on principle, even if we didn't really want it. Do you know what I mean?'

'You mean like when you nick things that you know you'll end up throwing away?'

'Yes,' Nicola managed a shy smile, perhaps feeling that at last she was getting through to Tiffany. 'We were like that, half drunk on excitement. We were working our way through cartons of it, forcing it down so that we could get to the next lot. Pretty soon we were both full, I could feel it sloshing about inside me and I was dying to go to the loo but didn't want to risk getting caught. Amanda suggesting using the sink, and just to show me how she climbed on to the worktop and squatted over the sink and started to have a pee. We were both laughing so hard that we didn't hear the door opening. The next thing I know Kasia and three of the prefects were standing next to us, watching Amanda emptying her bladder and me in hysterics.'

'I would love to have seen the look on your faces,' Tiffany laughed.

'That's just it, we were still laughing, we had no idea what to expect. Of course, Kasia's purple with rage, and she gives us the third degree to find out what we were on. She's sure that we're out of it on booze or something, but when we tell her that it's my birthday treat she just goes dead quiet. Then she tells me that as a special birthday treat she's going to give me one stroke of the strap for every year. Amanda's promised the same, just so that she's not left out. Both of us took that as a joke, but before you know it we're bending over the kitchen table, knickers around our ankles and skirts over the waist, still laughing.'

'Kasia must have loved that.'

'She did,' Nicola agreed, smiling at the memory. 'Her

face was doing the colours of the rainbow. I'm laughing like an idiot and then all of a sudden the two prefects are holding me in place and Kasia produces her strap, that long hard strip of leather that she loves so much. Then before I've had a chance to say anything she raises her arm and brings that strap down so hard the windows shook with my screams. Jesus, nothing had ever hurt like that, so hard and sharp and bitter. One stroke across the arse and I was on fire, the heat really spreading through me. Amanda starts screaming her head off, even before she's touched. The two other prefects just grab her and stuff something into her mouth to keep her quiet. The arm goes up and then I'm screaming again, each time that strap touches me I'm burning more and more.'

'Is this the embarrassing part?' Tiffany interrupted.

Nicola's face reddened again, as if she had only just remembered herself. 'The shame of being punished was bad enough. I'd never been chastised like that before. It was so hard and so painful, but that wasn't the worst of it. I was still bursting to go to the loo, and every stroke of that bloody strap was making me weaker, I tried so hard . . . My body was burning, and the pain was changing inside me . . . I can't explain it but it had gone beyond pain, all I could think about was the rhythm of the strap and the strange heat in my body and then it happened . . . I cried and I wept, but I couldn't stop myself. It came flooding out, dribbling down my sore thighs and around my ankles, a wet stream of piss.'

Tiffany was silent for a moment, her eyes fixed on Nicola, whose voice had trailed to silence. Her skirt was held high, but now it seemed as though she were holding it high to cover her face, to cover the red flush of shame that transformed her. The story had affected both of them. Tiffany could picture the scene, was able to imagine it all in glorious detail. She dropped the quilt that she had been holding and crawled forward, enjoying the wide-eyed look that her body elicited from Nicola. Her breasts, large and round and tipped with nipples that were dark chocolate, swayed as she crawled across the bed.

'Lie across here,' she commanded, taking Nicola's hands and pulling her over the edge of the bed. Nicola resisted for a moment, but one harsh look and she yielded. She fell across the length of the bed, somehow managing to hold the front of the skirt up even as she fell forward on to her front. Tiffany lifted the back of the skirt and looked down, admiring the view of nice round buttocks clothed in virginal white panties.

'Please . . . I'm sorry . . . Whatever it is I've done I'm sorry,' Nicola pleaded, her eyes sparkling with tears, her lower lip trembling.

'You woke me up in the middle of the night,' Tiffany reminded her coldly.

'But I was told to come here, I was told that you wanted to speak to me.'

'Who told you that?'

'Amanda,' Nicola whispered, looking up to see that Tiffany was smiling broadly, her full lips so sensuous and yet so cruel.

'Yes, Amanda, your dear little friend,' Tiffany taunted. 'Such a dear child, and boy, does she like to fuck. Do you like to fuck, Nicola?'

'No . . . Please.'

'No, please? Not very good grammar is it? Don't you mean yes, please?'

Before Nicola had a chance to say anything a hard slap landed on her backside, a full firm smack of flesh on flesh. She cried out and tried to turn over but it was too late, Tiffany was astride her, sitting firmly on her lower back.

'This is good,' Tiffany sighed, running her hands up and down Nicola's thighs and buttocks, pressing her fingers into the other girl's flesh and enjoying it. She grabbed the top of the panties and pulled them tight, forcing the crutch into a tight strip of white cotton and pulling it into the rear cleft, exposing the pink outline of a palm-print.

'Please . . . You're hurting me,' Nicola complained tearfully.

'There you go again,' Tiffany giggled, 'bad grammar again. The Mistresses won't like you talking like that. What you really mean is please, hurt me.'

Another hard slap, this time on the other bottom cheek, had Nicola squirming, trying desperately to push Tiffany off. It was to no avail, the more that she struggled the more Tiffany laughed and giggled, enjoying the struggle and pressing herself down firmly. In the dim light it was clear to see that Nicola's bottom was blushing pink, and a few more hard spanks soon had it matching the colour of her face. When Nicola stopped, breathless and weak, Tiffany was still firmly esconced, sitting comfortably on Nicola's lower back, looking down on a pair of suitably punished arse-cheeks.

Tiffany yawned, made a big show of stretching her arms out, bending backwards slightly. She could feel the warmth of Nicola's body under her, feel the nervous tension as she sat astride the weaker girl. Very slowly she reached down and began to stroke Nicola's thighs again, rubbing her hand up and down very deliberately, emphasising the mastery that she possessed. The panties were pulled tight into Nicola's rear cleft, a thin white sliver of material that separated and emphasised the shape of her bottom. Tiffany yanked tighter, feeling the material strain as it pulled into Nicola's body. Nicola caught her breath, Tiffany could feel her not breathing, holding still as the panties bit deep into her body.

'Does that feel good?' Tiffany teased, whispering hotly.

'I want to go to my room,' Nicola complained weakly, too afraid to move.

Tiffany knew that the panties were pulling tight between Nicola's thighs, pressing into the warm and sticky heat of her sex, creating desire when that was the last thing that Nicola wanted. It was a good little game to play, Tiffany decided, and began to rub the panties in and out, a teasing motion inside Nicola's pussy that could not be ignored. At the same time she began to slap the top of Nicola's thighs, short hard slaps against soft white skin that reddened quickly, spreading a glow that would merge with the sweet feeling in Nicola's pussy. In only a few moments Tiffany felt Nicola respond, a small sigh escaping from her lips, her body moving imperceptibly, lifting her bottom slightly.

'It's good, isn't it?' Tiffany whispered, aiming her smacks a little higher, aiming at the join of the thighs. Her fingers were smarting but that was nothing to the feeling that she knew Nicola was experiencing, a delicious feeling where the pleasure in her sex was merging with the red heat of punishment. Nicola moved languidly, parting her thighs slowly, unable to resist the strange mixture of sensations in her body.

A louder sigh escaped from Nicola, a tell-tale sign of the confused pleasures she was enjoying. It was what Tiffany had been waiting for. Without warning she yanked Nicola's panties down, fully exposing her punished backside, and slipped two fingers into the wetness. Nicola cried out, part shock, part horror and part pleasure. She tried to struggle but her heart wasn't in it, she lifted herself, parted her thighs involuntarily, and allowed herself to be fingered.

Tiffany pressed her two fingers in the other girl's pussy, enjoying the wetness and the feeling of pleasure as she took what it was she wanted. She smiled. Nicola was writhing, opening herself, silent and bewildered but lost to the pleasure of being finger fucked. Tiffany's fingers were coated with love juice, with the seeping fluid that poured from Nicola's sex. Nicola's cries and grunts of pleasure were wordless, animal noises from an animal feeling that she could not deny and could not control.

'Please,' Nicola moaned suddenly, opening her eyes and staring wide-eyed at Tiffany, who was now sitting cross-legged on the edge of the bed.

'Please what?' Tiffany asked innocently, looking for all the world as though nothing had happened.

There was confusion and anguish in Nicola's eyes. She didn't understand what was going on, she had no idea what Tiffany was up to. 'I don't understand,' she admitted finally.

'It's time for you to go to your room,' Tiffany explained sweetly. 'That is what you wanted, isn't it?'

'But . . . but . . . Why did you?'

'Why did I do what?'

There was a long pause while Nicola searched for the

right words. Her face was red again, and her eyes averted. Absently she lowered her skirt, covering up her backside that was patterned with fingermarks, though her panties were still a tight bundle stretched between her thighs. 'Why did you spank me and then touch me like that?'

'Did you like it?' Tiffany asked, smiling again, her eyes glittering with excitement. She was naked, her breasts pert and round, pressed forward enticingly.

'Yes,' Nicola whispered, sounding as though the sheer awfulness of it was shocking to her.

'Does your backside sting?'

'Yes, it stings like hell.'

'And do you like it?'

'Yes. I liked what you did afterwards.'

'Here,' Tiffany stretched out her hand, offering her pussy-soaked fingers.

Nicola turned away sharply, unable to face the evidence of her arousal and pleasure.

'Suck this,' Tiffany insisted. 'Suck your taste from my fingers, suck my fingers clean so that I can carry on.'

'Please, don't make me do this.'

'Do it and I'll carry on,' Tiffany promised, rocking her head to one side so that her long dark curls cascaded prettily over her shoulder.

Nicola edged forward, her eyes fixed on Tiffany's fingers glistening with droplets of pussy juice. She opened her mouth, poked out her tongue and touched the very tip of it to the jewels of fluid. Her eyes were closed, as though she couldn't watch what she was about to do. A flick of the tongue and then she swallowed, tasting herself from another woman's fingers, tasting the honey that flowed from her sex. Another flick of the tongue, another droplet of it to sit on her tongue and then be swallowed down.

'All of it,' Tiffany urged, her voice quivering slightly.

Nicola obeyed, she lapped at Tiffany's fingers repeatedly, then took the two fingers fully in her mouth. She swallowed her taste, her essence, licked it all and swallowed it without complaint. At last she opened her eyes, a look of shock on her face.

'Was that bad?' Tiffany asked, making it sound so reasonable.

'No,' Nicola confessed softly. It hadn't been bad, in fact she had almost enjoyed it, an odd thrill of pleasure passing through her as she had swallowed the last droplets.

'Good,' Tiffany declared, evidently satisfied, 'now bend over.'

Nicola obeyed without question, she moved across the bed on hands and knees, on all fours just as she had been commanded. She made no protest when her skirt was lifted high, nor when her panties were pulled off and discarded.

The renewed spanking on her backside was unexpected, and Tiffany relished the look of surprise and disappointment in Nicola's face. In fact it gave Tiffany an extra thrill, adding to the pleasure she felt in doling out the punishment. She dealt a series of hard smacks across the buttocks and then several hard strokes between the thighs. Nicola moaned and winced every time a stroke touched her pussy, the pain expressed on her face and in the twisting of her lips and the effort she put into fighting back the squeals of pain.

Tiffany pressed her fingers into the redness of Nicola's pussy, slipping easily into the inviting wetness, the juicy quim ready and open to the touch. Nicola sighed her pleasure, no longer bothering to deny that it was pleasure she sought. It was what Tiffany wanted, to make her accept the pleasure of pain despite her initial fears and disgust. Tiffany liked that, she liked forcing other girls to accept punishment at her hand. For a moment the memory of her sister returned, and with it the image of Chantel's face whenever the shame flared up when she responded to punishment or humiliation.

'Is this good?' Tiffany demanded, her hoarse whisper giving away her own excitement. She was hot too, her sex swimming with juices and aching to be touched and licked. Her nipples were hard points, dark beads that begged to be caressed and tongued.

'It's good. Oh Jesus, this is good.'

'Do you love Tiffany?'

Nicola gasped, she could hardly control herself any longer. Tiffany's fingers were sliding in and out of her sex, going deep and hard and causing powerful spasms of ecstasy to pass through her body. 'Yes, yes I love it.'

'You're a little slut really, aren't you?' Tiffany hissed, forcing her fingers in deep, harder, faster.

'Yes, yes, I'm a little slut,' Nicola agreed deliriously. She was pulling her stomach down low and her backside high, opening herself as much as possible to the deliciousness of being frigged.

'A horny little bitch.'

'Yes, I'm a horny little bitch, a slut, anything.'

'Good, because you can piss off back to your own room now,' Tiffany announced suddenly. She sat back on her pillow, looking down her nose at Nicola, still on all fours, her pussy and thighs glistening with sex juices.

'No!' Nicola cried, almost wild with panic. She hadn't reached the end, her body still ached with a deep unsatisfied want.

'Enough,' Tiffany warned her. 'I don't want you here, you can go back to your own room now.'

'But why Tiffany? Why?'

'Because that's the way I want it. If you don't go I'll call the landing prefect. Or better still I'll give your friend Kasia a shout.'

Nicola gritted her teeth. For the first time that night she felt real anger, an anger so raw that she wanted to scream and shout and do something, anything. 'You bitch, you dirty bitch!' she hissed.

'I'm the bitch? Look at you? Look at the fucking state of you. Get out, get out now.'

Nicola stood up, aware of the smarting of her behind and the raw heat in her pussy. She felt horror and shame, her face burning with humiliation. Tiffany was right – Nicola was in a terrible state and she hated it. She glared momentarily at Tiffany, vowing to get even, then turned on her heel and left.

Tiffany laughed, a full throaty laugh that she knew would cause the maximum reaction in Nicola, punished and abused and still aroused by it all. That was the best part of it. Tiffany knew that little sluts like Nicola were always aroused by the humiliation and self-abasement. They revelled in it, and Tiffany revelled in giving it out. She looked down and there, on the bed, were Nicola's panties, thin white cotton knickers that were soaked through. Tiffany reached out, picked them up and smiled, another trophy, another little souvenir for her to keep.

She had already planned the next step, and the soiled panties were going to be just right for it. Neatly folded over, the panties were going to go into the top pocket of her white shirt, a token of what she had done to Nicola, a badge to be displayed. Tiffany knew that Nicola would die of shame when she saw it, when she realised that all the other girls were going to find out what passed between them. Yes, Tiffany smiled at the thought, she was going to tell them all that she had spanked, fingered and then dismissed Nicola as though she were nothing.

Tiffany lay down, parted her thighs and touched herself, her fingers tantalisingly passing over her pussy lips. She closed her eyes, lost in fantasy, imagining everything she was going to do, and every image matched by a play of her fingers over her body. It hadn't just been Nicola aching for that touch, aching for that climax. A light touch of the fingernails across the nipples made her shiver with pleasure, her sigh like a whisper. Her body was responsive, all the excitement she felt in humiliating Nicola was there, pent up, a potential waiting to be released. She sighed again, parted her pussy lips and began to frig herself, with a delicacy that Nicola had not known, with the sort of touch that guaranteed a climax like no other.

Chapter Three

The most boring thing about university parties was the dull predictability of it all. There would be the petty jealousies to navigate, the departmental politics to unravel, the endless reiteration of personal vendettas dressed up as ideological battles, the tedium, the same mundane behaviour from academics who longed to leave academia but were afraid to take the step. All so drearily familiar that Simone had to remind herself why she even bothered. She herself had escaped from academia some years previously, rejoicing in her escape and finding in it a liberation from the sheer pettiness of it all, from the endless and dispiriting scrabbling for funds and from the tedium of weathering whatever ideological or scientific fad was in the ascendant. She had escaped and ultimately had helped to create the Institute, a new world in which to study and explore sexuality, but she had kept in touch with old colleagues and with the world of psychology as a whole. She returned to academia because it was still the primary recruiting ground for Institute staff. She had escaped and now she returned to help others make that same journey.

Simone looked down at the kitchen table stacked with drinks, a forest of green and brown bottles clustered together at random. It all looked pretty vile, every bottle potentially filled with stuff that could strip walls and pollute rivers. She was late and had arrived without a bottle so there was no excuse, but that didn't make the choice any easier. She settled for some red liquid in a plastic beaker, the bottle had proclaimed it as Albanian claret but most of the bottle had gone and so she hoped that it was an indication that the content was not too disgusting.

If the wine was bad, the food was worse. The dip looked like several herds of sheep had been through it, and the assorted crisps and crackers looked like they had been used to dry off the sheep afterwards. The kitchen was temporarily safe, and Simone took the opportunity to just shut her eyes and try to relax a little. She leaned against a counter and swallowed some of the wine, which turned out to be drinkable, and tried to shut out all her worries about what had been happening at work. It was a vain hope of course, no matter how hard she tried she just couldn't get it out of her mind. The Institute was too important to her, it was more than just a job, more than a career, it had out-grown all of that and was growing all the time. It was, she realised, more like a way of life, a belief and a vision of what she wanted.

'Hello there,' a cheery voice interrupted, 'had too much of the old vino, eh?'

Simone groaned. She recognised the voice at once. 'Hello Jerry,' she said, forcing a smile.

'What're you drinking my dear? Anything old Jerry ought to know about?' he asked, smiling like the idiot that he was. He looked older and shabbier than when Simone had last seen him, but then he had always looked pretty old and shabby, even when Simone had been a first year student and he had been a senior lecturer.

'Albanian claret,' she informed him, aware of the way his eyes could appear so watery and so lecherous at the same time.

'How very adventurous, my dear,' he slurred, swaying slightly. 'Mind if I try some? I'm always open to new experiences.'

Simone sighed wearily and fished out the bottle for him, poured it into his china mug and then made a hasty exit from the kitchen before he had a chance to say anything. She was amazed that Jerry was still around, he had long been moved from lecturing to admin, and even there he had struggled with the work. Over time he had become a permanent fixture, someone to be laughed at, sneered at, ignored, but part of the furniture.

From the kitchen Simone wound her way into the main room, where the CD player was blaring out some awful jazz over which everyone talked or shouted. How very different it was to some of the parties she had hosted at the Institute, where uniformed girls served drinks and were routinely spanked for infractions of the rules, where male slaves were kept at heel and Masters and Mistresses held court.

The room had already been staked out by mutually antagonistic groups, each occupying a given position and making sure that there would be no encroachments. For a roomful of psychologists, assorted shrinks and academics, for whom reading body language was a basic skill, the signals they were giving out were as basic and primitive as those of any less cerebral and more physical tribal grouping. Simone knew from past experience that once the drink had been flowing and the inhibitions were lowered the real bitching and screaming would start. Some of them seethed with secret resentments that would come bursting out in spectacular explosions of bilious hatred. A Masters and Slaves party was altogether more civilised, she reflected.

'Simone, how lovely to see you,' Marcia, one of a group of women standing close to the hi-fi system, called to her from across the room.

Simone made her way across the room, stopping a couple of times to say hello to acquaintances, to join Marcia's little gang. They were old friends, not very close but always glad to see each other. Marcia was a lecturer in industrial psychology, but over the years she had begun to focus more and more on gender issues, and her coterie of lecturers, students and hangers-on were all very political.

Marcia did the introductions, whizzing through the names of the four women who were with her. The smiles that Simone got back were all perfunctory, they were all waiting to see where she stood on the issues of the day before deciding whether she could be trusted or not. Simone knew that one wrong answer and she would be classed as one of *them* and not one of *us*, whatever that meant.

'Simone and I were students together,' Marcia explained, beaming happily. She looked slightly flustered, her face red and her eyes darting nervously, but when she looked at Simone she looked relieved more than anything else.

'What do you do now, Simone?' one of them asked. The name had gone, she was a dull-looking young woman, with a pinched face and suspicious eyes. Dressed as she was, in the same dreary uniform of shapeless clothes as her friends, it was impossible to say whether she was a student or a lecturer.

'I'm involved in a government research project,' Simone replied. It was her stock answer. 'How's the book going, Marcia?' she asked, turning quickly to her friend.

'Still going,' Marcia replied glumly. 'I suppose one day I'll finish the blasted thing.'

'What sort of research project?' one of the other women asked.

'Motivational psychology. Is the book still on industrial psychology or has it changed focus?'

'It's on gender approaches to applied psychology,' Marcia reported, with a distinct lack of enthusiasm. She peered around the room distractedly, looking over Simone's shoulder and towards the door. The lights had been dimmed and the music seemed to be getting louder.

'Drink?' one of the group asked, proffering a bottle of wine.

Simone had her plastic cup refilled, smiling politely at the group of young women around her, all of them regarding her with nothing but suspicion. 'Thanks,' she said, raising her voice above the music.

'You're not working for the Ministry of Defence are you?'

It was an accusation parading as a question, and its artlessness made Simone smile. 'No, it's not the MoD, the Home Office or the police. Oh, and there are no animal experiments involved.'

'We're sometimes so predictable,' Marcia laughed, drawing a warning glance from one of her friends.

'These things are so important,' the woman who had

asked the question asserted, as if there were any doubt about it.

'Oh shit! Beckie's just arrived,' another of the group hissed, and they all turned towards the door just as a young woman arrived.

Simone could feel the hackles rising of all around her; even Marcia looked distinctly unsettled. The young woman was superficially at least just like the rest of them, young, scruffily dressed, conventionally unconventional. The room seemed to part for her, the level of conversation dropped and the level of expectation rose. She walked confidently through the room, heading directly for Marcia, a determined look on her face.

'I've got all my stuff,' she announced, her voice rising above the music so that everyone could hear. She shook the heavy rucksack that she was carrying, lifting it so that her audience could see. 'I've cleaned all my stuff out, just as you ordered.'

'Please, Beckie,' Marcia whispered, her face red with shame. Her lieutenants had taken a step back, as if they too were embarrassed.

'Please what? Shut my mouth? Don't make a fuss because good girls don't?' Beckie continued, ignoring the sniggering that passed around the room.

'That's not what I meant and you know it,' Marcia countered defensively, her voice barely audible above the music.

'I don't know what you meant. I don't know what the fuck you mean any more, and neither do you. Property is theft, is it? A male invention to keep women subservient? Is that why you're evicting me? To teach me my place, to keep me from getting uppity.'

'Don't be stupid.'

'That's right, I'm only a stupid fucking woman, a dumb whore,' Beckie screamed indignantly. 'Well fuck you, hypocrite. So much for sisterly solidarity, so much for your bloody principles. I'm out of here, I don't want any more to do with you, any of you,' she cried, turning to face her silent audience.

'Beckie, please let's talk,' Marcia suggested weakly.

It was no use though. Beckie threw her keys to the floor and then stormed out, marching back the way she had come, head held high in righteous indignation, everyone else shrinking away from her.

'Ideological differences,' one of the women whispered to Simone, who had been struck dumb by the display.

'She needed to do that,' Marcia sighed wearily, turning back to face Simone. She looked exhausted, her eyes filled with tears which were held back by sheer force of will.

'At least she's gone,' Simone told her softly, trying to console her as best she could.

'She needed to ritually humiliate me, to get it out of her system and to announce to the world that she was leaving me,' Marcia added, adopting a clinical tone to cover up her emotions.

'I'm glad she's gone,' one of the group announced, smiling proudly. 'That's the most action we've ever seen from her. She talks a good fight but ideologically she's a complete dead loss.'

This drew nods of agreement from the other three, though Marcia herself made no comment. 'What were the ideological differences?' Simone asked.

'She was a bloody liberal,' the woman said, making it sound like a crime. There were more nods of agreement, the women sharing a vicious glee in the accusation.

'We had too many disagreements over basic principle,' Marcia reported softly, looking very unhappy.

Simone looked askance, unable to fathom what had happened to Marcia, but fully able to sense the unhappiness and sheer embarrassment that her friend felt. Instinctively, she turned away from the group, unable to mask her dislike of the arrogance and cruelty that they shared.

'You probably wouldn't understand . . .' one of the women was saying, the sneer in her voice echoed by the laughter of her friends.

'I don't like any of this,' Simone told Marcia and then walked away, ignoring the chorus of comments that her departure elicited from the group.

The party was beginning to gel, as though the scene between Beckie and Marcia had been the catalyst to set things going. On the way out Simone saw the scene being acted out again, Marcia's face being mimicked and Beckie's voice caricatured. There was nothing like someone else's misfortune to get people laughing, and here the professional jealousies and ideological baggage that people carried with them added to that pleasure. It was an ugly atmosphere, and Simone hated it completely.

Out in the open, where the air felt cool and fresh, Simone looked about quickly, hoping that Beckie had not disappeared yet. The street was lined with parked cars, and more people were arriving all the time. It was always certain that the end of term party was going to be wild, and that knowledge drew people like a magnet. Simone spotted Beckie at the other end of the street, sitting on the bonnet of one of the parked cars, holding her face in her hands.

'Are you OK?' Simone asked her.

Beckie looked up sharply, her face was still flushed red with emotion. 'Yes, thanks,' she mumbled dejectedly.

'What was that all about?'

'Sorry, but do I know you?' Beckie asked, looking sharply at Simone.

'Not exactly,' Simone smiled. 'I was in the party just now, I witnessed the little bust up you had with Marcia.'

'Did she send you?'

Simone shook her head. 'No, she didn't send me. I was just concerned, that's all.'

'Concerned for whom? Me or her?'

'For both of you. Marcia and I were students together, we've known each other a long time.'

'Well, she's a bitch, I can tell you that,' Beckie said coldly, though her voice lacked the passion that it had earlier. She looked as though she were comfortably seated on the bonnet of the car, one leg under her, the heavy rucksack dumped on the kerb side.

'I don't understand it,' Simone admitted. 'And, to be honest I don't really care.'

'Aren't you going to grill me on the ideology? Aren't you one of her little gang, one of the right thinking elect?'

Simone laughed. 'Do I look like one of her happy band?'

Beckie looked at her properly, dressed in tight black skirt, matching high heels, a jacket that was so tight it funnelled her breasts to prominence. Simone was smart and sexy, dressed powerfully in black clothes that were sharp and vivid, not in the sexless and shabby uniform that Marcia and her friends wore. Not in the same shabby uniform that Beckie herself wore. 'No, I guess not,' she admitted with a slight smile.

'So, what are you going to do now?'

Beckie shrugged hopelessly. 'I don't know. Find someone to put me up for a while, take time out to think about my future. I don't know . . . Sorry I don't even know your name.'

'Simone Shirer, and you are Beckie . . .'

'Rebecca Cassidy. Thanks for taking an interest and everything Simone, but I'm OK now.'

Simone looked at Rebecca for a moment, and then nodded to herself. 'Look,' she said, 'I've got a spare room at my place, if you're interested.'

'But we've only just met,' Rebecca laughed.

'That's true, and it's also true that I have a room going spare at the moment.'

'What's the catch?' Rebecca asked slyly.

'No catch. I'll expect you to pay some rent, but you can offset some of that by doing some cleaning for me,' Simone explained.

'You mean you want me to act as your skivvy?'

Simone laughed. 'It's a good deal. You get a room at a reasonable rent and you get to act as my maid.' She paused for a moment and her eyes met Rebecca's. 'Some people would jump at the chance.'

Rebecca looked at Simone quizzically, as though she had not fully understood what Simone was saying. 'If I don't like it?' she asked.

'Then you can leave once you've found somewhere else to go. Now,' she said briskly, 'are you interested or do I go home alone?'

'Sounds like I can't refuse,' Rebecca agreed, and then jumped down on to the pavement. 'You don't look like any of that lot in there,' she said, jerking her thumb in the direction of the party.

'No, but you do,' Simone replied, taking in the shabby clothes, the spiky blonde hair, the unadorned face. Yet Simone could see that Rebecca was different, that she was not one of the clones that had clustered around Marcia. She smiled to herself, her eyes sparkling with an excitement that Rebecca could not even guess at.

The hand over the mouth caused a feeling of absolute panic. Tina struggled, kicked out, gasping for air as she fought to regain control. It was still dark, and in that darkness she had no idea who it was that had crept up on her.

'Stop struggling you stupid bitch!' a voice in the darkness hissed.

The voice was female, a harsh whisper that Tina could not identify, other than that it did not come from one of the members of the Institute staff. The only thing she could do was comply, the hands that held her down and covered her mouth were too many and too strong. She stopped struggling, and lay back on her bed, heart pounding as she tried to figure out what was going on.

'If you scream . . .' the voice warned menacingly.

Tina could now dimly make out a figure standing by the side of her bed, no details, just a blurred figure standing next to her. The other assailants were on the bed, or on the other side, and Tina guessed that there were at least two or three of them. She nodded vigorously, fighting back the panic and trying to slow the breath that she was gasping through someone's fingers.

'Let her go,' the figure ordered curtly. At once Tina was free. She sat up slowly, curling into a ball at the top of the bed, unable to make out who the women around her were. They had used something to cover the crack under the door which would have let at least some light into the room. The intense darkness was frightening, giving cover and confidence to whoever it was that had entered her room.

'Good, you're quiet,' the voice continued. 'Stay like that if you know what's good for you.'

'What do you want from me?' Tina asked weakly, too afraid to risk defiance.

'What did Shirer get from you today?' the voice demanded.

'Nothing, nothing at all,' Tina whispered, racking her brains trying to remember what had passed between her and Mistress Shirer.

'You're a liar,' the voice told her coldly. 'That blonde bitch was in there today, ranting on about the other dorm. Wasn't she?'

Tina nodded quickly, then realised that the gesture was probably unseen in the pitch black. 'Yes,' she said softly.

'Well?'

'I wasn't in with them.'

'You know what goes on, so don't act the innocent.'

'There was a lot of arguing. Then Kasia left and I had to scoop up the haul that Kasia had found earlier. Mistress Shirer questioned me about the other dorm but I told her the truth, I don't know anything about it.' This failed to satisfy any of the intruders, Tina was grabbed again, this time her hair was pulled back sharply so that she cried out. She was shaking, her lower lip trembling.

'You'd better not be lying to me,' the leader of the unknown group cautioned.

'Honestly, I don't know anything,' Tina cried. She was released just as suddenly and just as mysteriously, no words or commands were passed between the figure in command and those who had grabbed her. It was perfectly choreographed, and, like the blanking out of the stray light, it further served to frighten and intimidate.

'Kasia's stash of make-up, what happened to it?'

'The stuff that was confiscated?'

'What else do you think I'm talking about?'

'It was put away for safe keeping.'

'How safe is that?'

Tina could see what was coming next and it frightened her. 'Very safe,' she lied, tensing up suddenly.

'Listen Tina,' the voice warned, and Tina could almost imagine a smile of pleasure on the unknown face, 'we know what goes on, there's no use pretending. Now, how much of it can you get back?'

'Please don't do this,' Tina wailed, knowing that it was futile to plead but unable to do anything else. They were asking her to steal things, to commit the very crime that had caused her to be sent to the Institute in the first place.

'You've done it before, we know you're a thief,' one of the other women said, the sound of her voice so close to Tina that it startled her.

'That was a long time ago. You know what'll happen to me if I get caught. Please.'

Tina was suddenly turned over on the bed, hands roughly grabbing her and pushing her face down. She tried to lash out but it was pointless, the women around her had full control, many hands keeping her in place. Each arm was held down, and as she twisted and turned something was forced over her face. There was panic again, and a feeling of drowning, of being suffocated. Her cries and screams became muffled as the tightness closed around her face, a cold, tight feeling forced onto her skin. With a supreme effort she stilled, the fear overriding the panic, making her come to her senses.

She was released, almost pushed away by the hands that had been holding her down, disembodied hands that belonged to the darkness. Her breathing was harsh but steady, to the same rhythm as the wild beating of her heart. She was masked, a leather covering forced over her face, over her eyes and wrapping her face in a cool embrace. But she could breathe, her mouth and nose were uncovered, and for that small mercy she was grateful. The drowning feeling had been unbearable, a nightmare experience that touched her to the core.

'Well, that's better,' the leader of the unknown intruders remarked, 'some light at last. Isn't that better, Tina?'

'Why are you doing this to me?' Tina begged, unable to see the light, not even to sense the soft glow through the mask.

'It's very simple,' the woman replied, with mock patience. 'You give us the cosmetics that Kasia gives to Shirer. Isn't that simple? So very straightforward I think. If you're good you get a little reward, if you're bad you get a little punishment. I like to think of this as the principle of the Institute extended down to us. So, what do you say?'

'How much of the cosmetics do I have to get back?' Tina asked, realising that defiance was no good and that self-preservation had to be her top priority.

'As much as you can, but that doesn't mean you take the piss,' the woman explained, sounding tough and business-like.

'What about Mistress Julie? She hates me, she's always looking over my shoulder,' Tina protested. It was true, Mistress Julie was the head girl, and intent on consolidating her position of authority. In many ways she was more zealous and ruthless than any of the staff.

'You'll just have to be extra careful, won't you? Now, just get as much stuff out as you can,' the woman ordered. 'We don't expect you to steal back the whole lot.'

'I'll do my best,' Tina promised, relaxing a little.

'Good girl.'

Tina winced, she felt movement on the bed and then a hand stroke her hair. There was somebody beside her, she could feel the warmth of the body and the weight on the mattress. The hand stroked her, playing gently with her long auburn hair, a relaxed, possessive gesture that caused Tina to grow tense once more. There was an almost palpable feeling of expectation in the room, a silent waiting for something to happen.

'Can you let me go now?' Tina whispered nervously, turning to face the body she could not see but which she knew was there.

'We haven't finished yet,' a voice informed her coldly.

'It's time for your little reward for being so good,' someone else cooed excitedly.

Before Tina hd time to react she felt her pyjamas being pulled down quickly, and underneath she was naked, her backside suddenly bared to invisible eyes. Her face was red, but the shame was hidden under the mask, a mask that was now hot and sticky. She felt unattached, disembodied, but more than anything she felt vulnerable.

Her backside was touched, a palm sliding up from the thigh and caressing the soft white skin of her buttocks. She was being touched possessively again, with the same relaxed and casual manner that had been apparent when her hair was stroked. The unknown woman was exploring, taking her time, enjoying herself. She rubbed her hand over Tina's buttocks, then smoothed her hand down the thigh again, rubbing firmly the soft flesh inside the thigh. Over and over, in absolute silence, Tina was rubbed and caressed, touched in front of an audience that she could not see and whom she did not know.

Despite herself Tina began to relax, unable to deny the pleasure of being caressed and fondled. One part of her hated what was happening, hated the mask and the feeling of exposure, but there was another part of her that was slowly beginning to enjoy the experience. Being masked meant that she could not see and could not resist, and if there was an audience of silent voyeurs she could do nothing to stop it.

She moaned softly, her voice a breathless whisper. She moved, lifted herself instinctively to the fingers that were stroking between her thighs. Her pussy was wet, her moisture drawn out by fingers that slid in and out between her pussy lips. What could she do? The pleasure was growing, becoming more intense, fired by the knowledge that she was helpless and exposed, and that she was being watched, that her exposure was somehow giving pleasure to others. She moaned more loudly, opened herself, lifting her backside high so that the skilful fingers playing in her sex could have her completely.

'Will you always be good?' the voice beside her teased, stretching out the word 'good' until it was obscene.

Tina's reply was to push herself on to hands and knees, to offer herself on all fours. Her pyjama top was loose and another pair of hands reached out for her, touching and caressing, playing with her breasts. The nipples were rubbed roughly, each stroke of the fingers sending spasms of pleasure through her. She was aware of the wetness leaking down her thigh, the nectar of her excitement pouring from her sex. It was good, the pleasure pulsing like a heartbeat through her body, her cries and sighs rising steadily as the expert fingers toyed with her pussy bud, other fingers on her breasts adding to that pleasure. She was blind to it, and behind the mask she could only focus on the physical sensation and the picture of herself in her mind.

She was being finger-fucked by a stranger, her breasts mauled by a stranger, her body displayed to numberless others. The image was so strong, the leather mask the symbol of her powerlessness but also the key to the images in her head. She screamed suddenly, climaxing powerfully as she was caressed and fondled from all sides. The pure pleasure blind in its intensity.

The screams of pleasure turned to pain, a transformation accomplished with the snap of a belt across the backside. Tina was momentarily bewildered, unable to understand where the intense red sensation on her behind had come from. A whistle of something through the air and then the snap of leather on soft flesh. Her cry was stifled, a hand covering up her mouth, fingers forced over her lips. The sensation of pleasure that had suffused her, the heat of ecstasy in her pussy was overlaid with the sharp red pain on her backside. She was on all fours, in the perfect position to receive the punishment being inflicted. Bewilderment begat confusion which begat pleasure. The boundaries were dissolving, she could not completely separate the pain from the pleasure, the two were so close together.

Three more strokes, delivered in silence and with cool efficiency, and she was lifting herself again, offering herself. Her long legs were taut as she curved her spine, making her bottom cheeks nice and round for the belt to land on. How good it felt, each stinging impact turning to a glow of heat that filtered through to her pussy. The hands on her breasts were insistent, playing with her nipples, crushing them between forefinger and thumb, pulling, teasing, causing eddies of ecstasy.

'That's it, girl,' one of the voices urged excitedly, 'cream yourself with pleasure.'

Tina could not control herself, it was almost as if she had to follow an order. She cried out again, her orgasmic cry of pleasure muffled by the hand over her mouth. On hands and knees, body exposed and red with stripes of pain across her arse-cheeks, she shuddered and climaxed again.

'Think of tonight as an experience of what the Sisterhood can offer,' a voice informed her calmly. 'There can be pleasure, there can be pain, there can be both. It's yours to choose. You know what we want, all you have to do is deliver. Do you see what I'm saying?'

Tina was too slow to respond, she was lying on her belly, face down, body tingling and smarting. She had hardly been listening, the words were outside of her, partly muffled by the close-fitting mask.

'She's out of it,' one of the other women remarked.

Tina allowed herself to be rolled over, she was too weak to resist had she wanted to. Her backside smarted under her, the stripes of pain blurred into one single sensation. She squealed suddenly, one of her nipples was being squeezed, fingers pressing tightly over the red button of flesh.

'Listen properly,' the voice beside her warned icily.

'I'm listening,' Tina cried.

'You'll deliver the cosmetics just as you're told. And if you think of talking to Shirer or any other bitch you'll have the Sisterhood to answer to. If you think Kasia's bad you just don't have any idea.'

'Who . . . What?'

'That's enough for now,' the voice warned. 'We'll be back in the next few days, so have our things ready for us.'

The disembodied hands grabbed her again, held her down forcefully. There was no resistance on her part, she felt afraid again, and this time there was no excitement or eroticism about her helplessness, that moment had passed. A hand reached round to the back of her head and grabbed the mask, with disorienting precision she felt the coolness of the air back on her face. For a moment she couldn't tell what had happened, were her eyes open in the darkness or closed under the mask?

Magically she was free again, still in her room, in the darkness that had always been so safe. She heard the door close and then she knew that she was alone, her body tingling with the faint memory of orgasm and her mind full of doubts and fears.

Chapter Four

The room was sparsely furnished, a bed, a chest of drawers, a bedside cabinet, a single shelf on one wall, yet for all that Andrea had turned it into her own. Simone noted the arrangement of books on the shelf, the box of pink tissues on the bedside cabinet, the fringe of ribbon that decorated the large mirror above the drawers. That was the way with every room in the Institute, the same functional furniture and arrangements subtly changed and enhanced to reflect the personality of the occupants.

Simone noted her reflection in the mirror, jet black hair that was almost glossy, full sensuous lips, deep brown oval eyes that scanned the room and missed nothing. It had been her idea to have a mirror in every room, despite the safety risk that the glass represented. A mirror was important: it reflected not only the truth but also the hopes and desires of people, it reflected back an idealised image when that was required, and it was required more often than imagined. Kasia, Simone remembered, had been outraged when she had first seen the mirrors in the rooms, they represented something altogether different to her. Her idea had been to convert the mirrors into two-way mirrors, to use them as a device to spy on the young women, and men, in her charge. The idea was rejected out of hand. Simone had been appalled by the idea of turning the looking glass into a surveillance device.

'Well, Andrea?' Simone began, stopping at the foot of the bed to look down at the strawberry blonde sitting miserably at the other end.

'I don't know anything, Mistress,' Andrea whispered, her voice trembling with emotion.

Simone sighed to herself, it was going to be another difficult session, though she had hoped that the mere fact of her presence would be enough to make Andrea more cooperative. 'As I understand it, Kasia has already punished you most severely,' she said.

'Yes, Mistress,' Andrea admitted softly, her face colouring, the striking red flush of shame contrasting to her pretty blue eyes.

'How?' Simone asked, knowing that the shame of confession would confuse Andrea, who would be fighting the pleasure she felt mingled with the shame.

'It was in the library, in front of some of the others. She had noticed my fingernails and wanted to know where I'd got the nail varnish from. I couldn't tell her, Mistress, honestly I couldn't. So she made me pull down my panties and expose my backside to everybody, it was just so embarrassing. I was bent over a chair and she used her strap across my backside and my thighs. I screamed and I cried, Mistress, but she just carried on regardless.'

Andrea's voice trailed to silence, and she looked up at Simone nervously, her eyes filled with tears that glittered like jewels. The imploring look was heightened by the evidence of her shame, the bright red sheen that touched her face and neck.

'Can you tell me where you got the nail varnish?' Simone asked, her tone quite neutral, neither threatening nor pleading.

Andrea choked back the tears, her voice was almost a sob. 'I can't,' she wailed, and buried her head in her hands, sliding across the length of the bed as she sobbed. Her short skirt had ridden up, exposing a length of white thigh, smooth and silky.

Simone could not allow herself to be taken in by the dramatic gesture, theatrical but obviously deeply felt. 'I will punish you also,' she pointed out quite reasonably. 'You know the rules, Andrea, you know the penalty for lying to a Mistress.'

The sobbing showed no signs of stopping, Andrea hid her face in the covers on the bed, hiding away the truth of her reaction. Simone knew what that reaction was, there would be a mounting excitement there, a fear that was tinged with the anticipation of pleasure.

'Stand up,' Simone ordered curtly. 'Up! This instant.'

Andrea's face was streaked with tears, wet trails of silvery liquid that poured from her eyes down to her chin. She bit on her lip, biting back more tears, and stood up by the edge of the bed. Her eyes were fixed on the stern vision before her, the dark-skinned Mistress dressed in short black skirt and blouse and high heels that were of glossy patent leather.

'Turn around, I want to examine you,' Simone continued, barking out the words with such authority that there could be no resistance. Andrea obeyed, turning around to face her bed, her arms hanging limply at her sides, fists clenched tightly.

Simone strode back across the room to the chest of drawers, keeping her eyes on Andrea, who was looking straight ahead, too afraid to turn around. The bright red hair-brush was neatly placed at an angle on top of the chest of drawers, the red handle pointing across the room, the wiry teeth of the brush pointing up to the ceiling. Simone picked it up, weighed it in her hand, gripping the handle tightly. It would do, she decided, walking back across the room, her high heels clicking sharply on the polished floor.

'You still have time,' Simone told Andrea. 'If you tell me all that you know I'll not punish you so harshly.'

'Mistress . . . Please, I can't tell you anything . . . honestly,' Andrea wailed, her voice utterly without hope.

'Bend over,' Simone ordered angrily. There would be no more chances, she decided, Andrea had been given all the chances she needed to recant.

The short skirt rode up high as Andrea bent over at the waist. She reached out with her hands to hold on to the edge of the bed for support. Her reddish blonde hair fell about her shoulders as she strained to look round, the fear shown so clearly on her face, her eyes wide with apprehension. The skirt went over quickly, Simone flipped it over Andrea's waist to expose the girl's snow-white panties pulled tightly into her rear cleft. The hair-brush was cool and smooth, Simone knew, as she used it to caress the long silky thighs and rounded backside before her.

'Mistress does not like liars,' Simone intoned coldly, enjoying the way she had free reign to touch and explore Andrea. Using the brush she stroked up and down Andrea's thigh, up and down the soft skin on the inside of the thigh, certain that it was inducing a feeling of delicious expectation in the recalcitrant creature. Andrea tensed, tightened her position in readiness for the punishment that she knew was certain to start.

Simone paused. The tension she liked to create was in stark contrast to so many of the other Mistresses, for whom punishment was a stark but enjoyable duty. She knew that it was the tension that counted, that the sensations and emotions of humiliation and punishment were as important as the pure physical effect of pain. She raised the brush high and held it there, holding her position as though in suspended animation. Then, when the moment had been stretched and contorted, she let it go, sweeping down with the brush to strike squarely on Andrea's pertly offered derrière. The sharp smacking sound was joined by a yelp of pain as Andrea winced and slipped forward.

In rapid succession Simone beat out three more strokes with the brush, each as heavy and as well-aimed as the first. The brush *had* been just right, the smooth head and the long plastic handle making it a perfect paddle to beat across Andrea's behind. Slipping her fingers under the elasticated band, Simone pulled the panties down quickly, exposing the reddened flesh of Andrea's round bottom-cheeks. The redness was centred on each buttock and was suffusing out, spreading across the white skin of her behind as though it were being soaked into her flesh. It would be spreading through her being, absorbed by senses, transformed from initial sharpness into something altogether more diffuse and sensual.

The red brush landed on the edge of the bed, just by Andrea's hands. She looked back sharply, her eyes a question. Was it really over so quickly?

'It's not over yet,' Simone explained, noting gladly that at least Andrea had not blurted out the question. Not for the first time she had the impression that Andrea was not being uncooperative for the sake of it, that there really was something stopping her from revealing what it was that she knew.

'Legs apart,' was the next order, and again Andrea obeyed without question. She moved her legs apart as far as the white panties between her knees would allow her. Simone reached out and caressed the punished bottom-cheeks with the flat of her hand, her dark fingers contrasting to the pinkness of Andrea's skin. Moving round slowly Simone touched and caressed, pressing her fingers firmly over soft yielding flesh, over the buttocks, up and down silky thighs, and then resting finally just under the join of Andrea's thighs.

'Do you enjoy being exhibited?' Simone asked casually, her wry smile caught in the reflection on the mirror.

'No, Mistress,' Andrea replied miserably.

'Do you enjoy showing this off?' Simone teased, moving her hand round quickly and closing tightly around Andrea's hard, erect cock. There was no doubt about the truth of the answer, the tears were falling from Andrea's face even before she tried miserably to whisper her answer. No, she hated being exposed because her hard cock gave her away, she was a he, Andrew not Andrea, and all her feminine desires and ambitions would be revealed as a sham.

Simone stroked the hard cock softly, her expert fingers causing shudders of pleasure that Andrea sighed away. The smooth thighs and pert backside, now losing the initial redness of the spanking, could not deny the masculine hardness that Simone held tightly in her fingers.

'Mistress has a special punishment in mind for you, Andrea,' Simone whispered hotly, leaning over to lift the front of Andrea's skirt so that the hard prick could no longer be hidden.

'Mistress, I'll do anything, you know I will,' Andrea pleaded, her beseeching eyes staring straight into Simone's.

'You know what Mistress wants, girl.'

'I can't . . . Anything but that.'

Simone picked up the brush in her free hand and began to smack Andrea, fast and furious strokes at the top of the thighs and on the arse-cheeks, the strokes merging, one into the other, hard and painful and showing no signs of stopping. At the same time Simone continued to play with and stroke the hard cock, flexing and twitching as each of the brushstrokes landed. The two sensations were merging becoming indistinguishable, pleasure and pain, pain and pleasure. Andrea's tears had stopped, her eyes were closed, and she was whimpering helplessly, sighing, aching, unable to control her reactions.

'No . . . No,' she gasped and then sighed, her eyes opening with horror. She was spurting thick white jets of come, her cock throbbing in the Mistress's hand. It had been too much, too confusing, the pleasure of being punished added to the pleasure of being wanked added to the pleasure of being a girl.

'I will have you tied up and exhibited in public,' Simone told her, 'your cock there for everyone to see, so that they know what a bad girl you really are.'

'Please, Mistress, anything but that,' Andrea cried, utterly appalled by the idea, shocked and horrified at the cruelty of her Mistress.

Simone picked up the brush, which she had dropped in the last few seconds before Andrea's climax. She looked at it for a moment, knowing that she had failed, that no matter how terrible the punishment she had outlined it had not been enough to break the girl's resolve. Her fingers were splattered with droplets of come, pearly jewels of liquid-like gel on her fingers.

'Clean me,' she ordered, offering her hand to Andrea.

The punished girl knelt down on the floor, her face was streaked with tears of confusion, her face flushed pink with pleasure and shame. She crawled forwards, aware that droplets of come were now sliding down her thigh. When she was close she scooped down quickly and planted a soft kiss on Mistress's heel, a quick peck of the lips against the cold hard heel. Then she looked up, saw the jewels of her own seed on Mistress Shirer's fingers. She knew what to do: she began to lap softly at Mistress's hand, licking away the droplets and swallowing them quickly, swallowing the emissions from her body from the holy body of a Mistress.

Rebecca sat in silence waiting for the key in the door that would signal Simone's return from work – wherever that might be. Simone had been very evasive about that when she and Rebecca had talked after they had arrived back from the party. They had talked for hours, about everything and anything, the two of them just getting to know each other. It was funny because they had got on so well almost immediately, quickly forming an easy relationship where Rebecca would have expected it to be much more strained. Perhaps Simone was used to picking up waifs and strays, or perhaps not. She had a very strange personality, Rebecca decided, quite open and relaxed, yet there was always the impression that there was so much going on behind Simone's almond eyes.

Initially they had talked about the university, about Marcia, about psychology and feminism, about the symbolism of clothes. Then they had talked about the living arrangements, and again Simone had been completely above board about what she required from her new lodger. Rebecca had smiled and called herself the new maid, which had prompted a smile from Simone that was unfathomable. Enigmatic or not, the duties that Simone had outlined for her were quite clear and precise: to ensure that the house remained clean and tidy at all times, to clean Simone's rooms three times a week, wash and iron Simone's clothes, do all small household repairs and do Simone's weekly shopping. It was a long list, but in return the rent that Simone asked was tiny, the sort of rent that even a penniless student, or ex-student, could afford.

Despite the banter and the bargaining, Rebecca had accepted the deal quite happily. Her room was spacious and the atmosphere of the house quite serene compared to the chaos of sharing Marcia's home. What was more, she realised, the nominal rent represented a kind of independence, she would no longer feel that she was living in somebody else's house as a special favour. There would be no repeat of the complicated and painful entanglements that living with Marcia had entailed. Besides, Simone's stand-offishness was welcome. They were going to be close friends but nothing more, and Rebecca was certain that both of them wished it that way.

The rattling of a key in the front door alerted Rebecca, she grabbed the bottle of wine and made straight for the hall. Simone looked startled to see her there, as though she had forgotten that she had rented out the bedroom on the ground floor. Her expression changed instantly however, from a look of surprise to a weary smile that lit up her oval face.

'You look bushed,' Rebecca told her, smiling keenly and waving the bottle in front of her.

'I feel it,' Simone sighed, trudging in and slamming the front door behind her.

'Well, a drink is just what you need then,' Rebecca announced in a voice that would brook no disagreement.

'What's the celebration?'

'This is my way of saying thank you,' Rebecca beamed. 'You saved my life last night, and for that I'll always be grateful.'

'In that case I can't say no,' Simone agreed.

Rebecca followed Simone up the stairs, noting the short skirt and the shiny high-heeled shoes that cracked hard on the wooden floor. They were not the sort of clothes that Rebecca wore. In fact none of her friends or acquaintances dressed that way. The clothes were too conventionally feminine, designed to show off a woman's body in the way that a man would like. The high heels contorted the leg, emphasising the shape of calf and thigh, drawing attention to the curves and lines of the body. Too overtly sexual, that was the trouble, Rebecca decided.

Simone showed her the way into the front room then disappeared into her bedroom for a moment. The front room was sparsely furnished, lots of open space and muted colours, books on the shelves and neatly stacked videos and CDs. Two upholstered armchairs dominated the room, facing each other across an open space that took up most of the room. It looked like the setting of a talk show, the open space that people would occupy with their thoughts and discussions, a space for people and not things. It was odd, really, Rebecca decided, hovering by one of the chairs as though afraid to take a seat.

'Glasses? Bottle opener?' Simone cried from her bedroom.

'Got those,' Rebecca called back, remembering why she was there.

The bottle was a struggle, but finally the cork came out with a satisfying pop and released the rich, fruity scent of the wine. She poured into each glass, the deep purple of the wine staining the glass as it was poured. It was a no-name red from the supermarket, the sort of wine that a snob would not deign to slosh around the mouth and yet it tasted perfect.

'Albanian red?' Simone asked, emerging from her room looking a little less tired than she had been when she had arrived.

'What?'

'Never mind, a private joke,' Simone laughed drily, taking her glass.

'It tastes good, smells nice too,' Rebecca judged quickly, hardly letting the flavour of it suffuse through. Suddenly she felt nervous, standing there in Simone's room, aware that she hardly knew her and yet was already deeply in her debt.

'It's OK, you can sit down,' Simone remarked, waving her glass in the direction of the chair.

'Yes, of course,' Rebecca said softly. She hesitated for a moment, unable to pin down exactly why she felt so nervous. The seat was welcoming, drawing her down comfortably, moulding itself to her body as she settled down.

'Tell me,' Simone began, also settling down in the other armchair across the room, 'what did you do today.'

'Not a lot,' Rebecca admitted apologetically. 'I put some

washing into the machine and had a quick spring-clean of my room ...'

'I didn't mean that,' Simone interrupted good-naturedly. 'I meant about Marcia and your course.'

Rebecca smiled sheepishly. Of course that was what Simone had meant, and yet she had found herself reacting differently. 'Nothing. Yet. Term's just finished, I've got the sumer vac to sort something out.'

'Any ideas?'

Rebecca shook her head sadly. 'Not really. It's a good course, but I can't go back to it. Marcia's the course director. If I went back I'd see her every day and that would be too much for either of us. Besides her little clique of Marcia clones would make my life a bloody misery.'

'What about transferring to another course?'

Another shrug. 'I don't know, Simone,' she said glumly. 'I don't really fancy doing any course any more. I'm sick of it, it's too bloody complicated all of a sudden.'

'You sound very weary for a young woman your age,' Simone remarked, taking a sip of her wine and savouring it. She shifted to one side, making herself more comfortable, and her skirt rode up slightly, the tightness of it lifting to reveal long smooth thighs. Rebecca found herself staring, her eyes drawn naturally to the attractive view of smooth flesh, the soft brown colour of Simone's skin seductive against the dark blackness of her skirt.

'Sorry,' Rebecca came back to life with a start, her face reddening as she realised that Simone had been talking to her and that she had been lost in contemplation of Simone's thighs. Damn! She felt stupid, confused. She wasn't like that, not normally, and she was never ever red-faced. Being embarrassed had never been part of her style.

'I was asking if you had any plans for the summer vacation,' Simone repeated, smiling knowingly, her dark eyes sparkling with her smile.

'No. None.'

'Not going home?'

'No. My parents don't approve of me,' she said. Forcing herself to act calmly, to deny the swirling confusion that she felt. If she concentrated hard enough, she thought, then she would regain her composure and the curious feelings she was suffering would go away.

'Really? What is it that they don't approve of, exactly?' Simone asked, still smiling. There was a hint of something in her smile, amusement perhaps, sardonic humour, enjoyment certainly.

'My politics. My way of life. Me really, the whole bloody package that is Rebecca Cassidy,' she declared grandly, then instantly regretted it. It had sounded better in the student union bar, or at one of the discussion meetings that she and Marcia used to attend. In front of Simone it sounded hollow, an adolescent certainty that came across as thoroughly immature in front of someone with more understanding and more experience of life.

'It's an interesting package though, this Rebecca Cassidy thing,' Simone remarked with a friendly smile.

At that instant Rebecca felt a surge of gratitude, an intense feeling of happiness and the certainty that she had never felt better. Simone understood. Simone could have sneered, she could have patronised, she could have devastated with a single choice put-down and yet she had done nothing of the sort. Rebecca felt herself blushing again, but this time she didn't care so much, this time she felt happy, happier than she had ever done with Marcia.

'Do you really think that?' she asked shyly.

Simone laughed joyfully. 'Of course I do, why else would I rescue you?'

'Simone Shirer, knight in shining armour, no I guess that doesn't sound right, does it?'

'No, that doesn't. You're looking again,' she added, catching Rebecca in the act of staring again.

'Sorry,' she whispered, embarrassed again. 'It's your clothes,' she added, desperately hoping to redeem herself.

'My clothes?'

Rebecca laughed. 'Why do you dress like that?' she asked, pointing at the short skirt and high heels.

'Because it makes me powerful,' Simone replied without having to think about it.

'No, you've got that wrong,' Rebecca told her, thrown by the answer. 'Sorry, I didn't mean it to sound like that. I mean you're dressing up like that because that's how men want to see women. As sex objects.'

'But what if I enjoy dressing like this because I like it? What if I dress like this because I'm in control of my sexuality and I enjoy looking sexy?'

Rebecca pondered for a moment. 'But that's such a stereotypical image of women, isn't it? Short skirt and high heels, I mean it's so . . . so . . . How does it make you look powerful?'

'Because I'm in control. I don't wear these clothes because I'm forced to. Do you think I look submissive? Do I look oppressed dressed like this?'

Rebecca poured herself more wine then realised that Simone's glass was in need of refilling too. She stood up and walked across the room, unable to decide how to continue the argument.

'Look at the heel,' Simone instructed. 'What is it? A symbol of power or a symbol of weakness?'

'Weakness,' Rebecca decided, stepping back to look at the sharp, tapering heel. It raised the instep high and curved slightly from the ankle down to a sharp point on the ground.

'Why?' Simone demanded, holding up her glass for more wine.

Rebecca poured the wine. 'Because you have to hobble about in high heels,' she explained, 'it makes you unstable, ready to topple over.'

'But the heel is sharp for stamping down on the ground, it explodes with every step. The stiletto is a phallic dagger, a symbol of power, the sexual imagery is all there,' Simone countered.

Rebecca stood back, viewing the heels again, unable to resist passing her eyes up from the heel, along the calves, over the knees and along the thighs. With a start she realised that she felt desire growing inside, that Simone's dress, her presence, provoked that desire. 'I don't understand,' she admitted, her eyes meeting Simone's.

'There's more than one way of seeing,' Simone explained

softly. 'Every image is laden with meaning, a multitude of meanings attached to every symbol, some private and some public. That's the mistake that is so easily made, to imagine that every person sees the same, to ignore the thousand different ways of seeing.'

'But that's so simple,' Rebecca exclaimed. Simone's explanation was seductive, but it was too simple and it conflicted with everything that Rebecca believed in.

'You mean it's *too* simple,' Simone corrected, as though reading Rebecca's mind.

'But it is.'

'Why don't you sit down,' Simone suggested, pointing to the floor close to her chair. 'The most powerful ideas are the simple ones,' she continued. 'Very complicated ideas are the ones that don't work. They're complicated because they don't have insight or meaning.'

Rebecca knelt down beside Simone, aware of the fact that they were now so close. Her eyes were at thigh level, and she could feast them on Simone's long legs, on the silky smooth skin that was revealed as the skirt slowly worked its way up. They were so close she could almost feel the warmth of Simone's body, already she could breathe the scent of her body.

'Do you still think I shouldn't dress like this?' Simone asked softly, her question leading on from where the discussion had stopped.

'I didn't say you shouldn't dress like that.'

Simone laughed. 'That's what you were implying. Aren't you saying that there's a correct way for us to dress?'

It was a leading question that couldn't be answered. Simone's arguments were tricky because they came from an alien territory that Rebecca had never encountered before. She had been used to arguments from other directions, and had been used to walking all over those, but these arguments were different. For a moment she wished that Marcia was beside her, because she would have known how to rebut Simone's arguments. Rebecca almost shook the thought away, Marcia was the last person she wanted to have on her side, especially not against Simone.

'You're very strange, do you know that,' she blurted out finally, unable to continue the argument any longer.

'I'll take that as a compliment,' Simone responded with a smile.

'I mean it,' Rebecca assured her earnestly. 'I don't understand you, I don't see where you're coming from.'

'Then that's a good thing. It means you'll have to take every argument as it comes, none of your preconceived ideas will fit any more.'

Rebecca thought about that for a while, her eyes returning to the shiny high heels, which had been miraculously transformed before her very eyes. It had almost been an act of magic, a few words spoken and the transformation had taken place, a transmutation of lead into gold. The two of them enjoyed the silence for a while, no longer needing words, both of them happy with each other's presence.

After a while Rebecca looked down at the bottle and saw that it was almost empty. 'I seem to have drunk most of this myself,' she giggled guiltily, showing the empty bottle to Simone, who merely smiled.

'If you don't mind,' Simone said and stood up, 'I have rather a lot of work to be getting on with.'

'Of course,' Rebecca agreed instantly. She felt dizzy for a moment, the wine suddenly filling her head with fuzziness. Simone was in front of her, legs slightly apart, balanced on those dangerous-looking heels, her thighs lithe and attractive and perfectly displayed by the tight-fitting skirt. Rebecca looked up from the floor where she was sitting, her eyes travelling from the heels up, taking in every inch of Simone's body. Their eyes meshed again, a look passing between them, something unspoken but powerful. An exhilarating feeling of excitement erupted in the pit of Rebecca's belly, a tight ball of emotion that matched the fuzzy feeling in her head.

Slowly, Rebecca rose to her feet, drawn up almost as much by the power of Simone's gaze as by her own volition. She straightened up, inches from Simone, facing her shyly, waiting excitedly, knowing that something was going to happen between them. It had to happen, the feeling was electric and she longed for it.

Simone reached out, elegant fingers, scarlet-painted nails, gold band around her wrist, and touched Rebecca's face. A soft touch, fleeting, gentle, inviting. Rebecca closed her eyes, felt herself floating, heart pounding with expectation. A touch again, a touch of fingers to flesh. Simone stroked Rebecca's face, a longer, more lingering touch.

Rebecca parted her lips for Simone, opened her mouth for the kiss that followed. Their lips touched for an instant, barely making contact yet it was enough. Simone's breath was warm on Rebecca's face, warm and sensual.

'Kiss me again,' Rebecca sighed, opening her eyes.

'Don't talk,' Simone whispered softly. Rebecca was standing awkwardly, arms at her side loosely, head cocked slightly to one side, eyes half open and filled with desire. Simone reached out and took Rebecca's arms, holding them in position, at her side.

They kissed again, more passionately, mouths twisting together, tongues touching and searching. Rebecca felt the breath flow from her, sucked into Simone's cool mouth. She felt hot and dizzy and excited. Her belly was somersaulting, fear and nerves and excitement all conspiring and merging with the desire firing in her sex. Her pussy was wet with expectation, with yearning.

Simone stopped, looked into Rebecca's eyes, and then kissed her again. A long slow kiss, extracting every ounce of pleasure from the simple act of joining mouths. Rebecca felt herself almost swooning, incredibly turned on by Simone's kisses, by Simone's presence. Her hands were pinned down at her sides, she could not embrace Simone, but somehow that made the searching caresses more potent. The thought flitted into her head that she had never been kissed like that before, no one else, male or female had ever been able to kindle such desire so easily. Her pussy was dripping wet, her panties warm and damp with sexy moisture, her nipples had hardened deliciously.

'Now,' Simone whispered, 'off you go. I've got things to do.'

Rebecca stood and stared, open mouthed with shock. Her breathing was ragged, an uneven rhythm that matched the beating of her heart. Her nipples were aching, her pussy wet. What was happening? 'I don't understand,' she managed to whisper, red-faced again.

'Tomorrow you can cook for me,' Simone suggested, though perhaps it was an order. There was fire in her eyes, and Rebecca could see that Simone's nipples were jutting visibly against her blouse, but for all that her tone was neutral, betraying nothing of what she felt.

'I don't understand,' she repeated. 'Don't you like me?'

Simone smiled, her full lips sensuously expressive. 'Of course I like you,' she said. 'I'll see you again tomorrow.'

'But . . . This isn't what I . . .'

Simone leaned forward and silenced the questions with a kiss, hard and passionate but all too quick to be anything but final. Rebecca turned away, moving through the fog of confusion and alcohol, dismissed at the height of her desire. She had been right, she understood for the first time just how alien and how strange Simone was. And yet, in spite of that, or because of it, she felt the desire and the love begin to blossom inside her.

Chapter Five

Tina limped from the gym, her leg aching and her body bathed in a thin layer of perspiration. Her breath was hard and ragged and, each time she inhaled, her leg seemed to scream its agony. Even her hands were trembling slightly, from the exertion and the excitement of the game she had been playing. Behind her the game of netball was in progress again, the shriek of the whistle restarting the game that her departure, forced by a foul, had stopped.

The door to the gym wouldn't budge and she was too tired to do anything, her fingers fumbled uselessly with the latch but it seemed to melt in her hand. As she struggled feebly, the door suddenly opened. She looked up and smiled at the young woman who had opened it for her. The young woman half-smiled back and then looked away, hiding her face by looking in the other direction.

'Thanks,' Tina said, stepping out of the gym and into the coolness of the corridor. The door slammed and blocked out the echo of the bouncing ball and the shouts and squeals of the rest of the girls involved in the game.

The other girl mumbled a reply and then began to edge away, stepping backwards towards the bench opposite the gym. There was another girl sitting on the bench, keenly watching everything that had happened. Tina recognised her at once – it was Tiffany. They had spoken on a number of occasions though they were hardly friends.

'What's going on?' Tina asked, shambling towards the bench, her limbs twitching with the after-shocks of the foul that had sent her sprawling across the polished floor of the gym.

'Nothing,' the girl who had opened the door mumbled, halting by the bench, her back to Tiffany.

'Don't lie,' Tiffany scolded, her pretty face breaking into a smile.

'What is it?' Tina repeated, drawing closer to the two young women. Tiffany was seated on the edge of the bench, her long legs splayed and stretched out, the short gym skirt barely covering her smooth dark thighs. It was an insolent sort of posture, taking up space in a manner that was almost aggressive.

'Turn around, Nick,' Tiffany ordered, her eyes flashing dark signals to the other girl.

Tina saw the beseeching look in the girl's eyes, but there was no yielding response from Tiffany. Reluctantly, slowly, the girl turned around. She had flowing light brown hair which reached a good way down her back, contrasting to the dark blue of her short-sleeved sports top. However it was not the long flowing locks that drew the eye, rather it was the short gym skirt which had been neatly turned up at the back to reveal that she was naked underneath it. Her round backside was fully displayed from the rear, the skirt carefully arranged to conceal everything from the front. The girl waited for a full second and then, her face scarlet with shame, she sat down on the pine bench, taking her place next to Tiffany.

'Who was it?' Tina asked sympathetically, trying not to let the excitement she felt show through. 'One of the Mistresses or a prefect?'

Tiffany laughed. 'Tell her,' she said, her smile and sparkling brown eyes making her seem sultry and sexy. Her full lips were sensual and slightly cruel, as though her mouth could shower with delightful kisses or wicked bites as the whim took her.

'I can't,' the girl mumbled, leaning forward to hide her head in her hands.

'It was neither,' Tiffany reported casually. 'She isn't being punished by a Mistress or a prefect. Nicola's just showing me how much she loves me, aren't you, darling?'

Nicola nodded, not with enthusiasm or delight, but with

a kind of weary stoicism. 'What if you get caught?' Tina asked her. The ache in her leg was a reminder for her to sit down and she took the end of the bench as her place, the smooth surface of polished pine cool against the sticky heat of her thighs.

'If she gets caught,' Tiffany replied for Tina, 'then she'll get a few strokes against that pretty little backside she's parading for me. Won't you, darling?'

Nicola nodded again, hardly daring to look up. Her long hair fell forward, covering her face and obscuring her blue eyes. Tina could see the side of the skirt where it was carefully folded over, the thick pleats bent over at an angle, the smooth thighs and bare bottom now flat against the bench.

'I suppose she'll do anything for you,' Tina sighed, smiling knowingly at Tiffany, who raised her eyebrows and smiled back in response.

'Of course she will,' Tiffany purred. 'That's why we have these little tests, just to see how much darling Nicky loves me.'

'And is it true that you used to fuck your sister?' Tina asked, finding the courage to ask the question that she had wanted to ask for so long. It was a rumour that she had heard more than once and, exciting though it was to think about it, she had never really believed it.

Tiffany seemed to hold her breath, as though weighing up what her reaction should be. 'My *twin* sister,' she confirmed with a proud smile.

Tina felt her heart beat faster, excited by the image that confirmation had conjured up. The fact that Tiffany and her sister were twins added an extra frisson of excitement, an exotic element that enhanced the feeling of lust that flared so powerfully. It was true, and Tiffany was proud to admit it. 'The cards?' she asked hotly, forgetting about Nicola's presence completely.

'Yes,' Tiffany purred wickedly, 'I played cards and staked my sister for the night. I lost too, but I honoured my bet, no matter how much it pained Chantel.'

The three young women fell silent, Tina unable to get the images out of her head, Nicola in embarrassment and

Tiffany lost in memories of her sister. There could be no denying the excitement, the pure physical reaction that Tina felt. Her nipples were becoming hard, straining against the coarse material of her sports top, and her pussy was hot and tingly. It must have been a hot sight, she thought, picturing Tiffany and her mirror image locked in an embrace.

'Do you play cards?' Tiffany asked after a few minutes, drawing a sharp look from Nicola and a hopeful smile from Tina.

'Sure, I can play cards,' Tina lied, swivelling round on the bench to get a closer look at Nicola.

'Don't,' Nicola warned, her voice low and adamant.

'But darling,' Tiffany whispered, leaning across and sweeping Nicola's hair back, 'it's what I want.'

'We'll play fair,' Tina added, trying to reassure the girl who was obviously going to be the game's highest stake. There was something extravagantly decadent about Tiffany, a wild and immoral sexuality that was completely exciting and difficult to resist. Tina didn't want to resist, rather she couldn't wait to arrange the game, eager to enter it even though she couldn't play cards and had nothing to stake in return. The game wasn't important, winning or losing were mere details. It was the action of staking Nicola which was important.

'Tina?'

'Yes?' she snapped, looking up at the girl who had appeared from nowhere.

'I've got a note from a Mistress,' the woman reported sullenly, handing over a slip of paper.

'Who was it?' Tina asked irritably, snatching the paper from the messenger's hand.

The girl made no reply. She glared at all three young women on the bench and then turned on her heel and left, walking back the way she had come, along the corridor that separated the two main gymnasia in the sports hall.

'Shit, I have to go upstairs,' Tina complained disappointedly.

'You're joking,' Tiffany complained, looking thoroughly piqued by the unwelcome intrusion.

'If only I was,' Tina sighed, noting the look of relief on Nicola's red face.

'We can arrange the game another time,' Tiffany suggested, sliding her hand along Nicola's thigh.

'Yes, let's do that,' Tina agreed. She stood up tentatively, not sure how much her leg would ache. She took a step and was pleased to find that the worst of the pain had subsided.

Nicola's skirt had been lifted by now, Tiffany's hand sliding smoothly up the naked thighs and taking the hem of the skirt with it. It allowed Tina a glimpse of heaven, the smooth thighs meeting at a copper-coloured triangle of curls, the full, plump pussy lips displayed for a moment, a tantalising image of the prize being offered.

'Sure,' Tiffany concurred lazily, her fingers tracing the groove between Nicola's thighs, dark fingers exploring light skin. Nicola opened her mouth to complain but her words were sucked away by a full throaty kiss that seemed to melt away all conviction.

Tina nodded. She could see that Nicola was completely in Tiffany's power, that she was beautifully submissive to the frizzy-haired young woman who was a Mistress in everything but name.

The note contained a peremptory summons, and as Tina trudged up the stairs to the changing rooms she hardly gave it a second thought. Being summoned by a Mistress was nothing new, it happened all the time, and she had already decided that it probably had something to do with the game of netball she had been playing. What she was really interested in was getting back to Tiffany, whom she now regarded in a new light.

Tiffany was one of those girls with a reputation, a bad reputation, which was the only sort to have. Tina had heard all the stories and discounted them, unwilling to believe that any one person could be as depraved as the rumours suggested. Now, Tina smiled to herself, she was willing to admit that perhaps, just perhaps, some of the stories were true.

The door to the changing room was closed, so Tina knocked softly and waited for the command to enter. She pushed the door open and went in, brushing down her skirt first just to make herself presentable. The changing room was dark, only the lights by the shower were on, and the smell of stale sweat and disinfectant was overpowering. In the poor light Tina could see that the benches were bare, the tiled floor was free of shoes and bags and there was nothing dangling from the hooks on the walls.

'Mistress?' she ventured softly, peering into the changing room.

'Here, girl!' a voice snapped in reply.

Tina noted the angry tone with trepidation. She swallowed hard and walked towards the last row of benches, close to the shower which was silent and dry. The game of netball had been hard fought, and both teams had been jostling and pushing, but it was her that had been fouled and she had done no more than swear in retaliation. The knowledge that she was the injured party should have given her confidence but it didn't. Sometimes a Mistress could be ruthless, and would punish the victim as well as the perpetrator, to teach everyone involved a lesson.

Tina screamed as she was pushed from behind. She fell forward, crashing painfully to the ground. Everything was a blur of sound and movement and pain. Her knee ached, and her head spun. She tried to get up but was pushed down forcefully, strong hands holding her, other hands twining in her hair and grabbing a handful. She screamed again, struggled to push herself up and away from her assailants.

'Stop it, you stupid bitch!' a voice hissed angrily, a voice that Tina recognised at once. The fear overtook her, she felt the strength flow from her body.

'That's better,' the same voice remarked when Tina had stopped struggling.

'I tried to do my best,' she whispered softly. She hardly dared to look up, afraid that if she did so she would be attacked again. The Sisterhood had returned for her, angry that she had failed to deliver as promised.

'Liar!' a voice spat angrily, a voice filled with hatred and violence. The very sound of the words was painful, the single word like a slap across the face.

'I'll try again, I promise,' she cried, hoping desperately that they would believe her. And it was true, she would try again, but she needed time. They didn't understand what it was like to have Mistress Julie looking over your shoulder.

'I'm sure you will,' the first woman replied, her voice tinged with amusement.

'I will, I will,' Tina repeated desperately. The fear was like a drug pumping through her veins, distorting everything, magnifying and amplifying and making everything spin.

'You've disappointed us,' another voice said.

'We hate to be disappointed,' still another added.

'Do you remember what we said would happen?'

'But I did try,' Tina cried.

'Trying isn't good enough, it's results that count, isn't that right, girls?'

There were murmurs of agreement. Tina tried to work out how many there were around her, how many holding her down, how many standing around watching. It had to be a half dozen, more perhaps. Her face was down, looking directly at the tiles on the floor, her hair fallen forward so that she could hardly see anything. She didn't want to look up. She knew that if she did she'd be even more frightened, and that she would be punished even more.

'You're filthy,' the first voice informed her, sounding completely disgusted.

'You stink,' another agreed.

'Don't you bathe? Don't you wash yourself, slut?'

'I've been playing netball,' Tina whispered, trying to excuse herself. The jets of water that sprang to life with a sharp hiss startled her. The sound of the showers filled the air, a harsh sound as the forceful jets of water struck the hard stone floor and fizzed and bubbled along the gutter.

She was slapped around the face hard as she was pulled up. Everything was a blur, and before she had time to focus she was in darkness, a blindfold was tied around her eyes.

'Keep it on,' the leader warned threateningly. Tina had no intention of removing it, no matter how much panic she felt. She knew that if she did her punishment would be doubled or re-doubled. They only needed to imagine that she could identify them and they would make her life hell. The hands that had been holding her down now pulled her roughly to her feet in one dizzying motion. She reached out blindly, hands stretched out in front of her, searching for something to steady her, afraid that she would topple over and really hurt herself.

The blindfold was checked again as she blundered across the changing room, unseen hands pushing and directing her. The sound of the water was close, she tried to turn back, knowing that she was being deliberately steered into the water. She was shoved from behind, two pairs of hands forcing her over the threshold and into the shower. Her screams merged with the sound of the water that cascaded over her body. It was freezing, the cold jets soaking through her thin clothes, soaking right down to the skin. As she moved, hands across the wall for safety, jet after jet of water spat at her, the nozzles all in line and gushing down over her.

Her teeth were chattering from the cold, body tensed and shivering, her nipples were hard puckered little points against the sodden skin that was her skirt. Stumbling blindly she made it from one end of the shower and out the other, her tears lost in the icy water coursing down through her hair and over her face.

'Check the blindfold,' the leader ordered as Tina stumbled out of the shower, raining water with every step.

The blindfold was tightened, not that Tina had been able to see anything through it, a thick wet bandage around her eyes. The taunts and the jeers from the other girls were like barbs,.biting into her freezing flesh. She tried not to cry but it was impossible to hold back the tears, even though she knew that it gave her tormentors a grim kind of satisfaction.

'Strip her,' was the next order, delivered in the harsh tones that came so naturally to the leader of the Sisterhood, whoever she might be.

Tina stood helpless as her wet clothes were quickly stripped away, leaving her body exposed, cold and glistening with a thousand stars of icy water. Her top was pulled over her head and she heard it plop to the floor, a soaked bundle of fabric that formed a puddle where it fell. Her skirt slipped heavily to her ankles, her panties were almost torn from her body. She stood for a moment, shivering, alone, vulnerable. She was standing naked and wet, in the middle of the changing room and surrounded by an unseen number of cruel young female tormentors.

'We obviously didn't impress you enough last time,' the voice explained seriously, 'otherwise you would've been a good girl, wouldn't you?'

'I tried . . . really I did . . .' Tina sobbed helplessly, trying to cover her breasts with her hands, unable to stop herself shivering.

'Well, you'll have to try harder, won't you. Much harder.'

'I will, I promise I will,' Tina cried earnestly, wishing that she could make them believe her. Her nipples were hard and she could feel slick droplets of water coursing down over her body and dripping from the erect buds.

'Hands and knees,' was the next order, and uttered in a tone which expected complete obedience.

Tina did not disappoint, she obeyed without question, kneeling down on the cold floor, feeling her way in the darkness. She inched forward, out of the squelching bundle of her clothes strewn around her. Her body was still wet, her cold skin pouring rivulets of water, her long hair matted against her flesh.

'That's it, bitch, move forward,' the voice hissed, hot breath close to her ears.

She was afraid but she crawled forward slowly, trying to open her senses to the darkness around her, as if she could find her way by sense alone. In her mind she struggled to remember the geography of the changing room, hoping desperately to picture it so that she would not crash into the low-slung benches or against the cold concrete walls. Her harsh breathing smothered the sounds, much as she sought to control her feelings. There was a rustle of clothing behind her, a murmur of voices filled with amusement at her predicament.

She cried out suddenly and almost fell forward, her elbows buckling under the unexpected strain of having to carry someone. Someone had straddled her, sitting down in the middle of her back and grabbing handfuls of wet hair to use as reins. Tina could feel the heat from the other woman's sex, could feel the warmth of thighs that wrapped themselves around her. The other woman was naked, her sex rubbing wetly against the small of Tina's back.

The strain was almost unbearable but she had no choice. Choking back the tears and in total darkness she had to allow herself to be ridden and steered by the rider on her back. The audience were cheering and laughing, encouraging the rider and ridiculing Tina. Hands slapped her on the behind and geed her on, hard slaps that made her backside sting sharply. Other hands milked her breasts, pulling tight on the puckered up nipples that throbbed painfully and sent spasms of sensation through her body. The rider leant back, keeping one hand knotted in Tina's hair as a rein with which to steer, and with the other hand she stroked Tina's side.

'I can't . . . Please.' Tina complained, her strength ebbing with every inch. Her arms and legs were shaking, her knees screaming pain, her back ached.

The rider responded instantly with a sharp slap on the behind and a direct order for silence. Tina complied, her breath was too short for talking anyway. The tweaking of her breasts was causing confusion. Again she found herself responding sexually to the humiliation and the pain. The blindfold, like the mask before it, was a barrier behind which she was hidden, creating a secret realm that could not otherwise exist. In her mind she could see herself, being ridden like a pony, wet and naked and surrounded by contemptuous young women who had complete access to her body.

She held her breath, afraid that her sighs would give her away. The hard smacks on the bottom had stopped, and now a heat suffused her flesh, a heat that radiated through her body and into her sex. Her pussy bud was a throbbing bulb of pleasure that burned with the same heat as the redness on her flesh. The rider leant back once more, and this time her hand began to play with the bulging pussy lips, slipping a cold finger into the wetness and warmth of the opening. Tina bit her lip as the fingers, so knowingly sensual, touched and caressed, tantalised and lingered. Jewels of wetness were drawn from within and smeared over the cold flesh, her clit was toyed with, touched lightly and then pressed more firmly.

The last few steps were a nightmare of pleasure and pain. Tina felt herself on edge, her body ready to collapse into the most glorious of climaxes as she carried her cruel and unknown Mistress across the room. A sharp pull of her hair and she stopped, her pussy weeping tears of sex juice, her body trembling with desire. She was pushed forward again. She allowed herself to be pushed and moved, powerless in her desire and in her blindness. Warm thighs wrapped around her head, the bouquet of sex, the tickling of soft downy hair, the feel of pussy lips against her mouth. There was no need for a command, her instincts were in the ascendant. She began to lap and lick, her tongue eagerly working between the labia of an unseen pussy. Unseen but slick with nectar that she licked into her mouth to savour and swallow.

As she sucked, her own quim was caressed from behind, fingers moving in and out quickly, while other fingers played with her pointed breasts. Like a dream, it was too much, too much sensation, too much pleasure, too much to resist. She cried her orgasm into the pussy that she sucked, her hot breath and wet tongue giving delight as she herself received a pleasure that was darker than any she had ever known.

The knocking on the door was tentative, a light touch of fingers of wood, a question and not a demand. Very nervously, Rebecca stood and walked across to the door, certain that only a face to face confrontation would do. All day she had brooded on the previous evening's events, running them over again and again in her mind, seeking an explanation that made sense. No explanation had been forthcoming, and there was nothing that could explain what it was that had happened. She and Simone were attracted to each other, that was certain, and when they had kissed the effect had been electric, that too was clear. But what followed made no sense to Rebecca. They had kissed, felt the shared desire swelling up like an electrical storm, and then she had been dismissed. There was no other word for it. Simone had dismissed her as though nothing had happened. What was worse, she had even asked Rebecca to cook dinner, as though Rebecca were a domestic to be ordered about as she saw fit.

There was no dinner, and now Rebecca was ready to open the door and give Simone a piece of her mind. She paused at the door for a moment, trying to summon the anger that had seethed all day, but it was gone. Instead she felt a strange sort of confusion that was toned with an inexplicable sense of excitement.

'Yes?' she demanded, acting out the anger she did not feel.

Simone looked at her coldly, her dark eyes and level gaze not in the least bit surprised by the angry tone. 'Such hostility,' she remarked.

'What do you expect?' Rebecca asked, standing by the door, barring the entrance to her room. Her knuckles were white where she gripped the door, afraid that if she relaxed for an instant Simone would barge in and . . . She didn't know what, and part of her was excited by that confusion and another part of her rebelled against it.

'I expect that you would rather kiss me,' Simone replied unsmilingly.

Rebecca swallowed hard. It wasn't the answer she expected, but it was so obviously true that it frightened her. How could Simone be so sure? How could she even guess what was going on Rebecca's mind? 'Why should I? So that you can send me away again?' she demanded, the hurt showing through.

Simone smiled at last, her dark eyes opening up, widening slightly. She was so beautiful, her dark skin flawlessly perfect, her lips sensual and inviting.

Rebecca was falling, dragged down by the seductive gaze of the other woman, a gaze that could see deep and understand. It was hard to resist, so easy to let herself go and fall into Simone's arms. So easy, but resist she did. 'Why do you play these mind games?' she asked softly.

'What makes you think I'm playing mind games?'

'What else were you doing last night?'

'It hadn't occurred to you that I was telling the truth? That I was tired, that I had too many things still to do?'

Simone sounded so reasonable, her words without rancour or emotion, that Rebecca suddenly felt quite foolish. That Simone had been acting honestly had not been one of the things she had considered. All day she had been brooding and sulking, imagining that Simone had been manipulative and devious which was apparently far from the truth. 'I'm sorry,' she apologised, her face blushing red with embarrassment, 'I was so put out that I imagined all sorts of things.'

'I see,' Simone said levelly. 'What makes you think I'm even capable of playing the sort of games that you imagined?'

A shrug and more blushes. 'I don't know. You're sort of . . . very strange, Simone. I'm sorry if that sounds bad, but I've never met anyone like you before.'

'Perhaps you're still thinking about Marcia?'

'No, definitely not!' Rebecca replied sharply. 'I haven't thought about her once all day.'

'Then you've been thinking of me,' Simone guessed, smiling.

Again Rebecca felt the heat touch her cheeks, her face glowing with a schoolgirl blush that was quite uncharacteristic. She was a woman and well versed in affairs of the heart, or so she had always assumed. 'If I were cynical I'd say that I'd just been manipulated again,' she said quietly, not daring to meet Simone's bewitchingly dark eyes.

'You have lipstick on,' Simone noted, her surprise tempered by delight.

'A small act of liberation,' Rebecca explained, trying to make it sound as if the act of applying red lip gloss were an important political act.

'You don't have to justify it,' Simone said. 'You're in my house now, you can do things for pleasure, you don't have to proclaim every act as being of fundamental political importance.'

'But . . .'

Simone pushed gently on the door and Rebecca stepped back. They stood inside the room, face to face. Simone reached out and touched Rebecca's face with the tips of her fingers, stroking the soft skin that had coloured red moments earlier. They moved together naturally, their lips meeting in a kiss that had Rebecca melting. She tried to reach up again, to take Simone's face in her hands but Simone wouldn't allow it. They kissed again and again, and all the time Rebecca's arms were at her sides, hanging limply as though excluded from the caress.

When they parted, Simone smiled and touched her again, fingertips barely registering on Rebecca's skin. Simone traced a line, from the eyes, over the high cheek-bones, past the mouth and down the soft skin of Rebecca's neck. It was a gentle exploration that seemed to mean more. For a moment Rebecca felt there was an almost possessive intent about it, that she were being possessed by Simone. Another kiss and Rebecca could feel the moistness of her panties, her body responding naturally to every whisper of every caress.

'Let's go to bed,' Rebecca whispered imploringly, taking Simone's hand and showering it with hot fevered kisses.

Simone looked at Rebecca for a second and then closed her eyes for a second and opened them again. Rebecca knelt down, obeying Simone's silent directions. She knelt down in front of her, looking up into Simone's eyes as though searching for meaning. Very slowly Simone began to unbutton the dress she was wearing, from the high collar downwards. Each button revealed a little more, first the throat and neck, then the swell of the breasts, the slight curve of her belly, the bulge of her mons. At last the dress was open, and Simone stood there, her full pert breasts cased in a satin bra that bulged at the nipples, the black panties that wore the shape of her sex.

'Suck me,' Simone whispered, pulling her panties down and exposing her sex, the fullness of her pussy lips fringed with jet black curls, the pink flesh of her pussy an enticing vision. She stepped out of her panties, placing feet apart, heels standing firmly on the ground. Rebecca moved forward, her hands sliding up the long smoothness of Simone's thighs, revelling in the feel of flesh on flesh. She breathed Simone's natural scent, her lips sowing soft kisses on the silky smooth skin.

'No. No hands,' Simone instructed as she bent down and kissed Rebecca's upturned mouth.

'I don't understand,' Rebecca whispered, looking up, the hurt and the confusion fighting through the pleasure of the kisses.

'Kiss me, give me pleasure, but don't touch,' Simone instructed. She reached out and touched her finger to Rebecca's mouth and then touched her own pussy lips, her dark finger pressing into herself.

Rebecca didn't understand, but that no longer mattered. She kissed Simone again on the inside of the thigh, her lips touching the warm soft flesh that was like heaven. Then she touched her tongue over the pussy lips, prising open the heart of Simone's sex. She kissed her there, a hard kiss that had her pushing her tongue into the heat of sex, into the moistness of pleasure. She licked hard, pushing her tongue deep and drawing in the honey that flowed. Simone tasted divine and in response she felt her own pleasure redoubled.

Moving up she lapped at the pussy bud, at the pulsing heart that she had exposed. Simone sighed, her voice soft and sweet. It was music to Rebecca's ears, she lapped harder, using her tongue to tease and delight. Nothing mattered any more, all that mattered was that she give pleasure, that she please Simone. On her hands and knees, not even allowed to touch Simone with her hands, she understood that to give pleasure was an even greater pleasure.

Simone gasped and grabbed Rebecca and forced her closer. Rebecca used her tongue, used her lips, used her teeth, and was rewarded with Simone's climax. As she sucked the nectar that poured from Simone's hot pussy, her own juices flowed. Again, she decided at that moment, she was going to make Simone climax again.

Chapter Six

The gentle knock on the door was not entirely unexpected. Simone smiled to herself before calling out to Rebecca to enter. She turned back to the dressing table, selected a bright red lipstick to apply, and watched a nervous-looking Rebecca enter the room. There was no need to act surprised, nor to indicate to Rebecca that her early morning visit was in any way unusual. Instead, she pursed her lips and applied a thick layer of sweet tasting red gloss.

Rebecca waited for a moment, her eyes meeting Simone's in the mirror and then turning away. When Simone made no move to open the conversation she took a step closer, stopping awkwardly by the bed, standing directly behind Simone, who was undressed and seated comfortably on the vanity chair by the dressing table. 'Simone?' she asked nervously, 'can we talk?'

Simone waited until her lips were perfect before replying with a nod to the mirror, her eyes catching the unease in Rebecca's expression.

'It's about last night,' Rebecca continued, her voice faltering.

'Of course,' Simone agreed.

'It's just that when we spoke you said that there would be no mind games, no screwing with each other's head. Isn't that right?'

'Is that what we said?' Simone asked, turning to face Rebecca, aware that her flimsy gown had fallen open and that the swell of her dark breasts was visible. 'Think carefully,' she added, moving back a little so that the fullness of her nipples was impressed on the silky gown, now partly open to the waist.

Rebecca hesitated, her eyes grew wider, focusing on Simone's breasts and on the dark thighs that the short gown barely covered. She seemed to struggle for a moment, her mouth opening wordlessly before she snapped back to attention. 'That's what you were implying,' she said firmly. She lifted her gaze, dragging her eyes from Simone's thighs, pausing at the open cleavage and then meeting Simone's questioning eyes.

'Perhaps you're right,' Simone conceded. 'Perhaps I gave that impression. Or perhaps you wanted me to give that impression. Is that why you're here?' she asked, a half-smile flickering on her freshly glossed lips. She liked the way that Rebecca was struggling with herself, trying to retain whatever feeling she had when she had knocked on the door and not to let herself be distracted by the sight of Simone's partly clothed body.

'You *are* playing games with me,' Rebecca stated sullenly. 'Why are you doing this? I thought you were . . .'

'I'd like you to bathe me tomorrow,' Simone said, seizing on Rebecca's hesitation. 'In the morning, before you do anything else.'

'There you go again!' Rebecca complained plaintively. Her eyes were ringed with dark shadows, the kind that only a sleepless night can produce. She sounded tired, as though the night had been spent wrestling demons or fighting with an unruly conscience.

'How would you like me to behave?' Simone retorted, smiling for the first time. Her expression was relaxed and she felt fully in control, knowing exactly what it was that Rebecca felt.

'I don't understand you,' Rebecca complained, taking a step nearer.

'Let me phrase the question for you. You want to know why you can't touch me. You want to know why you have to be on hands and knees, why you're not allowed to caress me with your hands. You want to know why I won't let you spend the night in my bed. Am I right?'

Rebecca looked as if her worst nightmares were coming to pass. For a moment she was very still, then she drew a sharp breath. 'Yes,' she whispered, letting the word escape with the breath that she sighed heavily.

'Because you respond to it,' Simone told her, letting her robe fall completely open. She was seated on the edge of the seat, legs crossed and elegant thighs fully displayed, leaning forward and resting her chin in the palm of her hand, her bare breasts caressed by the loose fold of her robe.

Rebecca made no reply for a moment, then, sitting heavily on the edge of the bed, she looked at Simone sharply. 'But I don't want it to be like this,' she explained softly. 'I want to be close to you, I don't want this distance.'

'Yes you do, I can see that the very idea of it arouses you. That's the part that you find so hard to take, that you are turned on by that distance.'

There was another pause while Rebecca reflected on what Simone had told her. Her face had lost its colour and she looked as though her whole world had collapsed. And yet she could not stop herself sneaking glances at Simone, admiring the perfection of her body, aroused by the sights of pert nipples and long smooth thighs.

Simone turned back to the mirror, checked her lips again and then stood up. The silence in the room was anxious, heavy, dragged down by Rebecca's sinking mood. Always the anguish, Simone reflected, always the pain of self-discovery. Why was it never easy? Why did no one ever accept their nature without question?

'I'm not the first, am I?' Rebecca asked suddenly, looking up, her eyes full of horror and fascination.

'No, not the first,' Simone admitted, her smile an attempt to defuse the situation. She felt tired, the trouble at the Institute was taking its toll. Formerly she would have had Rebecca punished, turned her over on hands and knees and applied a few brisk strokes to the backside, but now she could not summon up the energy. There was something different about Rebecca also, she was not a typical subservient, she was too wilful, too full of questions and ideas for that.

'I'm leaving,' Rebecca announced, without the histrionics that she had served up to Marcia. 'I trusted you, now I see that that was a mistake.'

'You're not the first,' Simone told her, sitting beside her on the bed, 'and you won't be the last. When I offered you a place to stay there were no ulterior motives, none at all. That something has developed between us is entirely accidental. If you want it to stop then it'll stop. The room is yours regardless. If you don't want it to stop then don't be surprised if our relationship develops in ways that you hadn't anticipated. Now, if you want to leave, then please do. However, if you were merely making an empty threat then I would ask you to leave immediately, I don't like empty gestures.'

Rebecca listened in silence and then stood up, her face was marked by indecision. Avoiding Simone's eyes she turned and walked to the door. 'I'll be packing my things,' she said, halting at the door and looking back.

Simone watched her go, listened to her footsteps on the stairs and finally heard the door downstairs close. She sighed heavily. For the first time she felt waves of exhaustion pass through her. Rebecca was different, her personality was complicated, her moods complex and baffling. In many ways she reminded Simone of herself. She could remember how she had been at the same age: headstrong, opinionated, angry, sensual, adventurous. It was that recognition, unconscious at first, that Simone had found so attractive about Rebecca, and which had drawn them together so quickly and unexpectedly.

As she dressed, her thoughts went back to all the others that had shared her house, male and female, each of them unique yet each of them yielding to her sexually. She could savour the memories, so powerful and affecting, as each had finally submitted to her, accepting for the first time that they were submissive and that she was their Mistress. Some, like Jaki, had lost themselves totally in her, finding their true nature at her heels.

Jaki. In that indefinable way that a fragment of memory can spark off a thousand associations and give birth to a hundred ideas everything fell into place.

She finished dressing and strode to the door. Rebecca would have to wait, she realised sadly, something far more urgent had occurred to her. Her heels on the wooden floor echoed throughout the house, sharp snaps of sound that had been music to Jaki's ears. That time had long passed, but it was a fond memory and she was certain that Jaki too savoured such memories. Their relationship had been so intense, a firestorm of passion and desire that had held Jaki in thrall.

'Simone?' Rebecca asked, standing at her door, waiting nervously for Simone to reach the bottom of the stairs.

Simone stopped and looked at her without emotion, waiting for whatever was to come next, good news or bad.

'I'm sorry,' Rebecca apologised earnestly, her face coloured red with emotion.

'Next time I'll punish you,' Simone threatened evenly, her face austere and unemotional.

'Punish?'

'I'll lay you across the armchair and beat you on the backside until you've had enough. Then you'll thank me by pleasuring me with your tongue. Think about that while I'm at work today.'

'Punish?' Rebecca repeated incredulously.

Simone smiled curtly and then continued on her way out. She wondered whether Rebecca would still be there on her return that evening. In her heart she knew that Rebecca would stay. The promise of punishment, which had come as such a shock, opened up a whole new world of possibilities that would be impossible to refuse.

Harriet buzzed for Jaki and Vicky, who appeared promptly moments later, a slight look of alarm in their eyes. Jaki was wearing a smart red skirt and loose blouse, an outfit that could light up even the dullest of rooms. In contrast Vicky's clothes were functional and sober, tight grey skirt and white polo neck top, tight enough to display the outline of her breasts but not enough to turn heads in the street.

'I've had an unexpected telephone call from a dear

friend,' Harriet announced, directing her gaze first to Vicky and then to Jaki. 'Mistress Shirer and I will be meeting for lunch,' she added, 'and there is every possibility that I will bring her back here after lunch.'

'She's not checking up on us, is she?' Vicky asked anxiously.

Harriet smiled. 'No, both of you have nothing to do with the Institute now, though naturally she'll be asking about your progress. However, if she does come back for a visit I want everything to be perfect, is that understood?'

'Don't worry,' Jaki assured her, 'everything will be fine.'

'Of course it will,' Vicky concurred. 'We both know what'll happen otherwise.'

Harriet seemed satisfied with the assurances. 'Good. Now Jaki you can look after the telephones while I'm out, and Vicky you can finish off all the paperwork in here. I'll be at the usual place for lunch, but no calls, not under any circumstances, OK?'

Jaki nodded. 'I'll just take messages,' she said, 'anything urgent will go to the top of the pile.'

All three walked to the top of the stairs, Harriet proffering last minute instructions even as she donned the jacket of her sharp, fashionable business suit. The taxi arrived before she reached the bottom of the stairs, and Vicky and Jaki had to urge her on the way by reminding her of the time.

'Right, coffee time,' Vicky announced briskly, 'and it's your turn to make it.'

'But it's always my turn,' Jaki complained, crossing her arms and walking back across the office.

'That's because you're good at coffee,' Vicky told her. 'Now, hurry up. Bring mine into the office when it's ready.'

Jaki shot her a look that was sharp enough to cut but it was ignored, Vicky breezing into Harriet's office with a proprietorial air. That was always her way, Jaki sighed to herself. As soon as Harriet was out of the way Vicky would always assume airs and graces, seeing herself as Harriet's heir apparent. She would bark orders, rush in and out, criticise, delegate her work to whoever else was there, which was often just Jaki or one or two of the others. All of them had passed through the Institute, but Vicky had been a prefect and the dominant attitude had never left her.

Vicky was sitting behind Harriet's desk when Jaki brought in the coffee a few minutes later. 'Round here,' she said, pointing to a space on the desk.

'If Harriet catches you . . .' Jaki warned, stepping round the side of the desk to deposit the cup where Vicky had pointed. The self-satisfied smirk on Vicky's face was expected, the hand on her thigh wasn't.

'You are a good girl, sometimes,' Vicky cooed, sliding her hand over Jaki's glassy thigh. She leaned back in her chair, enjoying the chance to take it easy for a while. The paperwork that she was supposed to be sorting out was still on her own desk, out in the main office.

'Stop that,' Jaki objected, smacking away Vicky's hand that had settled comfortably on the inside of her thigh. It wasn't that she did not enjoy the soft caresses under her skirt, but rather she was afraid of what Mistress Shirer's visit might mean for them.

'Don't snap,' Vicky replied coldly, placing her hand back where it had rested, on the inside of Jaki's lovely long thighs. 'Besides, I know you like it. Harriet's always touching you up.'

Jaki pulled away, stepping right back from the desk and Vicky's wandering hands. 'You are not Harriet,' she declared airily, 'and I've got work to be getting on with, even if you haven't.'

The phone was ringing when Jaki was back at her desk, she took a deep breath and answered in her best telephone voice, scribbling a message on a yellow notelet for Harriet. The office was quite busy that morning, and the flow of calls and messages soon mounted up. She barely had time to check the clock, nor time to worry too much about the visit of her first Mistress. When she did think about it she was filled with trepidation. Mistress Shirer did not usually arrange impromptu lunch appointments, and Jaki was certain that something important was happening. Thankfully the phone calls and the arrival of the post were welcome distractions to stop her dwelling on such thoughts.

Later on in the morning Vicky called for coffee and when none was forthcoming she stormed out to make her own, casting an angry look at Jaki who smiled back sweetly. Vicky swore under her breath, grabbed the pile of papers from her desk and decamped to Harriet's office, slamming the door angrily behind her.

By noon Jaki had sorted out the pile of notes into three neat bundles, ranked in order of urgency. Back in Harriet's office she was glad to see that Vicky had been getting on with her own work rather than lazing around acting high and mighty.

'Nearly finished?' she asked, walking across to the desk.

'Nearly,' Vicky mumbled sullenly, looking up from her work. The coffee cup beside her was full and had formed a skin where it had cooled down.

Jaki ignored the sullen tone, she hated it when people were upset with her and always did her best to smooth things over. 'Another coffee?' she asked, picking up the cup before Vicky had even nodded her assent. 'They might be back soon,' she remarked, walking towards the door again.

'If Mistress Shirer decides to come back,' Vicky called after her.

When Jaki returned with the coffee, Vicky was leaning back in Harriet's seat again, arms behind her head, looking relaxed and confident again. Jaki smiled at her and placed the coffee cup where it had rested earlier. The hand that touched her behind the knee was no surprise this time.

'What do you think this is all about?' Jaki asked, closing her eyes slightly as Vicky stroked her on the inner thigh. It felt good, she could not deny that. Her skirt was loosely flared, and, when she looked across to the punishment glass, she could see Vicky's hand sliding up and down. Their eyes met in the mirror, a possessive gleam in Vicky's and a look of pleasure in Jaki's.

'No idea,' Vicky said. 'Are you bothered by it?'

Jaki sighed, the outline of her tight silky panties was being traced, two fingers sliding under the crotch and between the rear cleft. 'I'm just curious, that's all,' she managed to lie. Without really wanting to she parted her thighs, the pleasure of being caressed was making her hot and excited. Vicky knew it too. She knew that Jaki would be unable to resist the pleasure.

'Is this what Harriet does to you?' Vicky asked, sliding her fingers under the silk, her fingers now pressed between the warmth of Jaki's arse-cheeks.

'They might come back . . .' Jaki sighed softly, closing her eyes dreamily. She leant forward, placing her arms on the edge of the desk to support herself.

'Forget them,' Vicky suggested, her voice a whisper that was insinuating and seductive. With her other hand she reached under Jaki's skirt and began to stroke the masculine hardness that was deliciously enmeshed in the silky panties. She loved to stroke Jaki, it was always a thrill to find a lovely hard prick under such pretty feminine finery.

'Don't do that,' Jaki purred in a tone that suggested she never wanted it to stop. She almost swooned when Vicky began to touch her finger against the tight anal bud.

'Don't you like me touching your pussy?' Vicky asked, pursing her lips like a spoilt child.

'You mustn't.'

'Oh, but I must,' Vicky insisted. She pulled Jaki round so that they were facing each other, Jaki standing up while she was comfortable in Harriet's chair. 'Now, what do we have under here?' she asked teasingly.

Jaki allowed herself to be pulled into place, said nothing when her skirt was pulled up to reveal her thick hard prick encased in soft red lace. Every whisper of silk against her erection was a sweep of pleasure, causing flutters of sensation that made her sigh feverishly. She was falling, lost in the most voluptuous of pleasures imaginable.

Vicky slipped off the chair and knelt down in front of Jaki, unable to take her eyes from the reddish glans that poked through the fine silk knickers. Already, tears of lubrication were dribbling down the thickly veined rod, touching silvery strands on to the silk. Jaki's thighs were soft and smooth, a feminine delight that Vicky loved to stroke and kiss.

'Don't do this,' Jaki sighed, her final resistance giving way when she felt Vicky's kisses on her skin.

Vicky kissed the inner thighs, her lips cool and soft against skin that felt as if it was on fire. As she kissed, her face rubbed against the hard cock, which flexed responsively, pressing against the tight panties. She worked her hands under the panties, pulling them down very slowly, revealing more and more of Jaki's hard prick and the smoothly shaved abdomen. Her tongue licked the glans, momentarily tasting the silvery fluid that glistened against the smooth skin.

Taking the glans fully into her mouth, Vicky also pressed the middle finger of her right hand into the tight roundness of Jaki's rear-hole. Jaki squirmed for a moment, trying to resist the irresistible, then she let out a loud sigh and allowed herself to be deliciously violated. Vicky felt the fires in her own belly, the juices running from her wet pussy, the excitement growing moment by moment. The middle fingers of her left hand snaked down under her own skirt, pressing against the white panties that covered her sex.

Jaki opened her eyes dreamily, saw herself caught in the mirror, body held stiffly, head thrown back with ecstasy, her skirt over Vicky's head which was bobbing up and down. Vicky was sucking expertly, using her mouth and tongue as she worked up and down, her tongue lashing the sensitive spot under the glans. The blissful feeling of having her cock mouthed was heightened by the way her backside was being caressed. For every moan of pleasure that was caused by Vicky's joyous cock sucking there was a sigh caused from the pleasure in her arsehole.

With her finger deep in the warm tightness of Jaki's anal passage and her own fingers playing with her clit, Vicky climaxed suddenly, the pleasure rippling from her sex in a wave that made her catch her breath. A second later she felt the explosion that pumped juicy wads of come into her mouth as Jaki climaxed too. Vicky sucked hard, drawing in every iota of the spurting juice that surged from the base of Jaki's cock and erupted from the tip. The orgasm shook

Jaki, her body trembling as she fell back a little, forcing Vicky's finger deeper into the rear-hole.

The sound of the front door carried up the stairs and through the building. Immediately Vicky was up, gathering her papers and trying to compose herself at the same time. Jaki felt dizzy but a surge of panic forced her to act quickly. Her panties were around her knees, she let them fall to her ankles and then quickly stepped out of them and dropped them into the bin under the desk. Glancing in the mirror she could see that her face was flushed and her hair out of place. There were voices on the stairs, two voices and getting closer. Vicky was out of Harriet's office before Jaki had even registered the fact, but that was good because it meant that Harriet and Mistress Shirer stopped to have a word with her. In those few seconds Jaki made herself presentable, tidied up the desk and struggled to catch her breath.

'It's been a long time, Jaki, hasn't it?' Mistress Shirer said, preceding Harriet into the office.

She looked as stunningly beautiful as ever, Jaki saw. Dressed impeccably, so stunningly elegant that it hurt to look at her, and as always that distant and austere look that caused excitement and desire in equal measure. For a moment Jaki didn't know how to react. Her first impulse was to fall to her knees and to kiss the heels of *the* Mistress. 'Yes, Mistress, a long time,' she uttered finally, almost tongue-tied with nerves.

'Have you been busy?' Harriet asked, striding across to her desk and the piles of messages.

'Yes, Mistress,' Jaki said, finding that in Mistress Shirer's presence she had to call Harriet Mistress too.

'Coffee?' Harriet asked Simone, who nodded her reply.

Jaki understood at once and turned to go, but Harriet stopped her. 'I'll get Vicky to make some coffee,' she said. 'Now, I'll leave you two alone, Simone.'

'Thank you, Harriet,' Mistress Shirer said with a smile. 'I doubt that we will be long,' she added, turning her dark eyes to Jaki.

* * *

After Mistress Shirer had gone, Harriet called Jaki into her office. Jaki looked flustered when she arrived, as though her interview with Mistress Shirer had been a traumatic affair. Harriet looked at her tenderly, her smile one of affection more than anything else.

'Simone says that you haven't agreed yet,' Harriet reported, her voice suggesting that she understood the decision.

'That's right,' Jaki agreed, her voice dulled by confusion. She stood in front of the desk, her back to the punishment glass, looking as though she were about to be punished for some office misdemeanour.

'That's understandable. When she first asked me I must admit that I was totally surprised by her request.' Harriet paused a moment before adding, 'But I can see that what she says makes sense.'

Jaki shook her head. 'Does it? Do you remember the last crisis at the Institute? Do you remember the panic when it seemed that the press had caught on to the story?'

'Of course I do,' Harriet said sombrely. 'We were all involved, not just you. But the problem was resolved in the end, and look what it did for you. Before Mistress Shirer and the Institute you were just J.K., a confused kid with an identity problem. If it wasn't for her, Jaki, you wouldn't be here.'

'It frightens me,' Jaki admitted softly, running a hand through her hair. It was the absolute truth. She was frightened of the Institute. The atmosphere there was almost of hysteria, a kind of pressure cooker waiting to explode – the perverse eroticism charged the atmosphere with an energy that was dangerously high. Yet it worked, against all the rules and common sense it worked. It changed people in ways that could not be imagined, using techniques that beggared belief.

'When do you have to decide by?'

'Tomorrow,' Jaki said, inhaling sharply.

'And have you made a decision?'

Another sad shake of the head. Jaki was torn by conflicting emotions. Yes, she wanted to help, Mistress Shirer meant so much to her. No, she was afraid of getting caught up again in the intrigues that surrounded something as secret and as important as the Institute. Harriet nodded understandingly and then lapsed into the same heavy silence as Jaki. The sudden visit from Simone had obviously unnerved her also, and Jaki guessed that she was wary of making her feelings known. The decision had to be Jaki's and hers alone and Harriet was kind enough not to let her own feelings interfere with that decision.

For several long seconds no one spoke, Jaki stood awkwardly in front of the desk, looking at nothing as she pondered on what to do next. 'I'd better do some work,' she finally sighed, looking up with a start when the shrill call of the telephone broke the silence.

The telephone stopped ringing before Harriet had time to pick it up. It had broken the silence but the tense atmosphere had not been so easily dispelled, Jaki looked ill at ease and nervous, and this seemed to be communicated to Harriet. 'If you prefer to go home early . . .' she suggested helpfully.

'No, I'd only mope about and worry,' Jaki replied, a tight-lipped smile on her face.

Harriet accepted this without comment. She flicked idly through the pile of telephone messages that Jaki had collected for her, marking off the ones that she wanted to follow up. The ones that she didn't want she began to put to one side, and as she worked through them she kept sneaking glances at Jaki, who had not taken a single step towards the door.

'You're moping about and worrying,' Harriet pointed out, not looking up from the papers on the desk.

'But at least I'm here with you.'

'This is no good,' Harriet said briskly, putting aside the papers. 'If you're going to brood then do it elsewhere. If you stay here then I want some work from you.'

Jaki smiled, the sharp tone was just what she wanted. 'Slave driver,' she complained softly, filled with gratitude for Harriet's firm good sense.

'There is just one thing though,' Harriet said, regarding Jaki sternly. 'Perhaps you could explain these?'

Jaki lost her smile. Harriet had fished into the bin and produced a pair of silky red knickers, a dainty little garment that she twirled in her fingers. 'It wasn't me,' Jaki cried instantly, remembering that under her skirt she wore nothing.

'Lift your skirt,' Harriet demanded, still dangling the panties from the end of her long painted finger-nails.

'When I said it wasn't me . . .' Jaki began to explain, the excitement making her voice quiver.

'Lift your skirt,' Harriet repeated, her voice harsh and cold.

There was no way out of it. Jaki lifted her skirt slightly, enough to display the tops of her smoothly shaved thighs and her cock that was slowly twitching to erection. 'I meant it wasn't my fault,' she protested.

'Are you saying that it was Vicky's fault?'

Jaki's eyes widened. 'No,' she murmured, averting her gaze.

Harriet shook her head sadly and leaned across to the telephone, pressing the buzzer that would summon Vicky instantly. 'Would you like to explain this?' she asked, waving the panties as soon as Vicky was through the door.

'I'm sorry, Miss,' Vicky told her earnestly, walking slowly towards the desk but making sure that her eyes did not meet Jaki's, 'but it's nothing to do with me.' To prove the point she stopped at the desk and lifted her skirt up, showing off creamy white panties that were almost transparent.

'Jaki?' Harriet asked.

Jaki looked away guiltily. She had nothing to say, there was no way to avoid the inevitable punishment. Telling the truth would mean that both she and Vicky would be punished by Harriet, and probably most severely. Later on she would also be punished by Vicky, who would accuse her of being a snitch and who would make sure that her hurt would be paid for in full.

'Then am I to assume that Vicky has nothing to do with this?' Harriet asked, though it was patently obvious to all of them that that was definitely not the case.

'Yes,' Jaki admitted softly. It wasn't fair, it was never

fair, never. She looked at Vicky who was wearing an expression of complete innocence.

'I find that difficult to believe,' Harriet admitted. 'Are you telling the truth, Jaki?'

'She is,' Vicky asserted, kicking Jaki in the ankle at the same time.

'I'm sorry, I . . . It was me, Vicky had nothing to do with it,' she confessed.

'Then I'll have to punish you,' Harriet decided promptly. 'I'll tan that pretty little backside that you are obviously so keen to display. I do not want my girls parading around without their knickers on, is that clear?'

'Yes, Miss,' Vicky parroted back the reply, eager to witness the punishment that she had managed to avoid.

'Over the desk,' Harriet instructed. She reached down and opened the bottom drawer. For a moment she dawdled over her choice of implement.

Jaki bent across the desk, pressing her face down flat on the cool surface of polished oak. The edges of the desk pressed against her body, a sharp line across the waist that was painful and unyielding. She waited anxiously, biting her lower lip and wondering what Harriet was going to choose.

'Shall I lift her skirt?' Vicky asked helpfully, hiding the smile that Jaki knew should have been there.

'Yes, you do that,' Harriet agreed. 'The cane I think,' she announced, sounding pleased with her choice.

Vicky moved quickly, lifting the short skirt to fully expose Jaki's naked posterior. At the same time she surreptitiously stroked a finger over the curves, enjoying the feel of a taut backside waiting to be chastised.

'The cane? But I wasn't so bad,' Jaki moaned, her eyes fixing on the long flexible rattan cane, the curved handle and slight arc speaking volumes for the efficacy of the cane as an instrument for correction. The cane hurt like nothing else, more direct and painful than the hand or a paddle, sharper than the strap and less bearable.

'The cane because you've been untruthful as well as naughty,' Harriet explained seriously.

'I haven't. Please, Mistress, I've been good,' Jaki begged, knowing it was pointless to beg but unable to stop herself. There was always the chance, the minute possibility, that Mistress would think again, would stop and reconsider. The strap, that would have been better, Jaki thought hopefully.

'Tell me what you were doing,' Harriet advised. She had taken her position, directly behind Jaki, the cane held comfortably in her right hand. Her eyes travelled over the exposed part of Jaki's body, from the ankles, over the long feminine legs, to the heavy ball sac at the join, to the bottom-cheeks that were slightly parted and almost obscured the dark rear opening.

'I was only posing,' Jaki cried, desperate to find a story that would deflect some of the punishment. 'I wasn't sure that these knicks were right for me,' she improvised, 'so I was looking at myself in the mirror. They're new, and they're too loose so I took them off, to take back and change. When I heard that you and Mistress Shirer were back I panicked and dropped them into the bin.'

'Do not insult my intelligence, girl,' Harriet cried scornfully. 'I had planned on six strokes, you've now earned yourself another three. Really, Jaki, you disappoint me so.'

'I'm sorry, Mistress,' Jaki whispered mournfully. Disappointing Harriet made her feel bad, far worse than the cane ever could because it hurt her emotionally. It was stupid, and she regretted piling lies on to lies, but it was too late for regrets.

'Count them out,' Harriet told Vicky, who was watching excitedly, her eyes moving from the whiteness of Jaki's behind to the end of the cane that swung menacingly from Harriet's hand.

Jaki tensed as the cane cut through the air with a whistle. The snap as it landed was lost in her cry of pain, the cutting pain biting through to the core. Vicky looked on, forgetting to count out the first stroke until reminded by a pointed look from Harriet. The second stroke followed, a swish as the cane sliced cleanly through the air, a sharp crack of sound and then a cry of pain and alarm, the count uttered in a whisper.

The third stroke landed as hard as the two first, Jaki could feel the individual lattice lines etched on her flesh, sharp red tracks that burned on her skin. A fourth stroke and then a fifth, an indeterminate pause between each stroke while the sharpest edges of the pain melted into the heat of punishment. The wait was terrible, the tension rising, trying to anticipate the slice of the cane, trying to second-guess a Mistress well versed in the arts of correction. As the strokes mounted up, the sixth a good length of time after the fifth, it became harder to tense, the muscles in the buttocks and thighs weakened, and the heat was spreading from the surface, winding down into the core.

'Seven,' Vicky whispered, watching open-mouthed as Harriet lifted the cane high, held it for an instant so that the tip flew up and then curved down in a swift and graceful arc.

It tore away at the defences, tore away the inhibitions and the thoughts, leaving nothing but the sensation, nothing but the pure physical essence of punishment. Jaki's cock was hard, throbbing as the pain became pain-pleasure, became pleasure-pain. She felt out of control, her whole being fixed on retaining the position across the desk so that her naked backside could be stroked by Mistress's cane.

With the eighth stroke Jaki was almost lifting her backside, gladly offering herself for correction. Her cry was mixed with a sigh of pleasure, the sharp pain linking with the tingling between her thighs, making her cock flex and throb. She was on the edge, afraid that the next stroke would push her into the abyss. She gritted her teeth, hoping beyond anything that she would not shame herself by climaxing over the polished surface of the desk.

The last stroke was delivered, hard and accurate, a slice across the top of the thighs. Daring to look back at last, Jaki saw herself framed in the wide reflection of the punishment glass. Her thighs stretched taut, arse-cheeks crossed with sharp lines of red that merged with a broader, pinker tan. Each line of the cane was clearly distinguishable, nine stripes arranged symmetrically across thighs and buttocks. She could see herself bent across the desk, her hands gripping the edge with white knuckles, her skirt arranged loosely above her waist. Below the redness of the punished area her thighs were still creamy white, flawlessly beautiful. At that moment she realised that she had never felt more desirable, more vulnerable and more devoted to Harriet.

'Thank you, Mistress,' she whispered lovingly, looking into Harriet's eyes with nothing but adoration. She was so unworthy and yet Mistress loved her enough to punish her, to give her attention when she deserved nothing but indifference.

'The punishment is not yet complete,' Harriet said emotionlessly. 'On your knees,' she directed Vicky, 'I want you to wet her.'

'Yes, Mistress,' Vicky gasped delightedly.

The cool touch of Vicky's tongue seemed to draw away the fire and yet add to the pleasure. Jaki perked herself up, straining her body so that it would present a more perfect picture for Mistress's delectation. The pain and the hurt did not matter, they could be endured, Mistress's displeasure could not.

Jaki wished that her panties had been used as a gag, to stop the sing-song of her sighs and moans. Vicky's tongue was smoothing across the striations, cooling and caressing the smarting redness. She was almost under Jaki, sliding her hands up and down the thighs before gently parting the bottom cheeks with her fingers. For a moment she seemed to study the dark anal hole, her eyes fixing on the pursed ring, and then she kissed it. Her lips barely touched the sensitive opening, sending butterflies of pleasure spiralling through Jaki, who moaned deliriously in response.

'Wet her properly,' Harriet instructed, stowing away the cane back in the drawer.

Vicky eagerly lapped between the parted arse-cheeks, wetting the base of the prick, under the balls and across the flexing anal hole. She kissed and licked, her tongue exploring every inch under the skirt. Her movements became more restricted, focused more on the tight anal ring, tracing the rim with the very tip of her tongue. As Jaki pushed herself back, opening herself to the caresses, Vicky pressed her tongue into the anus.

'Quiet, girl,' Harriet admonished sternly, looking up from the drawer.

Jaki bit her lip, wanting to hold back her sobs of pleasure. She was so close to orgasm, every twitch of her cock was dangerous. For one terrible moment she felt herself falling, the ecstatic joy of climax was there but thankfully she did not come. Vicky's tongue went in deeper, pushing in wetly, exploring Jaki's anal passage with enthusiasm.

'Enough of that,' Harriet commanded.

Jaki murmured her complaint as she felt Vicky withdraw and crawl back out of the way. The feel of Vicky's tongue inside her was like a ghostly image, she could feel the echoes of the pleasure still tingling in her behind. She closed her eyes, relishing the feelings that merged with the stinging across her backside.

'Well, as you are so enamoured of your backside that you need to look at it in the mirror,' Harriet lectured, standing with hands on hips behind Jaki, 'then perhaps we need to give it some attention.'

Jaki opened her eyes, the cold, cruel tone striking with all the power of the cane. Harriet was holding a thick black object, the smooth surface ribbed and curved in an arc, like the letter 'J' in an alphabet of heavy black plastic. She moved forward, using her fingers to part Jaki's buttocks and then sliding the long end into the well-lubricated rear opening.

Jaki exhaled heavily, fear taking away her voice. She was being violated, her arsehole fucked by a cold inanimate object that went deep inside her. She was too afraid to move. It seemed to take for ever to enter her, opening and stretching the tightness of her hole. It was splitting her, filling her completely, unyielding hardness against her yielding body. Harriet pushed it in as far as it would go, the curved end lodging between her bottom cheeks, tracing the curve of her backside.

In the mirror it was clearly visible, a dark strip that separated her arse-cheeks, pushing them aside before disappearing into her hole. Jaki's eyes were wide with sick fascination, excited by the peculiar device that seemed moulded to her body, fucking her and yet displaying her at the same time. Her cock seemed to swell even harder, as though the hardness inside her was protruding from her body.

'Is the post ready?' Harriet asked, turning to Vicky.

'In ten minutes,' Vicky replied incredulously, unable to tear her eyes from Jacki's punished body.

'Until then Jaki will stand in the corner, on display,' Harriet decided. 'Then she can go down to the post office to send off the post.'

'Mistress?' Jaki whispered, her heart pounding excitedly.

'Stand up and go to the corner,' Harriet instructed.

'Yes, Mistress,' Jaki obeyed, straightening up very slowly, aware of the stinging of the cane and the strange feel of the object inside her. It felt so very strange, as though she were being controlled, at the mercy of the black object that held her so tightly between the arse-cheeks. Every step was a combination of fearful pain and secret delight. In the corner she lifted her skirt and positioned herself with respect to the punishment glass. The dark shape held up her buttock cheeks, emphasising the roundness and the deep red of the tracks of chastisement.

'Sort the post out now,' Harriet told Vicky, who appeared reluctant to leave. She took one last, lingering look at Jaki and then left the office to prepare the stack of letters and packages that was to be taken to the post office for posting.

'Mistress?' Jaki ventured to ask, turning from her reflection to meet Harriet's uncompromising stare.

'Yes?' Harriet asked, returning to her seat behind the desk, the only clue as to her own excitement the slight pink flush of her face.

'When I go to the post office . . .' Jaki could not complete the sentence because she feared the answer.

'Yes,' Harriet confirmed, the faintest flicker of a smile across her lips, 'you will go to the post office with that still inside you. I want to teach you a lesson you'll not easily forget.'

'Yes, Mistress,' Jaki whispered, appalled and excited, frightened and elated. The skirt would barely cover her, every whisper of the breeze would threaten to expose her, every step would be a danger. She could think of no greater torment, but with that torment there would be the secret thrill of knowing she was helpless and under Mistress's command.

Chapter Seven

After the delicious agony of punishment there had to be the agony of exposure. Standing with hands on her head, back straight, chest out, Jaki was posed specially for the punishment glass. Her long, tapering legs looked so delightful, her bottom criss-crossed with vivid stripes, her flesh marked red and pink where it still smarted. The thick black strip that parted her arse-cheeks added to the humiliation, the cool object like a hard prick opening her backside, one end of it going deep inside her.

Harriet enjoyed the view for a few moments, looking at the reflection in the mirror and then crossing the room to touch and feel for herself. Jaki sighed when Harriet's fingers caressed the reddest parts of her backside, held her breath when the solid black phallus was pushed a fraction further into her anal hole. She felt faint with excitement and humiliation, delighting in her self-abasement, in the glorious degradation of her condition.

'Post's ready,' Vicky reported, poking her head round the door. Her eyes were alight with excitement, looking first at the reflection in the punishment glass and then again at the real thing.

'Good. Jaki will take it now,' Harriet responded, resuming her position behind the desk, as though she had just assigned some routine piece of office work. The fact that Jaki was to go to the post office as she was, her bottom red with cane marks and her rear filled with the black dildo, seemed entirely natural and good. 'I'd better call some of these people back,' she added, pointing to the list of messages that Jaki had prepared earlier.

'Come on then,' Vicky urged Jaki, her broad smile betraying her excitement. 'I'll tell you what needs to be done.'

Jaki turned to Harriet, miserable face and tear-filled eyes hoping for a reprieve, but there was to be none. Harriet had already picked up the telephone and was tapping out a number, her mind clearly on her work and not on anything else. Utterly crestfallen, Jaki had no option but to do as commanded. She walked, slowly and uncomfortably, out of Harriet's office, taking one last hopeful glance at her before softly closing the door.

'I can't go out like this,' she sighed tearfully, looking beseechingly at Vicky.

'Can you walk?' Vicky asked excitedly, taking Jaki by the hand sympathetically.

'With difficulty,' she admitted. 'Each step is a reminder that Mistress has filled me with this . . . this thing.'

'Let me see,' Vicky suggested, stepping back and folding arms across her chest.

Jaki walked to the office door and back, trying to get used to the phallus in her arsehole, trying also to walk as naturally as possible. Her short skirt suddenly seemed to have shrunk, and she felt exposed, as every swish of movement seemed to reveal the nature of her punishment. 'Well?' she asked nervously.

'The tops of your thighs are red,' Vicky reported, 'and you can see that even when you're standing still. As for that prick thing. Well, you only need to bend over a little and they'll get an eyeful they won't forget.'

'That's awful,' Jaki wailed. Awful, but there was no choice. She could not disobey. A slave did not disobey, and she was a slave first, last and always.

'What about your jacket?' Vicky suggested helpfully.

'Yes, that might be better,' Jaki responded eagerly, seizing at the chance offered. Her jacket was slightly longer than the skirt, and when she wrapped it tightly she felt better. It covered the redness at the top of her thighs, and wrapped so tight it did not swish as much as she walked. Not for the first time, she wished for a mirror in the main office too, but she accepted Vicky's assurances that she looked OK.

'All the foreign ones are in Europe,' Vicky explained, handing over the thick pile of letters for posting. 'The rest go first class. Except for the package which has to go registered. Got that?'

Jaki nodded, barely understanding the instructions she was given. The dildo inside her was hard and unyielding, pressing deep and sending spasms of pleasure that made her sigh uncontrollably. Her cock was hard, achingly hard, and the sensations from her caned backside and from her invaded arsehole were a heady mixture that caused waves of orgasmic pleasure that passed through her.

'Are you OK?' Vicky asked, taking Jaki by the shoulders and giving her a shake.

'Yes, I just feel . . . I'm fine,' she said, trying a smile that almost made it to her lips.

'Be careful,' Vicky whispered. 'And thanks for not telling.' She pulled Jaki closer and kissed her, their lips melting into one.

Jaki responded deliriously, as though sucking for sweet breath. She felt Vicky's arms around her, holding tightly and lovingly before moving down. She was unable to resist. She felt Vicky's hands travelling lower, sliding under the jacket and the skirt. Cool fingers stroked her backside, caressing the smarting pain before homing in on the dark plastic band between her thighs. A finger touched her prick, a light caress that had her moaning her ecstasy into Vicky's ear.

'Better get going,' Vicky sighed, reluctantly releasing Jaki.

'Will you wait for me?' Jaki asked, stopping at the top of the stairs.

Vicky nodded. 'Be careful,' she added.

The sharp breath of air was like a slap in the face. Jaki gasped for breath, the shock of her situation punctuating the daze that she had fallen into. Now she was out, away from the warmth of the office, away from the safety of Mistress and the strange rituals of punishment and display. The sound of the passing traffic, the dull colours of the street, the dreadful reality of everyday life were far removed from the cosseted world of her devotion to Mistress.

The sharp sound of her heels, usually so comforting, was lost in the unfocused sound of the street around her. She walked awkwardly, wrapping herself up in the protection of her jacket, looking straight ahead or else down at the ground. Once, she remembered, she had been punished by Mistress Harriet by being sent home on the train wearing nothing but her coat. The journey home had been an ordeal of excitement, especially when an unseen hand had stroked her naked behind.

But that journey was nothing as to that which she was presently suffering. She was torn by the fear that the thing lodged between the firm flesh of her bottom would begin to inch out, the dildo working loose until it threatened to fall to her feet. Or else she feared that the letters she clutched so tightly would fall from her grasp and that she would have to bend down to pick them up, threatening exposure as she did so. Or else she feared a sharp gust would whip away her jacket and lift her skirt. Or else . . .

There were so many things to fear, and all of them ended with her exposure, her shameful condition uncovered for all to see. She was aware that she drew glances wherever she went, sometimes admiring, sometimes hostile, always quizzical. With her short jacket, bare thighs and high heels she would be inviting interest anyway. The question would always be whether she wore anything under her coat. It had been asked before, and had been a chance to flirt coyly, but now she feared the question, and had no answer to it if it came.

The post office was full. A long, straggly queue was taped in and waiting for service from the few counters that were working. She joined the line, inching down her jacket and ignoring the smile of a man in front of her. As she smoothed down her jacket she felt the hardness of her prick, could feel the wetness where droplets of fluid had poured from the slit. How she ached to climax, longed for that release of tension into pure joy, but the reward was not for her to give – only Mistress could do that.

The queue shuffled forward slowly, silent, sullen, passive. Jaki tensed and felt the hardness deep inside her, the solid object controlling and possessing. She was being fucked even as she stood, fucked and caressed by the unfamiliar object which Harriet had produced. Jaki had never seen it before. Had it been a present from Mistress Shirer? The question triggered other questions, more immediately urgent. What was she to do about the Institute?

The queue shuffled forward again and, as it did so, Jaki caught sight of herself in the mirror by the photo booth in one corner of the post office. She looked flustered but beautiful, her full lips so red and kissable, her slim body wrapped tight, her long legs shapely and attractive, high heels accentuating the curve of calf and thigh. For a moment she wanted to scream, to tell them all who she was and what she was, to glory in herself and in her condition. She was Jaki, feminine, beautiful and belonging to a Mistress. The idea increased her excitement, made her trace her lips with the tip of her tongue.

She felt a secret thrill of exhilaration: all those around her, all those ordinary, humdrum people, they had no idea about her. If they knew . . . She knew that they would feel outrage and disgust if they knew the truth about her. They would look upon her as some disgusting and degraded being, feeling shock and revulsion in equal measure. The thought made her quiver with pleasure, she would bask in the glow of their disgust, accept it as a prize worth having. She was a *slave* and they had no idea what rewards that offered.

At last her turn came. She stepped across the line and moved to the counter with the light flashing. The man behind the counter looked at her, and for a moment she saw the questions behind his watery blue eyes, but the moment passed and then he stared at her with tired eyes that hid nothing. Hurriedly she off-loaded the letters, working automatically, her consciousness taking a back seat while she worked out what was needed. With typical efficiency everything was stamped and labelled and back in her hands ready for the post-box.

The relief washed through her, she grabbed her letters and marched through the crowded post office, head held high, and thrilling to the feeling of the dildo pressing hard and yielding pleasures and delights of sensuousness. The post-box was outside the post office, and in her rush to finish things two of the letters fluttered to the floor while the others made it into the belly of the red beast. Without thinking she bent down quickly to retrieve them, and squealed with the sudden shock of remembering.

The cool breeze touched her, stroked her bare thighs and hard prick. With sickening certainty she realised that most of her lower body was exposed. Very slowly she looked back, able to feel the quizzical eyes that had locked onto her. A couple was watching her, a young woman and her boyfriend. Jaki straightened up quickly, smoothing down her jacket and covering herself up again. When she turned the man and woman were still watching her, a look of fascination animating their smiles. She hesitated and then smiled back nervously, wondering just how much they had seen. When the woman pulled away from her boyfriend, lightly touching her lips to his, and approached her, Jaki stepped away, overcome by fear and panic. She fled quickly, despite the woman's pleasant smile, which soon turned into a look of disappointment. Jaki felt her face shamed into redness she walked as fast as she could, wishing only to be back in the safety of the office.

It had been an ordeal. A torment. But now she was safe. She struggled for breath as she closed the front door of the office and leaned back against it. The world outside was shut away again, never to intrude, never to threaten. She reached down and traced the groove of the plastic object between her arse-cheeks, delighting in the feel of it snuggled so tight. As she explored the join of it with her flesh, tendrils of erotic sensation passed through her. It felt so good, the tightness of her rear hole gripping tightly the hardness that violated her. She liked the feel of it, so hard, so powerful and dominating.

She stopped for a moment, knowing that if she continued she would climax powerfully, shooting thick spray of come over her skirt. Back upstairs she could find no sign of Vicky, but then the door to Harriet's office was closed, which could only mean one thing.

'Mistress?' she asked, knocking softly on the door.

'Come in,' Vicky called from inside.

Pushing the door open, Jaki was not surprised by what she saw. Harriet was sitting on the edge of her desk, legs parted and pussy exposed. On hands and knees in front of her was Vicky, greedily lapping at Harriet's wet sex.

'Good, I'm glad you're back,' Harriet sighed, running her hands lovingly through Vicky's hair. 'I think it's time you showed Mistress just how much you love her.'

'Yes, Mistress,' Jaki sighed hotly. She slipped off her jacket and got down on hands and knees. The thing inside her stretched her arsehole but that felt good, and besides it was Mistress's to remove, if she so wished. She crawled forward, certain that Vicky was sucking Mistress only because Mistress had been so excited by the earlier punishment session.

'Mistress?' Jaki whispered, looking up appealingly.

'Yes?' Harriet whispered in return, closing her eyes as Vicky's tongue caressed her swollen bud.

'I have to do it, I have to go back into the Institute,' Jaki said, sounding both elated and afraid at the same time.

'That is what Mistress Shirer and I both desire,' Harriet said, her smile and her breath lost in the pleasures that Vicky was giving so generously.

Jaki knelt down, Mistress's long heels were sharp and dangerous, and she kissed them lovingly.

Jaki waited pensively, trying to focus on Mistress Shirer's instructions and not the shiny black heels that glistened as she paced back and forth. They were in Harriet's office, and Mistress Shirer was delivering instructions in a clipped and precise voice. Her face matched the tone, stern and commanding, beautiful but utterly remote.

'A suitable cover story will be manufactured for you,' Mistress Shirer continued. 'Under no circumstances do we want to arouse suspicion. As far as everyone else is concerned you are just another new arrival.'

'I understand,' Jaki murmured, lifting her eyes from the heels that acted like a magnet, drawing her attention completely.

'If it were just a case of a few cosmetics or things smuggled from one dorm to the next I would not be too concerned,' Mistress explained, voicing aloud the disquiet that had been growing for so long. 'I think that what we have uncovered is just the tip of the iceberg. I am concerned that a culture of deceit is taking root, and that in the end it will destroy the Institute completely. Even exposure in the press would be preferable to this infiltration of deception and dishonesty.'

'I'm sure that I'll be able to find out what's going on, Mistress,' Jaki said, wanting to reassure Mistress Shirer. The plan that had been outlined was exceedingly simple: arrive at the Institute, find out the truth and report back. There was nothing that sounded remotely difficult or problematical, the only problem had been to find a suitable candidate to go back, and Jaki had to admit that she was the perfect choice.

Mistress stopped and looked at Jaki, who was standing by Harriet's desk, hands held politely in front of her, eyes lowered respectfully. 'I won't be able to have much contact with you,' she said. 'To do otherwise will draw attention to you. Mistress Kasia is the person you will have most contact with, although she will be unaware of your true identity. I warn you now, Mistress Kasia is very strict and I am certain that you will be punished quite severely should you merit it.'

Jaki nodded but said nothing. She had not really considered the possibility of being punished, but if that was what she had to do to please Mistress Shirer then that was what she was going to do.

'Don't imagine that this is going to be easy, Jaki,' Mistress warned, turning her dark eyes on Jaki. 'You may well find yourself in great difficulties, so be prepared.'

'Yes, Mistress,' Jaki said.

Mistress Shirer returned to the seat behind the desk. 'Are you sure you want to do this?' she asked wearily.

'Yes, Mistress,' Jaki replied firmly.

'I am no longer your Mistress, you belong to Harriet. If you choose to help me then you become mine again, to do with as I please, is that clear?'

'Very clear, Mistress,' Jaki said. Her heart was pounding with excitement. She felt so alive, free to give herself completely to Mistress Shirer once more.

'Then you're mine once more, Jaki, and I don't think I need remind you just how strict my rule is,' Mistress affirmed. 'I have already started things, and in two days you'll be arriving at the Institute. You will be arriving as J.K., a young man found guilty of theft, and about to undergo the trials and tribulations of the Institute. There you will submit to the domination of many Mistresses and accept the need to be feminised when you receive your just punishment. You will cease to be a free agent, understand that from the beginning. When you pass into the Institute you become nothing more than a slave.'

'I understand, Mistress,' Jaki said gravely, her excitement dampened by the grim warnings of her Mistress.

'Now,' Mistress Shirer stood up again, 'I suppose you remember how to thank your Mistress?'

Jaki nodded eagerly. She needed no other bidding, her mouth was already tingling with anticipation. She fell to her knees and crawled towards Mistress, her eyes fixed on the shiny black shoes, and on the sharp heels that were symbols of her own submission and of Mistress's dominance.

Had it been a dream? J.K. stirred, opening his eyes to the darkness before dawn, the nebulous sleepiness dissolving instantly. It had not been a dream, the pounding of his heart testament to the excitement of the days just past. The excitement of Mistress Shirer's surprise visit, the strict punishment inflicted by Harriet, the trip to the post office . . .

It had not been a dream, rather it had been a revelation, another glimpse into the darkness of Jaki's sexuality. After the heat of punishment and the ordeal of having to risk exposure, Jaki had returned to the office with the knowledge that she had to do as Mistress Shirer asked. To return to the Institute.

The memories of the previous few days merged with the vivid, dream-like memories of the Institute. J.K. closed his eyes again, losing himself in the powerful recollection of events that were for ever on the edge of consciousness. He remembered the moment of rebirth, when he had cast his previous life aside and fully accepted his new existence as Jaki.

It had been in the main hall, during a party, surrounded by Institute staff, guests and a number of young female slaves. Lucy had been there, a slave to her beloved Mistress Diana, who worked with Mistress Shirer in the Institute. An accident had occurred, and, much to her initial confusion and horror, Jaki was held to blame. The punishment was in public, precariously balanced on a table top, a leather switch used mercilessly by Mistress Shirer. The memory was exciting, and J.K. pulled the duvet aside, revealing his smooth thighs and hard prick. Reaching down to touch himself, he closed his eyes again, concentrating once more on the dream-like memories and images of that day . . .

After the cruel and merciless lash of the switch, Jaki opened her eyes. There was a light smattering of applause from the audience. Biting back the pain, she felt a rush of pride. Her bottom-cheeks were sore and aflame from top to bottom, and fingers of jabbing pain throbbed with a delicious pleasurable rhythm on her behind. Through tear-filled eyes she turned and looked back with adoration at Mistress Shirer, stern and demanding and completely beautiful.

The mass of people, still largely silent and gazing with approval at Jaki's punished form, parted suddenly. The murmur of conversation was silenced and replaced by an expectant hush. They watched Mistress Diana stride elegantly through the room, poised on steel-tipped red ankle boots, naked apart from those boots and a stiff leather bra that raised her breasts enticingly. The neatly shaved triangle of hair above her sex was exposed, and the lips of her other mouth were roused and slightly parted.

Mistress Diana was followed obediently by one of the serving girls, carrying a silver platter. From her low position on the table top Jaki was unable to discern what lay on the platter. Instead, her eyes were fixed firmly on the young Mistress, trying to drink in the full picture: the securely laced ankle boots, the spiky heel a shining threat, the long agile legs reaching up to the bare sex, the full ripe breasts cupped temptingly by the stiff matt leather bra.

At that moment Mistress Shirer leaned forward and exchanged a light delicate kiss with Diana, their lips fusing momentarily. It was a lovers' kiss, certain, open and filled with the sweetest of promises. They parted, fingertips touching as they smiled to each other.

Mistress Diana turned to the silver platter and picked up a number of straps and chains. These were passed to one of the girls who took them with a shy and grateful smile. She had needed no instructions and approached Jaki directly.

Jaki looked around, thoroughly confused, looking imploringly at the girl with the chains, who merely smiled back knowingly. She had fallen to her knees by the side of the coffee table and lay the bundle of straps and clinking chains by her side. Carefully, she retrieved a single strap and chain. Jaki watched with rising horror as the girl applied one strap to the table leg, pulling the buckle tight and tugging at it to test it. The strap was connected to a short silver chain which was in turn connected to another strap. The second strap was applied around Jaki's wrist and pulled tight. The bond was adjusted diligently, and Jaki realised that she had been firmly tied to the table. The other arm was also attached to a table leg. Jaki tried to pull free, knowing she was secure but wanting to see how much room she had to manoeuvre. There was none. She was bound tightly to the table, as though she were an inanimate object tethered safely like a treasure about to be stowed.

Mistress Shirer watched approvingly as Jaki's heels were similarly chained to the coffee table. She ignored Jaki's beseeching look, not even deigning to acknowledge it. The girl bound Jaki's heels in the same way, pausing only to stare for a second at the bulging prick crying a single tear of glistening fluid.

Unable to move, Jaki strained to look back, her arse was still smarting and alive with an intense tingling ache. She would never forget the hot feeling. Her prick was aching and she knew that she could hardly contain herself.

Mistress Diana coolly picked her chosen implement from the silver platter. It looked a little like the kind of thing that her slave, Lucy, wore: a complex cradle of straps and chains. However, firmly embedded in the weave was a long black object, like an upturned arch. Mistress Diana smiled as she undid the straps and carefully climbed into the costume. She stepped into it and slowly pulled it up from the knees. She took the central device in one hand and with the other had parted the opening to her sex. Very slowly she eased one end of the thing deep into herself. There was a delicious thrill of pleasure as she forced the thing into place, forcing it against the walls of her moist pussy and letting it rest against her centre of bliss, her pleasure expressed in the fluttering sigh of her breath.

Jaki stared wide-eyed with disbelief. Mistress Diana proudly showed off the massive false penis that emerged from between her thighs. She held it proudly while Lucy pulled all the straps tight, so that the penis was firmly positioned under the thighs and held fast by straps around the waist and another strap between the buttocks.

The penis was large and thick, much bigger than any man could be. It's matt black surface was smooth, and at the end there was a hard spherical head standing out menacingly. Jaki tried to pull away, frightened by the dangerous-looking object, shocked by the size and the obvious look of intent that had shone in Mistress Diana's eyes. The chains clinked and the table rocked a little, but Jaki knew that there was no escape.

Lucy had crawled forward on her hands and knees, eyeing the false rod with fear and respect. She was handed a tube, and obediently she squeezed out a thick wad of clear translucent jelly on to her fingers. Very slowly she had applied the jelly to her tongue, it was cool and tasteless but it seemed to glow in the dancing light of the fire. At last, when her tongue was heavy with the thick jelly, she raised herself up and be-

gan to smear the jelly over the hard prick jutting proudly from Mistress Diana's engorged sex.

Mistress Diana closed her eyes and enjoyed the reciprocal feel of the pretend prick deep in her sex. Lucy mouthed it expertly, taking as much as she could between her lips and using her tongue to spread the jelly over the surface. Lucy had squeezed more jelly on to her tongue and then spread it lazily over the hardness, ensuring that every inch of the massive object was wet with a glistening layer of lubricating jelly, from the bulbous globe at the head to the very base where the jelly had flowed with the first golden drops of juice from Mistress Diana's tightly filled cunt.

Lucy then sat back and looked at Jaki, bound tightly on to the table, her arse quivering from the afterburn of punishment. Their eyes had met for a second. Jaki didn't seem to recognise her at first, but then recognition did come. She nodded hopefully, expectantly. Then Lucy shook her head. For a second, a half-smile flickered on Jaki's pale withered face. They knew then that there was no turning back. Neither Jaki nor Lucy could deliver the story of the Institute to the press. They were the story and whilst they were willing to sacrifice themselves for their Mistresses' pleasure, they were unprepared to sacrifice themselves for other motives.

The audience was silent, stunned by the perversity of the exhibition underway before them. A number of the serving girls were being quietly touched, some by staff, others by the guests and some by other girls. The sexual tension in the room was electric and was centred on the view of Jaki and Mistress Diana.

Jaki wanted to cry out. She was petrified of the lustrous penis that Mistress Diana sported. It was unnatural and frightening. But Jaki was also filled with an excitement that she could hardly contain, the pretend penis was both a promise and a threat. She knew that Mistress Shirer would expect her to give herself fully, and that was the sole purpose of existence. To resist would have been to deny herself and to deny Mistress Shirer.

Mistress Diana took Jaki by the waist, placing one knee on the edge of the coffee table and positioned herself behind

Jaki's tormented and marked backside. With her hand she pressed the head of prick at the entrance to the jewel that she had wanted from the first. Jaki gasped when the head of the monster was pressed against her tight anal hole. She froze. The slippery globe rested at the entrance to her hole. She held her breath, unable to believe that the thing could enter without tearing her. Mistress Diana leaned forward in a single slow movement and somehow Jaki's arsehole opened and took the full circumference of the lubricated pole.

Jaki cried out once, a shrill cry of pain as the immense prick was prised into her accommodating rear hole. She felt the urge to fight the intrusion, to push against the cool shaft that slid deep between the walls of her arse. It took for ever to fill her, a single long action that forced deep into her insides. Mistress Diana halted when the thick rod had been pushed as far as it could go. She rested a second, catching her breath, her heart pounding wildly. Every subtle movement in Jaki's bum-hole was amplified by the long tool into a delicious pattern on her pussy, the two poles of the tool an integral whole.

Jaki felt as if she had been cleaved in two. Her buttocks were spread fully apart, her bum-hole gripped tightly around the base of the prick. There had been a feeling of discomfort, a pain that wouldn't go away. But this was complemented by the delight of feeling the thick base of the prick wedged firmly into her wide arsehole. She had taken the fullness of the monster without tearing, and the pleasure of acceptance had been mixed with a sense of pride.

Mistress Diana began to pump the penis in and out of Jaki's hole, pressing herself back and forth in long slow fluid strokes. She savoured the feel of fucking the servant girl fully in the arse, the pleasure of sodomy had its own special thrill. She felt Jaki responding under her, doing her best to take the hardness without pain. She began to pump harder, gyrating her pelvis, thrusting the heaviness faster and faster, somehow managing to drive deeper into Jaki's virginal backside.

Jaki turned back to see Mistress Shirer laughing with one of the guests; they were enjoying the view. With that, Jaki closed her eyes, relaxed, secure that her Mistress was happy *with the performance. Mistress Diana was thrusting harder and harder, Jaki could hear the Mistress panting and releasing short gasps of delight. Each push lasted an age, the oiled weapon gliding smoothly in and out of her arsehole, which expanded and contracted over the thickness of the beast.*

She also began to moan. Each thrust, and they were becoming rapid piercing drives, seemed to inject a greater degree of pleasure into her. Her own prick had seemed to be directly connected to the force driving pleasurably into her arse-pussy. She realised at last that she was being fucked like a woman, the thrusting tool in her arse-pussy was pressing against a secret place that had caused her to wilt with pleasure. Her buttocks were still painful from the thrashing, but that only added to the excitement and the delight. She had suffered her secret joy in public, glad that so many eyes had seen her being so expertly buggered by a beautiful Mistress. Most of all she wanted the glory, and what wondrous glory it was, to reflect on her Mistress.

Jaki opened her eyes suddenly, she had been disturbed by an unexpected caress on the face. She was surprised to find that a stranger stood before her. It was a man, and he stood directly in front of her face, naked and holding his strong hard prick in his hand.

For a second Jaki studied the length of flesh that he held for her. She saw that the head was a dark gleaming purple, the length slightly ribbed and it was twitching noticeably. Without stopping to think, she passed her tongue over the glans, tasting the salty taste of prick for the first time. She turned to Mistress Shirer who nodded her assent, her eyes glowing with pleasure, and, Jaki hoped, pride.

The stranger inched closer. Jaki pressed her lips and tongue over the full length of the warm flesh. There was a strange contrast between the cool hardness fucking her in the arse with the more pliant hardness of the real thing. She opened her mouth and took it fully, sucking immediately at the dewdrops of fluid that were dribbling from the eye. The stranger began to move back and forth, and she rose and fell over his prick.

Jaki was overwhelmed with sensations. She was sucking at

the prick being forced into her mouth, alive to the different textures of it on her mouth and against her cheek, and to its taste that filled her mouth. From behind. Mistress Diana was fucking her vigorously, impaling her with the double prick that pleasured them both. She wanted to cry out with pleasure, but her sobs were stifled by the urgent fucking in her mouth.

A great cry brought silence to the room. Mistress Diana was seized by a wild swirl of bliss. Her soaking pussy exploded with delight. She climaxed with a headlong rush into the valley of oblivion and elation. At the same instant the stranger took Jaki's head in his hands and forced his prick deep into the back of her throat. She almost gagged as the man began to spurt thick wads of jism. She felt the velvet purity of the come on her tongue and in her mouth, and swallowed it down, feeling the honey glide down her throat smoothly.

She was unable to contain her pleasure any longer. Her mouth was still sucking at the last drops of come from the prick that had fucked her there. Her arsehole was still wedged tightly over the thick rigid pole that had buggered her so well, and had brought Mistress Diana to climax.

She began to sob. Tears had streamed down her face. Her prick was pumping thick globules of spunk over her belly and on to the table. She felt as if she were falling through space.

When she finally opened her eyes, she looked round at her Mistress who gave her the faintest hint of a smile.

And for the first time in her life Jaki experienced the elation of being totally happy . . .

Would that elation be repeated, he wondered? Already he was afraid of what the day was to bring. The dawn that broke, flooding the darkness with a pale watery light, heralded the start of the day when he was to return to the Institute.

Chapter Eight

The traffic would not move, no matter how much J.K. willed it to, nor how much the driver cursed it. It had straggled its way from central London and out through the suburbs, moving at the same interminable pace, in fits and starts, and never picked up speed or led to an open road. The driver, uniformed and sullen, stared at the road ahead without enthusiasm, his eyes darting to the rear-view mirror and back. J.K. guessed he was searching for that elusive gap in the traffic that would allow them to break free of the pack and make their destination on time. In any case the driver seemed to prefer to study the patterns of the traffic to talking either to J.K. or to the social worker who sat in the forward passenger seat.

'I wish this paperwork had been correctly processed,' the social worker grumbled, not for the first time. He appeared to be more concerned with the irregular paperwork than with the fact that he was delivering a young man to the Institute.

'What's this place like?' J.K. asked him, exasperated by the whining tone and the sheer pettymindedness of the man.

'Jim, call me Jim,' he insisted, twisting round in his seat to peer through the head-rest at J.K. 'It's a place like any other,' he added. 'Can't say that I've been here before, but then I'm not at all familiar with your details either. You see, this one was rather foisted on me, not my case at all.'

'We got far to go?' J.K. asked the driver, depressed by the social worker's attitude. The driver replied with a shrug that could have been a yes, a no or a don't ask me.

'Do you think you can get me back to the district office by three?' Jim asked, removing the heavy-rimmed spectacles that had been pushed well back on the bridge of his nose. He squinted hopefully at the driver, a thin smile forming on his lips, the facial muscles struggling to keep up the unfamiliar expression. 'Case conference, very important,' he added when the driver ignored the request.

'You got hours yet,' the driver said coldly.

'So we should make it then,' Jim concluded, though it sounded more of a hope than a certainty.

They settled back into a listless silence, the dull throb of the engine a blanket of sound that smothered everything else. At last the traffic began to thin out and the gaps between cars lengthened as they picked up speed. The horizon turned from grey to brown to green as the suburbs gave way, eventually, to the countryside. Jim had settled back in his seat and was studying the contents of his battered briefcase, picking through the papers and shaking his head sadly. The driver seized his chance and steered the car into the outside lane of the motorway and put on a sustained burst of speed.

J.K. sat alone on the back seat, feet up and arms across his chest, casually insolent – the way he was supposed to act. The morning had begun with being picked up by Mistress Shirer, who delivered him to a local magistrates court, from whence he'd been picked up by the social worker and the driver. Papers had been signed, checked and signed again, and then he was theirs, a body to be delivered to a secure place for punishment. J.K. had been content to observe. The procedure seemed to have been designed to exclude him, turning him into an object without power. For a moment the procedure in the court had been like an elaborate game of dominance and submission, except that everything was veiled and the erotic content removed.

The car pulled off the road sharply, decelerating suddenly and turning from the busy carriageway on to an unmarked exit, shielded from the main traffic by a dense thicket.

'Bit of a dangerous one back there,' Jim exclaimed, turning to look back at the sharp junction which had already disappeared.

J.K. could vaguely remember the way, but in the past his journeys had been very different. Every time he had ever been to the Institute, and there had been very few occasions, he had been in a fever of anticipation and excitement. He felt nothing of that, instead he was trying hard to appear calm and composed. Mistress Shirer had warned him not to show any signs of recognition. It was vital that he give the strong impression that it was his first journey to the Institute. Even more importantly, once he was there he had to express shock and horror at the regime, even though it was understood that he was psychologically predisposed to respond to it sexually.

The car continued on the road for a while, passing no other vehicles as it made its way. The turning off the country lane was as sharp as that from the main road, but this time it led on to a gravel track through a thickly wooded avenue of trees. Jim stared ahead, quite obviously puzzled as to where the track was leading. Then, suddenly, the Institute was there in front of them: an imposing building of dark brown brick, tall and square, looking for all the world like a minor public school, in well tended lawn and surrounded on all sides by dense woods.

There were evenly spaced windows on each of the six floors, with old-fashioned wooden frames that looked grey with age. The slanting, slate grey roof gave the impression of solidity but J.K. knew that the building was arranged around an inner courtyard, so that the Institute building appeared to be looking inwards rather than outwards.

'I'd say you've landed yourself a cushy little number,' Jim remarked approvingly. 'If I were you I'd behave myself here. I've seen much worse than this, I can tell you.'

'Thanks, I'll bear that in mind,' J.K. replied sarcastically.

'That attitude will get you nowhere,' Jim sighed, with a sad but resigned shake of the head.

The car pulled up in front of the unattended entrance, and, even before anyone had disembarked from the car, the heavy black front door creaked open. A figure emerged, female, clad in stark white uniform, hair curled up in a severe bun, blue eyes without emotion. She waited at the top of the worn, granite steps, arms locked across her chest.

'This shouldn't take too long,' Jim said, speaking to himself. He grabbed his tattered briefcase and hopped out of the car.

J.K. watched him go, a thin smile on his face as he climbed the steps to meet the impassive woman waiting at the top. 'Been here before?' J.K. asked the driver, who had taken the opportunity to light a cigarette.

'A couple of times.'

'What's it like?'

The driver exhaled a swirling grey cloud of bitter smoke. 'Dunno,' he said, 'I only deliver.'

'It's not like other places though, is it?' J.K. persisted, wondering what the rest of the world made of the strange place he was about to enter.

'There's women here,' the driver said, smiling through the smoke that wafted around him.

'Like her?' J.K. asked, gesturing towards the severe looking woman, impatiently going through the bureaucratic niceties with Jim.

The driver inhaled sharply. 'No. Inmates. In a separate wing from what I can make out.'

'That can't be right,' J.K. laughed, affecting incredulity to see if he could glean any more.

'You don't get it, do you?'

'Get what?'

The driver smiled. Jim was returning to the car, the pages safely stowed in his case. 'This is a bin. A nuthouse,' the driver whispered firmly. 'They've committed you and you don't even know about it.'

'That's not true . . .' J.K. cried, a look of alarm in his eyes.

'What's going on here then?' Jim asked, smiling happily as though he'd just walked in on a joke.

'He says that this is a loony bin,' J.K. cried.

'I didn't say nothing,' the driver countered.

'Don't be silly,' Jim laughed. 'How can they send you to a place like that? For a bit of petty thieving? No, there's been some mistake.'

J.K. exchanged an angry look with the driver and then got out of the car. 'I ain't even seen a doctor,' he shouted as the car door was closed.

'Forget that,' Jim advised quietly, 'he was just having a joke. Now, follow me and I'll introduce you to . . . To her.'

'You mean you'll hand me over,' J.K. whispered sullenly. Together he and Jim climbed the steps towards the woman, who was staring at them with cold blue eyes. Her skin was very pale, and the lightness of colour was heightened by the platinum blonde hair and light pink lips.

'Follow me,' she ordered, before Jim had a chance to attempt an introduction. 'The paperwork is finished,' she added, dismissing him instantly.

'Yes. Well . . . er . . . Good luck . . . I'll see you again, sometime . . . Or perhaps not, eh?' Jim said, excusing himself and backing slowly down the steps towards the car.

'Is this a nuthouse?' J.K. asked, the hostility of his tone matched by the coldness with which he returned the woman's stare.

'Is that where you feel you belong?' she asked.

'No.'

'Then it isn't. Now, you will follow me.'

She turned and walked towards the door, not even waiting to see if her command had been obeyed. J.K. heard the crunch of gravel as the car turned, then followed her into the forbidding building.

The entrance to the Institute had been changed. J.K. noted. The front door led to a small room, windowless and without markings, almost like an empty cell. Doors led to right and left, each of them unmarked and featureless. J.K. could remember the old lobby, airy, spacious, heavy with silence and yet alive with an unmistakable atmosphere of excitement. That was gone – one of the casualties created by the addition of a male dorm. The woman, and she had yet to introduce herself, stopped at the door on the left and unlocked it using one of a heavy bunch of keys that she carried in her pocket.

The door opened on to a long corridor, formed by the addition of a plasterboard wall which partitioned off part of the old lobby. J.K. walked through the open door and waited for the woman to lock the door behind her. The artificial corridor made sense. Mistress Shirer had explained the need to segregate strictly the male and female sections of the Institute – unfortunately the borders were being breached in some way. The woman locked up and proceeded to lead the way again, walking with chin high and an obvious air of authority about her.

The corridor led to a flight of steps, through a second locked door and then into a small lobby. A young woman was waiting there, dressed in the standard Institute uniform of blue skirt and white top. Her face was pretty, despite the lack of a smile and the cold manner with which she regarded J.K.

'The arrangements have been completed, Mistress Kasia,' she reported soberly to the woman with J.K.

'Good, Louise, I don't think that this will take too long,' was the reply. 'You can wait for him outside my room.'

Kasia's room was at the far end of the lobby, and J.K. fell into step behind her as she strode towards it. He was aware of Louise behind him, following closely and watching him with a cold and impersonal look.

'Stand there,' Kasia ordered when J.K. had followed her into the cramped little office that was hers. She pointed to a spot in front of her desk and waited. He looked at her for a moment, then shrugged and walked to the desk, slouching across the office insolently.

'Do I get the lecture now?' he asked, looking bored.

'You are not going to be troublesome,' she said and, with her odd, slightly accented way of speaking, it was impossible for him to tell whether it was a statement of fact or an order. 'The first thing you must understand,' she continued, taking her place behind the desk, 'is that everything you have ever known and experienced is to be eclipsed by what you will experience here. The Institute is not like any other institution. It is not just another place to lock people away. When you understand this you will appreciate your good fortune in being assigned a place here.'

'I'm overwhelmed,' he mumbled.

'I will ignore that remark,' she said sharply, her tone several degrees colder. Her eyes were ice, and he saw the threat in them at once. 'In days to come you will think back and marvel at my leniency. You will soon see that we do things in an entirely different way here, entirely different, and initially perhaps not to your liking. But, fear not, you have been psychologically profiled and assessed, that you are here at all means that you are suited to our methods. Do you understand that?'

'I filled in some questionnaires,' he admitted, parroting the instructions issued by Mistress Shirer.

'There is more to it than that. Many of the people in authority that you spoke with prior to sentencing were assessing your personality. Suffice it to say that we have a very good idea of what makes you tick.'

'Like fuck you do,' he snorted derisively. His scorn was not for the sake of the act. He hated the idea that people knew who, or what, he was. Nobody knew, nobody. Except for his Mistress, only she could know.

'That was your last chance, one more outburst and . . . Here we do not lock people in their room, here we do not separate them from their peers. We impose other sanctions. Our punishments are more direct and more physical. And punishments there will be, as you are to discover for yourself. Our rules are complex but unwritten. You will learn to navigate our little society, and in doing so will acquire the skills required to navigate the infinitely more complicated society outside our walls. For every rule you break you will be punished physically.'

'What does that mean?' J.K. asked suspiciously.

'It means that you will be physically chastised.'

'You mean hit?'

Kasia ignored the question. 'The first rule is that you

address all females as Mistress. Every female that you come into contact with has authority over you, and you will show her respect at all times. Every female has the right to punish infractions of the rules, no matter how inconsequential that infraction may be. Among females there is also a hierarchy. The young women in uniform, such as Louise, have graduated through the Institute and have voluntarily elected to serve with us for a further period. Louise is the head prefect in this dorm, and has authority over the girls serving here. The professional staff make up the next level in the hierarchy, they have authority over all the young women and over young men such as yourself. The staff, in this section of the Institute, report to me directly. In turn I report to Mistress Shirer, who is the director here. Clear?'

'You're saying I'm at the bottom of the pile,' J.K. said. 'That's very new, never happened to me before.'

'Perhaps if I outline the punishments you will not be so flippant. The girls here have the power to punish you by setting you to work, the more menial the task the better. They may also punish you with up to six strokes on the backside, applied with the hand only . . .'

'What?'

'Louise, as head girl may punish you with as many strokes as she feels necessary, again using the hand only, and in public if she wants to. She may also apply three strokes of a strap in extreme circumstances. A member of staff may beat you with a paddle, a strap or a cane. She may also apply restraints in extreme cases. Do not look so shocked,' Kasia warned coldly. 'These are facts which you will discover shortly. Do not imagine that you can resist. You will be overpowered and the punishments applied will cause you the greatest humiliation imaginable.'

'How can you overpower me?' J.K. asked, though his tone was less aggressive than it had been.

'Many of the other young men here will gladly help,' she explained, a slight smile greeting his look of surprise. 'To serve is the greatest duty, and so any order is obeyed without question. Clear?'

'Yes.'

'Yes, Mistress,' she corrected.

He hesitated. 'Yes, Mistress,' he echoed, though not with feeling.

'I hope you will adapt,' she concluded, seating back in her seat and searching his eyes for a clue to his reaction. 'In fact, I think I am right in judging that you will adapt very quickly. I am a good judge of character, there is an outward show of resistance but underneath you have already accepted the dominion of women. This is true.'

J.K. shook his head. 'Not true, Mistress,' he said. 'I'll keep my head down until my time's up and then I'll be out of here.'

Kasia smiled, for the first time her eyes sparkling with amusement. 'That is a fantasy, the Institute does not operate in that way. Remember, always address us as Mistress. It will save you much anguish in the next few days. Now, Louise will take you to the medical unit. You are dismissed.'

'Before I go, I've got one question, Mistress. Is this place a psychiatric unit or something?'

'No. But do not be surprised if things are a little strange. Louise is waiting, join her now,' Kasia waved her hand towards the door. Her eyes were cold again, as though the emotions had died down again and she were functioning without them.

Louise wasted no time with idle chat. She barked an order to follow and then turned on her heel. J.K. obeyed, trying hard to put himself in the shoes of a genuine newcomer to the Institute. How would it appear to the novice, to the young man who had yet to submit to a Mistress? It would appear as a lunatic asylum, or else a place where his most repressed desires had suddenly blossomed in the light of day. In either case the only understandable, and believable, response had to be a kind of dazed shock.

He followed meekly, hardly daring to deviate from the brisk pace, too afraid to bother her with any questions. Everything was strange. He passed a group of young women, who all ignored him and directed their attention to Louise, who hardly bothered to even notice their existence. At one point she led J.K. along a corridor with classrooms on either side of it, but she was going too fast for him to stop and stare. The blurred glimpses that he got of the classes told him nothing.

The medical unit was at the top of several flights of steps, which Louise took at the same brisk pace. There were no signs anywhere, and J.K. guessed that that was part of a deliberate policy to create disorientation in new arrivals.

'Wait here,' Louise ordered, indicating a stiff wooden bench outside the plain blue door which he hoped was the entrance to the medical unit. She started to push the door open but stopped. 'What are you supposed to say?' she asked.

'I'm supposed to say, "Yes, Mistress",' he said, sitting on the bench in the corner.

'Well?'

'I just said it,' he said, smiling.

'I won't forget that impertinence,' she promised, smiling in return.

She went in and he settled down on the bench, his back against the brick wall. For a building of its size, and with the number of occupants it contained, there was remarkably little background noise. The atmosphere was quiet and restrained, unnaturally subdued given the function of the Institute. He had, despite his previous visits, expected to find a non-stop orgy of sexual excess, a veritable Roman orgy of lust and passion.

'You can come in now,' Louise told him, poking her head round the door.

He stood up and ambled over, hands deep in pockets, looking bored by the whole thing. Louise's face was now full of excitement, as though she knew that what would come next would unsettle him.

The medical unit was all white light and gleaming chrome, a fully equipped unit that seemed well able to cope with any emergency that was likely to occur. A small desk sat in one corner, under a shelf full of thick medical volumes. Beside it stood the usual paraphernalia of a consulting room: scales, blood pressure kit, a monitor of some sort, charts on the walls. A padded couch dominated the other side of the room, soft black leather and steel tubing, with bolts and sliders all along the frame. An open door led to another room. The light was off but J.K. thought that it might be a shower or a bathroom of some sort.

He looked up and saw her, their eyes met, locked for a moment and then he turned away. In that single, lingering look he understood perfectly who she was, and she in turn seemed to suck meaning from his uncertain eyes. She was so unlike Louise, and very different from Kasia.

'Welcome to the Institute,' she said, her voice cool and refined, matching to perfection the natural authority of her uniform.

'Thank Nurse for welcoming you,' Louise chided, a touch angry at J.K.'s perceived insolence.

'Thank you, Mistress,' he whispered, unable to lift his gaze from the ground. He did not need another look, already her image had been imprinted vividly onto his imagination. Black shoes that sported stiletto heels that glistened, black stockings of fine mesh, short white nurse's uniform, cinched at the waist, short sleeves, white cap. Her face was pure ice: white flawless skin, dark brown eyes, lips that were full, pursed, glossy scarlet and enticingly sensual.

'You can address me as Nurse,' she told him.

'Yes, Nurse,' he whispered. The desire that had flared up was sudden and powerful, ignited by the powerful Mistress that stood before him. She understood, she was a Mistress, and carried herself accordingly. Hers was a natural understanding, she was a Mistress by instinct and, in a way that was completely intuitive, she could see that J.K. was ready to fall to his knees in adoration. Nurse. Even her title was perfect. In his mind J.K. spelt it with a capital, repeating it lovingly and let the connotations echo through his excitement.

'Undress,' she ordered, snapping the single word with curt authority.

'Yes, Nurse,' he repeated, thrilling to the sound of his

submission. There would be no pretending with her, she would know what was going on in his mind better than he did. The contrast with Kasia could not be more marked.

Quickly he pulled off his sweatshirt and dropped it to the floor, shoes he kicked off eagerly, socks came off at once. Then he stopped, Louise was behind him, watching intently, fascinated by what she was witnessing. He could tell that she too had divined his true nature, saw it clearly in the way he could not meet Nurse's eyes and in the quiver of his voice.

'Don't be bashful,' she told him, laughing lightly at his obvious discomfort.

'Undress, now,' Nurse repeated, her voice unhurried, the threat unspoken but evident to J.K.

His heart was thumping, and the blood seemed to rush to his face. He could feel the red flush of shame and confusion, and that only added to the feeling. Closing his eyes he unzipped his trousers and pulled them down, stepping out of his jeans and then picking them up to cover himself.

'Well, well,' Nurse smiled. 'This is a surprise. There was nothing in your record about this.'

'What does . . .' Louise began to ask but was cut off by a sharp look from Nurse.

'Is there something you'd like to tell us?'

J.K. ventured to look up once more. Her hair was reddish brown, neatly arranged under her cap, thick eyebrows above eyes that were fixed intently on him. 'No, nothing,' he told her, before looking down again once more. Her heels were high, the curve tapering down to a point, and he longed to kneel before her and press his lips to them.

'Undress completely,' she commanded, pointing a long red fingernail at the trousers he was using to shield himself.

He obeyed because it was the only thing he could do. The trousers fell to the floor and all eyes in the room fixed on his smooth thighs. He dropped his shorts and stood before Nurse, completely naked, his stiffening cock rising from a neatly shaved triangle of hair.

'How often do you cross-dress?' she asked, the question precisely worded and without doubt.

'I don't,' he lied miserably.

'Lies are punished here,' she responded. 'How often?'

He swallowed hard. 'Not very often,' he whispered, his voice barely audible in its shame.

'Have you ever been punished for it?'

He shook his head. 'No, Nurse, I've never been caught.' He wished fervently that the lie sounded true.

'That I do not believe,' she stated harshly. 'But you have nothing to fear. At the Institute you're not punished for that.'

'What?' he looked up sharply, as though unable to believe his ears.

'That's right,' Louise added.

'There is usually an induction process, and feminisation is a part of that,' Nurse explained. 'I think that in this case we can afford to dispense with that. I shall have to clear it with Mistress Kadia, but if it is approved then you will be allowed to adopt a female persona immediately.'

'I don't want that!' J.K. cried, his voice suddenly powerful again. He stepped forward, his eyes wide with fear and confusion, as though the world were spinning manically about him.

Nurse stepped forward too, snapping her feet apart, heels cracking hard on the stone floor. She slapped hard, her wrist a blur as it struck J.K. full across the face. Her eyes were narrowed, anger expressed as pursed lips and a cold look. Her slap had momentarily shocked J.K., and she seized the chance to grab his arm and twist it expertly behind him. It happened quickly, and before J.K. really had a chance to see what was going on it was too late.

'The lessons must begin early for you,' Nurse hissed.

J.K. moaned, his arm was pulled up behind him, her long nails digging into his flesh adding to the pain. He was a prisoner, held tight and unresisting.

Louise was in front of him, her excited eyes all over him, a smile on her lips. 'You have to be punished,' she reported. She reached out and stroked his cock, and it was only then that he realised the degree of excitement that he felt.

He was pushed across the room, pressed flat across the leather couch. Nurse handled him as though he were a silly child, a slap here, a pinch there, humiliating with the minimum of fuss. He was bent over at the waist, his chest pressed flat against the cool surface of the couch. Her heels dug into his calves and forced his legs apart. A clink of steel and his ankles were fettered and chained to the legs of the couch. Nurse grabbed a handful of hair and forced his face down against the leather. The sound of more chains, the feel of her starched white uniform across his back, the snap of cuffs on his wrists. In a moment he was secured, restrained, fettered across the couch, legs apart, arms apart, face down and unable to move.

'That wasn't too bad, was it?' Louise remarked, happy with the way she and Nurse had manhandled him.

'I've never cross-dressed, never!' he insisted. His hard prick was pressed down against the leather, the coolness of hide sensuous against his flesh.

'Lies are severely punished,' Nurse told him.

'I'm not lying,' he continued, though without the necessary conviction to carry on the pretence.

'Get him a uniform,' Nurse ordered Louise, 'while I teach him the value of the truth.'

'Yes, Nurse,' Louise replied enthusiastically. As she stepped away her fingers stroked the inside of J.K.'s smooth thigh, making him shiver with excitement.

He strained to turn around but he was too well secured to have much freedom of movement. From the corner of his eyes he could see Nurse preparing. She was pulling on sleek black gloves, shiny black rubber and reaching to her elbows, a stark contrast compared to the purity of her white uniform. She smoothed down the gloves and then turned towards him, her eyes scanning his prostrated form with a cool and impersonal eye. She crossed the room to her desk. Her skirt was short and curved tightly around the firm roundness of her backside. At the desk she reached up on to a shelf, her skirt rising and revealing the thick black band of the stockings, the suspenders pulling at them, a glimpse of white flesh between stocking and skirt. J.K. admired her shape, the curvaceous legs so long and supple, the seams of her stockings very straight.

'At the Institute you will learn to obey,' she promised, turning to face him. She held a paddle, rounded, sculpted, hard and unyielding, the padded handle gripped tightly.

'What are you going to do to me?' he asked, even in his excitement remembering to pretend ignorance.

'I'm going to spank that lovely, feminine backside of yours,' she said, smiling. 'And then, when Louise returns, you'll be ready to don your uniform.'

She crossed the room quickly, the determined look on her face silencing him. She positioned herself behind him, ran her gloved hand over his skin, up across the thigh, touching his balls, across the cleavage of his backside and finally over his lower back. The feel of her fingers, clothed in tight black rubber, made him catch his breath.

The scream of pain died in his throat. The sharp smack of the paddle across his backside echoed in the room. It felt like fire on his flesh, a wicked red heat that seared and smarted. Another smack, and then another. Aimed quickly and hitting hard on his sweating skin. She beat expertly, at the top of the thigh, across the buttocks, a touch across the anal hole, on the inside of the thigh. Deft movements, light touches of the paddle that had him squirming and moaning, clenching and twisting in an effort to get away. At last he could hold back no longer, she was beating harder and harder, until the cries escaped from his open lips. He screamed as she smacked hard, wielding the paddle as an instrument of revenge and pain.

It was a while after it stopped that he regained his footing. He had slipped at the height of the punishment, when blows rained down on his martyred form. The blaze on his skin was still acid, and yet he had lost himself in the rhythm of cruel chastisement, accepting it with pleasure in the midst of the pain. He righted himself, wincing as he realised just how much she had inflicted on him.

'He's hard,' he heard Louise say, reaching down to stroke his cock, which was wet with fluid pouring from the glans.

'I've spoken with Mistress Kasia,' Nurse said, walking back into the room.

J.K. felt dazed, things were still hazy, but he understood that the prolonged beating across the backside had taken him out of himself. The insistent smack of the paddle across his skin, the heat of punishment at the Nth degree, had been enough to disorient him completely. Lost in the world of sensations, he had lost track of time and place. His cock ached, as though the red heat on his arse-cheeks and thighs had burned through to the underside of his body. The feel of the leather under him was a tantalising frenzy that now threatened to bring him to the peak of pleasure.

'I have the uniform ready, Nurse,' Louise reported delightedly.

Nurse nodded and Louise sprang into action. With a few deft movements she had loosed the bonds and released J.K. from his prostrated position. He moved slowly, every muscle in his body screaming its protest. The weakness and the dizziness were overwhelming and he feared that he would collapse to the floor.

'This is what you will wear from now on,' Nurse told him, gesturing to the blue skirt and white top that Louise held for him.

'Yes, Nurse,' he croaked. He was to be dressed like one of the girls from the Institute, and the idea of it filled him with an indescribable delight. Despite the pain which she had so viciously inflicted, at that moment J.K. felt nothing but gratitude to Nurse. She understood him, she had punished him so severely precisely because she understood him.

Shakily he reached out and took the clothes. The loose top he pulled over his head and then stepped into the skirt. The cotton material felt sharp across his reddened arse-cheeks, but when he turned he saw how short it was and that too filled him with paroxysms of delight.

'We need a name, too,' Louise said, reaching under J.K.'s skirt and stroking her cool fingers between his burning rear cheeks.

'Jaki,' Nurse decided instantly.

'Yes,' Louise agreed, 'that sort of fits with his real name, doesn't it?'

'Welcome to Institute, Jaki,' Nurse smiled.

'Thank you, Nurse,' Jaki responded, her voice soft and yielding, as though the punishment had taken the male edge from it.

'Now, thank Nurse properly for being so kind to you,' Louise instructed.

'How?'

'On your hands and knees,' Louise explained, pointing to the floor.

Jaki knelt down at once, on all fours where she knew she belonged. The burning on her backside was insistent, and when she crawled forward the hem of the skirt flapped back and forth over her naked backside.

'Good, Jaki, that's very good,' Nurse said approvingly. 'Now, a good girl like you is always ready to pleasure her Mistress. Do you know what I mean?'

'No, Nurse,' Jaki lied, her greedy eyes were already fixed on the hem of the uniform. She longed to be commanded to pleasure Nurse, to lift the skirt and apply her tongue to her new Mistress's hot pussy. She had been named Jaki again, and it felt like a rebirth, a rediscovery of her true self under the cold exterior that was J.K.

'I want you to use your tongue on me,' Nurse told her. 'I want you to give me pleasure. That is your reward for being good, the punishment for being bad you have already experienced.'

Nurse retreated back to the couch. She skipped up on to the edge of it and parted her thighs, lifting her skirt at the same time. Under the crisp white uniform she was wearing lacy black briefs, almost transparent against the voluptuousness of her sex. Jaki crawled forward eagerly, watched with excitement by Louise. Nurse pulled the crotch of her panties aside, opening the redness of her pussy to Jaki's searching tongue.

Jaki was lost in pleasure, her mouth suffused with the distinctive taste of Nurse's quim, enjoying the bouquet and the slick juices that she licked on to her tongue. She lapped up and down, drinking in the dew from Nurse's sex, before searching for the jewel. Nurse teased herself for a second and then clutched a handful of Jaki's hair and steered her into place. The moans of delight and the sighs of pleasure were music to Jaki's ears. She used Nurse's mewing pleasure song to guide the movement of her tongue. She toyed and played with Nurse's swollen clit, until at last Nurse screamed her orgasm, her body going limp as she peaked ecstatically.

'Now it's my turn,' Louise declared jealously.

Nurse released Jaki and turned to Louise. 'Careful, girl,' she warned coldly, 'don't forget your place here.'

'Yes, Nurse,' Louise replied contritely.

'On your knees,' Nurse ordered. 'I want you to show Jaki where else Nurse likes to be pleasured.'

Louise obeyed, though it was hard for Jaki to understand what the story between the two women was. She watched as Nurse turned over, adopting the same position that Jaki herself had adopted for punishment. Nurse's backside was firm and round, the fullness of the flesh bulging against the black suspender belt she wore. Louise inched forward and then used her hands to part the lovely round arse-cheeks, exposing to view the round anal bud. Jaki understood at once, and she ached with passion as she watched Louise move forward and begin to joyously mouth the rear hole. Nurse sighed softly, lost in sensual pleasure once more.

Chapter Nine

'Is this what you do?' Rebecca demanded, angry tears filling her eyes. She waved the book in front of her, a heavy tome thick with a layer of dust, the dull green of the cover and the academic title turning it into an icon of respectability.

'You had no right going through my things,' Simone countered, though without the screaming hysterics that Rebecca had claimed as her own.

'*Erotic Motivation: An Inquiry Into The Nature of Desire*,' Rebecca said, reading from the cover of the book. 'Makes it sound all so respectable, doesn't it? Doesn't it?'

'Put the book down,' Simone told her. 'You're upset about something and . . .'

'Upset? You've used me, haven't you? I'm just another one of your sick experiments. What academic journal am I going to end up in? Why don't you stick a fucking label around my neck, Specimen Number 99, Rebecca Cassidy.'

'Why are you upset?' Simone asked reasonably. 'What is it that you find so objectionable?'

Rebecca threw the book down on the armchair beside her. Earlier in the day she had been doing her household chores when she had found the book by Simone's bed. At first intrigued, especially as Simone had authored one or two of the chapters in the book, her initial interest became excited fascination and then sick horror. The book described in great detail all manner of sexual perversions and variations, from sado-masochism and bondage to lesbian dominas and their slaves, cross-dressing submissives and drag queen Mistresses. The cool academic tone, the language of science stripping away the language of desire, could not disguise the deviancy of the acts, and their players. Above all of this, and for Rebecca the very idea of normality was as suspect as the idea of deviancy, there was the emphasis on 'motivation'.

Motivation seemed to be Simone's speciality, her own contributions to the book were on that subject, and she was heavily quoted by other authors. Rebecca had been excited at first to discover more about Simone, the more so as strong feelings were developing between them. It was only when she read about the conditioning of erotic responses, and when hypothetical scenarios of conditioning were described, that her feelings turned to shock and horror.

Suddenly, and with alarming clarity, it all became clear. The no-touching rules, the desire thwarted, the disappointments and the fostering of insecurity, all were part of a process of erotic conditioning. Simone was indeed engaged in mind games of a high order, and Rebecca was their subject. She felt sick with the realisation, because she could see how easily she had fallen, how strongly she had reacted to the situation. The hypotheses described by Simone in the academic journal had been turned into reality, and the actuality of it was far stronger than the dry scholastic language had suggested.

'I object to being treated like a fucking laboratory specimen. That's what I object to,' she managed to say, controlling her anger with the greatest of effort.

'If that is what you've concluded from reading the book then I can only say you are very much mistaken,' Simone told her calmly. She walked across the room and picked the book up.

'What else can it be? We kiss but I cannot touch you. You excite me and then send me away. You've already got me doing the housework for you. You're trying to condition me, just as you describe in your paper.'

'Aren't you going to accuse me of brainwashing you? Or is the next charge to be one of exploitation?'

'That's right,' Rebecca snapped, 'treat me like a child. Isn't that another of your techniques?'

'If you insist on acting like a child then . . .' Simone stopped. 'This is going nowhere, Rebecca. If you read carefully you'll see that nowhere do I describe a situation where a person is made to do something that is against their nature. Everything we have done together has brought us pleasure. If it hadn't then I assume you would have been woman enough to tell me. If you find the situation uncomfortable then it is because you don't like to accept your own desires. Many people prefer to bury their desires, to suppress the things that excite them the most. I had simply imagined that you would have preferred to liberate desire rather than to shackle it.'

Rebecca listened, but the anger was still strong and the hurt too raw. 'Shackle desire? So you call it liberation to have real physical shackles applied? You call it liberation to give yourself completely to another person? You've got everything mixed up, Simone, it's all the wrong way round.'

'Is life really that simple for you?' Simone asked, the weariness coming through at last. 'If life were only so simple, so that what looked right *was* right. If the look of things was so important then we'd only have to worry about the superficial, about the surface detail. But unfortunately life is never that simple.'

'What makes you such an authority on life? What gives you the right to lecture me and tell me what to do?'

Simone shook her head sadly. She crossed the room and slipped the book back on the shelf, one of many such volumes. 'I leave the choice to you,' she said finally, turning to face Rebecca, 'you can leave or you can accept the punishment that I mentioned to you before.'

Rebecca's face coloured sharply. Simone had threatened it before, and at the time Rebecca had been confused by it, but now she understood what it was about. The book had been explicit, and provided the context which had been missing earlier. 'You mean you'll beat me?' she asked. The question had meant to come out as a sneer, instead it had sounded genuine.

'I'll expect you later this evening,' said Simone. 'If you

come up to my room I will punish you with my hairbrush, across the backside. If you stay in your room then I'll take that as meaning our relationship is over.'

Rebecca made no reply. She glared at Simone stonily and then marched out of the room.

Jaki stared up at the ceiling, unable to get to sleep, the events of the day circling in her mind endlessly. She had arrived at the Institute as J.K., been threatened with dire punishments, and been introduced to Nurse who had divined his true nature and had punished him severely. Nurse had then dressed him in the feminine uniform of the Institute, turning him from J.K. back into Jaki and had then extracted her pleasure. The rest of the day had been a blur after that. All her thoughts had been of Nurse, clothed in her uniform of power and pleasure, and fully aware of the raw animal desire she provoked.

After being feminised, Jaki had been shown to her room, then taken down to one of the classrooms. There she had been introduced to a bewildering number of new people, some of them in male attire and some feminised as she was. The teacher had been a strict young woman, who ruled her class with a rod of iron but without the passion that Nurse had inspired. The lesson had been meaningless. Jaki had been unable to pay attention, and had floated along dreamily for the afternoon. Free moments had been few and far between, and she had hardly been able to swap more than names and room numbers with her classmates.

The day had ended with a meal in a communal dining room, where female prefects kept a stern eye on things, and then she had been shown to her room. Her classmates were allowed more time, but being new it had been decided to keep her relatively isolated until she had settled into the strange routine of life at the Institute. It was understandable, but annoying because she had so many questions to ask and so much to find out.

Her room was sparse but comfortable and there was no need for anything else. She had half hoped that she would be sharing, but it seemed that no one in the male dorm was allowed to share. Every room was a single. Thinking back he was certain that in the female dorm that was not the case, but there were bound to be differences in the way that these things were organised. He remembered once that Mistress Shirer had explained that the fetish element was more pronounced in young men than in young women, and that a male dorm would have to accentuate that. If that was the case, and Jaki was uncertain whether the generalisation had been valid or not, it would explain the presence of Nurse completely.

Without wanting to, Jaki's thoughts went back to Nurse. Jaki had ached with jealousy as she watched Louise tonguing Nurse's anal hole. She had imagined herself doing that, on hands and knees, paying homage to Nurse's rear bud, licking and sucking, pressing her tongue deep into the tight sheath of muscle. Just the thought of it made her feel faint with desire, the pit of her belly swirling with excitement. In her mind's eye she saw the picture clearly: on all fours, her skirt high at the back and displaying her own rear end, her face buried in the softness of Nurse's backside, her mouth suffused with the taste as her tongue pierced the tight knot of muscle.

Involuntarily she reached down and stroked her cock, almost climaxing at the first touch. The images were so strong, the desire raging like a fire inside her. She regretted not bending down and kissing Nurse's heels when she'd had the chance, but that would have been too much of a give-away. As it was, she was lucky that more suspicions had not been aroused, but perhaps it had not been the first time that a new arrival had been happy to cross-dress.

Jaki's musings were interrupted by a sound from the door. She leaned over and clicked on the bedside lamp, throwing a pale orange light across the room. Instinctively she covered herself, just as the door to her room was flung open.

'Nurse,' Jaki whispered incredulously, her eyes opening completely to gaze on the object of her fantasy.

'Well, Jaki, I just wanted to check up to see how you were,' Nurse announced, closing the door behind her and striding purposefully across the room. She was still in uniform, high collar, short sleeves, white cap, sheer black stockings and shiny high heels.

'Thank you, Nurse,' Jaki whimpered. She felt weak and terribly happy that Nurse had arrived, but afraid of what the visit might mean.

'I like to keep a close eye on all new arrivals,' Nurse explained, sitting on the edge of the bed, crossing her long legs and showing an expanse of beautiful, stockinged thigh.

'Yes, Nurse,' Jaki sighed. She wanted to call her Mistress, or Mistress Nurse, or Goddess or . . . Nurse was all of those and more.

'Especially arrivals as pretty as you are.' Nurse smiled. She reached out and touched her cool fingers to Jaki's brow.

'Thank you, Nurse,' she repeated, resisting the impulse to grab Nurse's hand and to shower her fingers with kisses.

'You enjoyed being punished, didn't you,' Nurse stated unequivocally. 'And you have no objection to being a good little girl, do you?'

'No, Nurse,' Jaki confessed, as if there had been any doubt.

'Do you like Nurse very much?'

'Yes! Very much, Nurse,' Jaki cried, her feelings bubbling up excitedly.

'Good,' she smiled. In the pale orange light her lips were even more seductive. 'In that case I'll be keeping an even closer eye on you, just to make sure that you're a good girl, and a cooperative one at that.'

'I will be good, honestly, Nurse,' Jaki gushed, in a fever of excitment.

'I'm sure you will,' Nurse said, smiling once more. She reached across the bed and touched Jaki over the duvet, her hand finding the hardness that Jaki had been hoping to keep hidden.

'I haven't been touching myself, Nurse,' Jaki lied, trying to swallow but finding her throat was dry.

'What did I say about lies?' Nurse demanded, throwing back the cover and exposing Jaki's nakedness.

Jaki fell silent, a jewel of fluid glistened on her belly where it had fallen from the slit in her cock. She could feel the pressure in her balls, on the edge of climax even before Nurse had done anything.

'What did I say?' Nurse demanded, slapping Jaki hard on the tip of her cock.

'You punish liars, Nurse,' Jaki said quickly, the pain biting through her silence.

'You've been a bad girl, Jaki,' Nurse told her sternly, 'and I think it's time you had some of my special medicine.'

'Medicine?'

Nurse reached into her pocket and produced a plastic medicine spoon, the gradations of dose marked out on its mouth. Without smiling, she turned back to Jaki and took hold of her cock. Her movements were precise but sensual, stroking the hard cock quickly, measuring every stroke by the rhythm of Jaki's breath. In moments Jaki had closed her eyes and was squirming, her hand clutching at the bed as waves of pleasure washed through her. Nurse wanked her expertly, brushing her thumb over the glans, holding tightly at the base, making Jaki sigh breathlessly. With her other hand she stroked the inside of Jaki's thighs, as though enjoying the contrasting feel of feminine thigh with male flesh.

'Oh,' Jaki whispered as her arsehole was caressed by Nurse, and then she shot her spume of white come. She bucked and writhed, and Nurse continued with the up-down motion, pumping out every last drop of spunk from Jaki's sweaty body.

'What a mess you've made, girl,' Nurse scolded, slapping Jaki's face forcefully.

'Sorry, Nurse,' Jaki whimpered, clutching her burning face and looking down at her semen-splattered body. Her belly was glistening with pools of thick creamy juice, which had arced from her cock in fountains of bliss.

'You have to take your medicine now,' Nurse told her.

Jaki watched silently, unable to believe what she was seeing. Nurse scooped up the thickest droplets of semen into the medicine spoon, the whitish cream filling it to the highest measure. Nurse smiled and slowly brought the first spoonful to Jaki's mouth. For a moment Jaki remained still, her mouth firmly closed, but a sharp look from Nurse broke her resistance. She opened her mouth, and trembling with humiliated delight, swallowed her medicine, the taste of her own orgasm filling her mouth and sliding down her throat.

Simone waited impatiently as the phone rang and rang at the other end, the electronic purr maddening because it did not cease. She was just about to put the receiver down when the ringing at the end stopped and Kasia picked it up.

'We had a new arrival today, I understand,' Simone said, hoping that a late night call would not arouse too many suspicions.

'That is correct,' Kasia reported. 'This one seems to have been an emergency case of some sort. I haven't had time to consult you on it yet.'

'What sort of emergency case?' Simone asked. She knew that Kasia enjoyed working late, she seemed to thrive on the long hours through to dawn.

'I haven't all the details. But having spoken to Nurse it is clear why he was referred to us.'

'Why?'

'A practising cross-dresser according to Nurse's report, his legs were clean shaven and he responded positively to the feminisation.'

'You mean he's in female uniform already?' Simone asked, astounded by the quick transition and half afraid that Jaki had ruined the plan by it.

'She has accepted a femme name also. I think that this one will respond very well to our treatment. I do not think that this one will be any trouble at all,' Kasia reported with evident satisfaction.

'I hope you're right.'

'I am certain, Miss Shirer. Tomorrow I will arrange for you to meet Jaki. I think a good talking to from you at this stage may be very beneficial.'

'As you wish, Kasia,' Simone accepted gracefully, thankful that she had not needed to suggest such a meeting herself. 'Don't work too late,' she added.

'There's so much to be done,' Kasia sighed conscientiously. 'Good night, Miss Shirer.'

'Good night, Kasia, and I'll see you tomorrow.'

Simone put the phone down and sank into the enveloping arms of her chair. All day she had been on tenterhooks, worried that in some way her plan would misfire. Jaki was a good girl and could be trusted, but the Institute had a tendency to tap into the deepest parts of a psyche. Now it was up to Jaki to observe all she could, and if there was anything wrong to investigate it as far as possible.

The diversion with Rebecca had been unwelcome, and now that the dust had settled she wondered whether she had handled it at all well. Perhaps Rebecca was simply not the sort of person to get entangled with. She was too sure of herself, too opinionated and angry to be happy as a submissive, even though there was a part of her that responded to that. Simone walked across the room and selected the book that had started the argument. The pages were starting to grey, and the style of the book was old-fashioned, but there was still much that was of value locked in the close print and obscure terminology.

She returned to her seat with the book in hand, thinking back to the time when she had written her contribution to it. That had been long before the Institute had been built, at a time when she had only just graduated and was looking around to find the path that suited her best. The sexual angle had been an accident, a chance encounter with Fiona Schafer had led to her becoming interested in the study of desire. How strange it had been to discover her own needs whilst researching the needs of others, but that is how it had happened. Her first few papers for the learned journals had been tentative, questioning, a mirror of her self-development. But those few papers, the first faltering steps in her career as a psychologist, had been critically accepted by her peers. Her contributions to the book, which had filled Rebecca with such loathing, had also been her route back to Fiona Schafer. And together they had forged the theories that led directly to the Institute.

Fiona knew nothing of the present troubles at the Institute. Simone had not the heart to tell her. Whilst she was busy on a similar project in the United States, Fiona kept in regular contact, phoning Simone once or twice a week. The Institute was their joint creation, and nothing, not even the width of the Atlantic could keep her away. The time had come, Simone realised heavy-heartedly, to tell Fiona the truth, no matter how difficult that might be. What would Fiona advise? She would advise Simone to do as she thought fit, implicitly trusting her to know what was best.

That was the trouble. For the first time in her life Simone did not know what was best. The problem was that she did not know the full extent of the problems in the male dorm. Nobody did. It was as though there were a secret life that was hidden from the staff, an underground society that functioned despite the close watch and firm control. What form that society took was as much a mystery as to who was involved, and that too was a worry.

The knock on the door startled her. She looked up and saw Rebecca standing there, a nervous, anxious look on her pretty face. Simone placed the book on the floor beside her and waited, encouraging Rebecca to speak.

'If I don't like it,' Rebecca began, 'do you promise to stop?'

'I do.'

'If it hurts then I don't want to do it.'

Simone raised her eyebrows. 'How can you have a punishment that doesn't hurt?'

Rebecca accepted that with a nod. 'If it hurts too much then you'll stop. We can make a deal, can't we? I read once that we can have a secret word, and when I say the word you stop. Does it work like that?'

Simone smiled. 'No safe-word,' she said. 'I'll know when to stop. I'll judge when you've been punished enough. You have to trust me completely, you have to trust me and not false props like safe-words and special signals.'

'But how will you know?' Rebecca persisted.

'Because I'm going to be your *Mistress*,' Simone deliberately laid stress on the word, 'and that means I'll know. Call it intuition, understanding, insight, whatever, when the time is right I'll know. As my slave you will have to trust yourself to my judgement.'

'I've never done this before.'

'I have. Take your panties off,' she snapped the order, and was pleased by the startled look in Rebecca's eyes.

'Have we started?' she asked.

'You will speak when spoken to. Knickers down, now.'

Rebecca was still standing nervously in the doorway, one hand on the handle as if she were about to slam the door shut. She breathed suddenly, almost gasping for air and then took a step into the room, letting the door close behind her. Her face was pale, the colour drained from her lips and skin. Slowly she reached under her long, loose skirt and pulled her panties down to her knees before releasing the thin garment so that it fell to her ankles.

'Bring your knickers with you,' Simone instructed, gesturing from the comfort of her chair.

'Simone?' Rebecca asked, bending down to retrieve her knickers.

'You'll be punished for that,' Simone warned calmly.

'May I ask one question?'

'One question,' Simone agreed, feeling generous.

'Why am I to be punished?' Rebecca asked, stopping in front of Simone.

'Because you need to be.'

Rebecca nodded and subsided into a tense silence. Her panties were held tightly in hand, a frilly white bundle that was warm with a moist heat from her sex. She stood waiting, trembling slightly with nervous apprehension.

'Squat down in front of me,' Simone ordered.

Rebecca's long skirt covered her completely as she squatted before Simone, the folds of material scraping the floor and hiding the nakedness of her sex. She felt excited, her thighs were parted and her sex vulnerable, although well hidden. Simone sat forward and reached under the skirt, careful not to lift the shroud and expose Rebecca's body. Her hand slid smoothly over the warmth of calf and thigh, stroking the silky skin, enjoying the feel of it. She could sense her tension, feel the way Rebecca was trembling nervously. For a few moments she stroked Rebecca's thighs, relishing the softness of skin under her fingertips.

Simone reached down further, her hand travelling across the inner thigh to stroke Rebecca's sex, her palm cupping the labia and fingers closing round them. She held Rebecca for a few seconds, fingers squeezing the pussy lips together. Their eyes met, faces close enough for their breath to mingle. Simone noted the look of bewilderment, and the slight flush of embarrassment, and then Rebecca turned her eyes away. Simone suppressed her smile, controlled her own feelings of arousal, as she began to stroke Rebecca's thighs again, rubbing her hands back and forth of the smooth expanse of flesh.

When she stroked the pussy lips again, Simone felt the heat, the moistness that oozed from within Rebecca's sex. This time she teased the pussy lips open, parting the mouth of Rebecca's sex but not penetrating. It was a game she always enjoyed, teasing, and stroking, tantalising with lingering caresses. She knew that Rebecca's excitement would be growing by the second, that she would be aching to have her pussy stroked and rubbed, to have her clit massaged.

Back to stroke the inner thigh, and then down, grazing the sensitive folds of the pussy and reaching underneath. Simone teased the perineum, fingering the join between Rebecca's pussy and her anus, toying, not touching either sensitive zone. And then the thigh, and again she brushed her fingers over Rebecca's pussy, now slick with juices, before touching, very softly, the flexed anal bud. Rebecca let out a low moan of desire, her eyes were half closed as the pleasure pulsed through her. As Simone removed her hand, going back to stroke the warmth of the thigh, she let her fingers slip across the aching wetness of Rebecca's pussy.

For ages Simone just touched and caressed, moving as the mood took her, enjoying her complete control of the pliant and thoroughly aroused young woman before her.

She pressed a finger into the tightness of the arsehole, testing Rebecca's reaction, who moaned deliriously and moved to accept the anal penetration as best she could. She massaged Rebecca's swollen clit, which seemed to throb and pulse as it was teased. Her fingers entered deep into Rebecca's sex, seeping with nectar and raging with the heat of her longing.

When her fingers were thoroughly soaked with Rebecca's wetness, Simone stroked harder, sliding her hand between the arse-crack and finding the tightness she desired. Her finger waited, resting against the sensitive rear hole, and then, when she judged that Rebecca could stand it no longer, she penetrated roughly. Rebecca screamed, an animal sound that tore from her lips, and then she fell forward, her anal hole opening to the slick finger that entered deeply. Simone began to frig the rear hole, taking her time and relishing every second of it. Rebecca was sobbing wordlessly, tears streaming down her face as wave after wave of orgasm surged through her. Simone pressed her finger deep, down to the lowest knuckle, forcefully taking Rebecca's arsehole and claiming it as her prize.

'Follow me,' she ordered, her voice betraying none of her emotions. She removed her finger and trailed it between Rebecca's bottom cheeks, stroking between the pussy lips which were soaked with the honey of her climax. When she stood up Rebecca fell forward, as though too weak to support herself.

Simone crossed the room, not bothering to look back, certain that Rebecca would summon up every reserve of energy and will in order to obey. She sought the long-tailed lash for a moment, finding it just as Rebecca entered the bedroom.

'Undress,' Simone told her, turning to watch, holding the lash in her hand as she did so.

Rebecca's eyes focused on the lash, on the stiff handle, bound in rough suede, to the thong of black leather that hung stiffly from the end. She undressed, her hands moving automatically across her body. The long skirt fell away, and then the top was pulled over her head. Her breasts were free, nipples erect and excited, her breasts patterned pink by the orgasm she had experienced moments earlier.

'Do you obey without question?' Simone asked, her eyes stone cold as she watched Rebecca struggling with inner demons of doubt and denial.

Rebecca closed her eyes, then she shook her head as though trying to clear the fog in her mind. 'No,' she said at last. 'The questions are there, I can't help that, but I obey in spite of that. That doesn't make sense. But I'll do anything you ask me to, anything.'

'I want you to use this on yourself,' Simone told her, a smile breaking the stern look on her face, brightening the darkness of her eyes.

Rebecca nodded, stepped forward and took the lash. She held it gingerly, loosely, afraid to grip it with the firmness it so obviously required. For a moment everything was still; the two women in the room, the lash that was yet to uncurl properly, the pale light that cast their shadows on the wall. When Rebecca moved it was with a fluid motion that seemed choreographed and stylised. She turned her back to Simone, a back that was smooth and flawless, white skin without blemish. Her right hand was raised high, a fist of defiance clutching the black snake of the lash. The hand dipped and then swept back, the lash swishing sharply through the air and then biting hard against the lower back. Rebecca caught her cry of pain, swallowed it, gritted her teeth and let the sensation burn through her.

Simone watched her, lashing sharply, left and right in turn, every stroke biting bitterly into pale white skin. Soon the red tracks were crossed over Rebecca's backside and lower back, never cutting the skin but raising a lattice of pain as eloquent as it was beautiful. Not once did Simone say anything. She watched, in rapture, as Rebecca beat herself with a finesse that was exquisite and without equal. She noted the sighs of pleasure that infiltrated the moans of pain, listened and understood the journey that Rebecca was making. The cry of orgasm as the lash landed between the arse-cheeks and whipped under to touch the wetness of Rebecca's pussy signalled the end.

Rebecca collapsed on to the bed, her body shaken by sobs of weakness and delight. She had beaten herself with a severity that Simone would never have attempted, lashed herself with a cruelty that only she could deliver. Her body ached with pain, and yet she felt more alive and more sensual than at any other time in her life. She reached out and found Simone's welcoming arms. The two women held each other, Rebecca seeking solace and comfort in the arms of Simone. She ached, and yet she felt nothing but desire as she was cradled and hugged, as soft kisses took away the pain from her body.

'Have I done well?' Rebecca asked, looking up through tear-soaked eyes.

'Very well, my darling,' Simone answered, sweeping back Rebecca's hair and kissing her softly on the brow.

'Will you punish me next time?'

Simone reached down, seeking the raw heat in Rebecca's sex. 'Yes,' she whispered, pushing her fingers into the yielding, open, desirable pussy of her new slave, 'I'll punish you next time.'

Chapter Ten

The first class of the morning was for one of the vocational courses that had been set up in order to justify the Institute's existence. Jaki could remember Mistress Shirer explaining it once to Mistress Diana, how the vocational classes were necessary to bring in government funding, and that the various classes in social skills and politics were paid for on the back of that funding. It made for an interesting mixture of courses, Mistress had explained: a girl might study Erich Fromm in the morning and mathematics in the afternoon.

Unfortunately for Jaki her vocational class was in computers, a subject which she, in her other personality, knew inside and out. Much as she would have preferred not to, she found herself in a room full of computers with a dozen other unfortunates. The familiar buzz of the printers, and the tapping of keyboards, did nothing to excite her interest. Computers were the province of J.K., and any interest in the subject disappeared when Jaki was herself. She sat at one of the terminals and stared blankly at the computer screen, and only the threatening looks from the Mistress in charge of the class induced her to switch the computer on.

However, once the class started she feigned ignorance, taking the opportunity to study the environment around her. It soon became apparent that everyone in her class, those dressed as males and those as females, was more interested in attracting the attention of the prefects, or the Mistress in charge, than in learning the ins and outs of spreadsheets and databases. Jaki noted the way they vied for attention, turning even the slightest difficulties into mighty dramas. She also saw that the prefects and the young Mistress in charge of the class, were well aware of these games and tended to devote most of their attention to those few that had real questions to ask.

As the new girl in the class Jaki attracted attention from her peers, half of whom looked down their nose at her and the other half were eager to make friends. Of the ones that wanted to make friends Andrea seemed the nicest, with her glossy black hair, fiery blue eyes and a smile that was captivating. When she spoke, her voice was soft, husky, and she acted every inch a girl. It was hard to tell that under her skirt she was masculine. With her pretend ignorance it was easy for Jaki to ask for Andrea's help, and there was no objection from the prefects.

Andrea was very friendly, managing to gossip, laugh and show Jaki how to use the computer all at the same time. Jaki merely listened and smiled, unable to concentrate on what she was supposed to be learning. Despite her own double life as a female, she had enjoyed very little contact with other people with the same predisposition, and those that she had met had all been very disappointing. Instead she had always felt most at ease surrounded by powerful and attractive young women, who treated her as a flighty young woman in need of a firm hand. That was what she enjoyed the most, to be punished as a young woman, and even flirting with men who did not know her secret could not compare with that pleasure.

At one point during the lesson Jaki had noticed that Andrea's long fingernails were glossed, the varnish bright and shiny and freshly painted. When she asked about it, Andrea became very tense and her voice dropped to a whisper. Looking round furtively she confided that she had hidden a bottle of nail gloss in her room, and that cosmetics of all sorts were in short supply, unless you knew the right people. Who the right people might be she did not reveal, but Jaki's heart beat with excitement at the realisation that she had unwittingly found her first lead.

Any more conversation on the matter was cut dead by a sudden cry from the other side of the classroom. All eyes turned to the source of the cry: the two girls sitting in the furthest corner of the class. Jaki had noticed them earlier, seemingly engrossed in their work and studiously avoiding all contact with the others in the class. Now, however, the Mistress had grabbed them by the hair and was pulling them across the room.

'Oh shit,' Andrea sighed, shaking her head sadly but knowingly.

'What is it?' Jaki asked her, watching with unconcealed interest as the two young women were dragged across the room and to the whiteboard at the front.

'They've been cheating again,' Andrea explained, putting her hand on Jaki's arm and pulling her closer. 'They're working for their assessments but we all know that they've been swapping answers.'

'What happens now?' Jaki asked, although she was certain of the answer.

'You get to see what punishment means to us here.'

Jaki watched, vaguely aware that every pair of eyes in the room was on the Mistress and the two cheats. The Mistress turned to face the class, her eyes fired with anger and her mouth clenched tightly. Her victims stood beside her, arms hanging loosely at their sides, heads bowed miserably, tops bedraggled and hanging from their skirts.

'How many times must I warn against cheating?' the Mistress demanded. 'How many times do I have to tell you that these assessments are not for fun? Yet again I catch two people cheating and I intend to teach them, and you, a lesson. I hope this is the last time I do this, because next time the punishment will be twice as severe.'

She waited for her words to sink in before snapping her fingers and getting a prefect to jump to attention. She was handed a well worn belt, the leather soft and supple, folded over and ready to be applied.

'Paula,' the Mistress said, speaking to the prettier of the two, 'ten strokes across Pattie's rear. Make them good strokes. If you hold back you'll have to beat her the full ten strokes again, and get twenty in return yourself. Pattie, knickers down, legs apart and touch the floor.'

Pattie looked nervously at her friend and then slipped her knickers down to her knees, chastely reaching under her skirt so as not to expose herself. She turned and faced the whiteboard, covered with the day's instructions in red ink, parted her legs as far as the panties would allow and then bent over. Her legs were straight, and as she bent over the skirt revealed finely shaped thighs that were glossly and smooth. The Mistress gestured to a prefect who smiled and flipped the skirt over the waist, revealing Pattie's plump backside, the dark anal crack leading down to a heavy pair of balls, showing that her cock was building to erection.

Paula stared dumbly, her eyes fixed on her friend's behind, the belt hanging loose in her hand. A prefect had to nudge her before she seemed to wake up. Jaki saw her smile apologetically to Pattie, giving a slight shrug as if to say it wasn't her fault. Pattie looked back, her eyes begging for mercy though she could say nothing. Instead she fell forward a little, her hands flat on the floor in front of her for support.

'Ten strokes, which you'll count out, Pattie,' the Mistress said, crossing her arms across her chest impatiently.

Paula moved into position, standing to one side of her friend so as not to impede the view for everyone else. She lifted the belt and held it high above her head, letting the moment drag on while she feasted on the sight of Pattie, straining to keep her position, her backside rounded and perfect for chastisement. The belt whistled and snapped down hard, making Pattie wince with shock at the impact. She exhaled heavily before calling out, 'One'.

There was a pause before the next stroke, during which Jaki's eyes were drawn to the redness striped across Pattie's bottom cheeks. The second and third strokes were counted out through gritted teeth, the red stripes standing out distinctly against the paler skin. From where she sat, Jaki could see that Pattie's prick had hardened, that the thrashing of the belt was doing nothing to dampen her excitement. Paula was following orders precisely, swinging the belt down as hard as she could, letting the lash sting fully on her friend's backside. Soon, as the number of strokes was counted out by the victim, the red lines began to merge into circles of pain, tanning the skin scarlet and pink at the centre.

At last Paula finished. She stepped back, her face flushed with excitement and exertion. She half-smiled to the class, a smile of complicity as she enjoyed the view of her handiwork: Pattie's bottom and thighs pink with strap marks. Mistress nodded her approval, but only after massaging the reddest part of Pattie's backside, as though checking the full extent of the punishment. She stroked the naked buttocks, touched her fingers along the arse crack and even touched Pattie's stiff prick.

'Now it's Pattie's turn with the belt,' Mistress announced, apparently satisfied with the treatment Paula had meted out.

Pattie had to push herself back to a standing position, and then she carefully rearranged her skirt before turning round. Her face was as red as her backside had been, and she hobbled the few steps necessary to get into position. She glared angrily at Paula, and Jaki realised that revenge was going to be instant. Paula realised it too, for she took her time in assuming the correct position, fidgeting nervously whilst pulling down her pale pink panties and then bending over very slowly.

'Make that twelves strokes,' Mistress snapped impatiently, and drew a contrite look from Paula.

Jaki decided that she had been right, Paula was by far the prettier of the two, her thighs were smoother, shapelier, less muscular than Pattie's, and her buttocks were more feminine and attractive too. In essence she looked more like a girl than Paula did, much more, and even the glimpsed view of her erect penis did nothing to dispel the vision. Once in position there was no dallying by Pattie, who looked intent on extracting the maximum amount of revenge. She was stronger than Paula, and when the belt hissed through the air the snap of impact was that much louder, Paula cried out in pain, her horror overwhelming any other considerations. The red imprint of the belt was a vivid track, and Jaki could well imagine the pulses of sensation that it had caused, could easily imagine the welt that it raised on the skin.

'She didn't count it out,' Pattie reported maliciously, turning to face Mistress.

'Then you didn't strike her,' Mistress said, her imperious face showing not the slightest trace of mercy.

Pattie used the belt again, with the same power and aim as the first stroke, Paula cried out again, but this time she did not forget to yell out the number of the stroke. Her skin coloured easily, it was so pale that every blemish on it would show up, and the two strap marks were paralleled across her full round bottom cheeks. Pattie allowed no time for recovery, she issued the next two strokes in quick succession, swishing the belt and striking hard and painfully.

Jaki turned away from the public chastisement, appalled by the severity of punishment and ashamed at her own reaction. Despite her sympathy for the unfortunate Paula, who now seemed to her the true victim of the display, she could not resist the desire and the excitement within her. She could not control her physical reaction, nor could she control the red heat that swelled in the pit of her belly. Looking around her she could see that many others shared her reaction, there were many faces that showed a mixture of delight and horror, sharing with her a morbid fascination for the exhibition of correction. Beside her she saw that Andrea was watching closely, her attention riveted as Paula called out 'nine' when the belt landed, the whiplash of sound resounding around the room. Paula's beautiful rear was marked with distinct lines, each one burning with a heat that seemed to radiate sexual excitement.

Andrea turned, becoming aware that Jaki was watching her. She smiled coyly and then lifted her skirt, exposing her fully erect cock. Jaki's face flushed red with embarrassment but she could not turn away. She watched, fascinated and afraid, as Andrea reached out for her. Hardly daring to breathe, Jaki felt Andrea's hand touch her on the thigh, sneak up under the skirt and then stop. Andrea leaned back a little and stroked Jaki's thigh, and then, becoming bolder, she touched Jaki's prick. Jaki sighed, inched forward without wanting to.

'Let me,' Andrea whispered, detecting Jaki's nervousness.

Jaki complied, secretly thrilled but hardly daring to think about what it was that was happening. She sighed inwardly as her cock was stroked, squeezed, caressed lovingly, Andrea having a light touch that felt like heaven.

'Both of you will stay on display for the rest of the morning,' Mistress instructed sternly.

Jaki looked up and saw that the two girls had been disciplined, and that both of them were facing the wall, with hands on heads and skirts around their ankles, punished bottoms on display to all. The view was immensely erotic, and she knew that it would be impossible to do any work as her eyes would be drawn to the display all the time.

The door opened and Louise, the head prefect, arrived, causing Andrea to remove her hand quickly from under Jaki's skirt. Louise went across directly to the Mistress, not even stopping to admire the two punished backsides on display to the class.

'Look,' Andrea whispered, and she showed Jaki her hand, the fingers wet with the sticky juice she had milked from Jaki's cock. Without another word she then put her fingers to her mouth and licked away the wetness, smiling wickedly when she saw Jaki blushing furiously.

'Jaki! Here girl!' Mistress snapped, sending a jolt of panic through both Andrea and Jaki.

Jaki felt weak, she knew at that instant that her flirting with Andrea had been observed by one of the prefects. She wanted to burst into tears, to say that it had not been her idea, to affirm that she had not enjoyed it. But that would have been a lie, and one that her body would give away.

'Mistress Kasia wishes to see you,' the Mistress said sombrely. 'I hope for your sake,' she added darkly, 'that you've not broken any of the rules.'

'No, Mistress, I haven't,' Jaki reported breathlessly. She felt relief tinged with more nerves. She had not been caught out with Andrea, but now she was afraid that she had unwittingly broken some other, far more important rule.

'Louise will take you there,' Mistress replied, and her tone suggested that she did not believe Jaki one bit.

Louise gave no sign that she had ever set eyes on Jaki before, nor that she would lower herself by doing so at any point in time. She turned on her heel and marched across the room to the door, pausing only to make sure the other prefects in the room were behaving themselves. Jaki chased after her, in the blur of the moment not even bothering to look back across the room to see if Andrea was OK.

Jaki tried hard to adopt the same brisk stride and pace as Louise but couldn't quite manage it. Too many thoughts ran through her mind – fears that she had broken a cardinal rule and was to be severely punished for it, or, much worse, that her reason for being at the Institute had been discovered. She followed Louise along the silent corridors, unable to gain her bearings in the large, rambling building.

'Wait here,' Louise muttered, leaving her outside the door to Kasia's office.

'Yes, Mistress,' she responded, wanting to be on her best behaviour in case of the worst. Louise smiled, losing the icy untouchability that she had projected. Jaki smiled back instantly, gratified by the friendly smile and taking it as a sign that the worst of her scenarios had not come to fruition.

Louise knocked on the office door and went in. A second later she was out again and gestured for Jaki to go in. Taking a deep breath Jaki did as she was told, and entered once again the cramped confines to Kasia's office.

'You are here,' Kasia announced stiffly. 'This is Mistress Shirer, the Director of the Institute.'

'Hello, Jaki,' Mistress Shirer said, her voice emotionless and her face impassive.

Jaki gave no sign of recognition, and she stilled the fear that made her heart pound violently. 'Hello, Mistress,' she whispered.

'Mistress Shirer is interested in your case,' Kasia explained. She was standing by the desk, which was occupied by Mistress Shirer. A thick folder full of papers was spread out on the desktop, and it was obvious that it had been studied in detail.

Mistress Shirer took up the explanation. 'After speaking with Mistress Kasia and Nurse, I think that there is perhaps more to you than meets the eye. Is that not so?'

'We want the truth, now,' Kasia added menacingly. Her hair was arranged in a tight bun, pinching in her face and making her seem cold and heartless.

'I . . . don't know what you mean,' Jaki murmured hesitantly, her eyes seeking direction from Mistress Shirer's expressionless countenance.

'You have admitted to the cross-dressing,' Mistress Shirer began, 'something which you managed to conceal during your assessment. We have also noted that you have accepted the idea of female dominance remarkably quickly. It is as though the idea of it is not new to you.'

'You submit too willingly,' Kasia observed.

Jaki denied the charges. 'I don't, that isn't true,' she said.

'Lies are punished most severely,' Kasia warned.

'Have you had a Mistress before?'

'No, never,' Jaki stated flatly.

'Tell me how it is that you began to accept the feminine side to your character?' Mistress Shirer asked. She gave a curt, almost imperceptible nod, a look that Jaki understood and which she saw that Kasia has missed completely.

Jaki understood. The bare bones of a story had been sketched out previously, but Mistress Shirer had not supplied the details, which Jaki now had to supply, and supply them convincingly.

'It was an ex-girlfriend,' she whispered softly, deliberately bowing, looking down at the bare floor of scratched tiles. 'She was a bit wild, into all sorts of kinky stuff, and once I got involved with her I sort of got pushed into it too. One night we were both a bit drunk, feeling really sexy and laughing and joking and she just picked up a tube of lipstick and applied it to my lips. It was a joke at first. She said it made my lips look really sexy and kissable. That turned us both on even more, and I liked the feel of it on me, and she liked the taste of it, and kissing was really sexy. That's how it started.'

'It is a long journey from that to where you now stand,' Kasia pointed out sceptically.

'Well, we were both so turned on that first time, that soon it became a regular part of our love-making. I used to really look forward to her making-up my lips, and then applying a little bit of rouge. One day she used her silk panties to wank me off, wrapping my prick in them and stroking it till I spunked my load. The next step was for her to suggest I try on her knickers, and that was a real turn on too. She was absolutely crazy,' he added wistfully.

'There is more,' Kasia said, confusing question and statement in her odd kind of way.

'There is,' Jaki admitted. 'I tried on her lingerie, and liked it, we used to fuck like animals when we were turned on like that. Then she wanted me to go the whole way, pretend to be a real girl, she had this lesbian fantasy she wanted to act out.'

'She didn't have female lovers?' Mistress Shirer interrupted.

Jaki nodded. 'Yes, she did, though I didn't find out till later. I liked playing games, but I didn't want to go as far as she did. One night she suggested something different and produced a pair of handcuffs, which she'd borrowed from somewhere. It was just another game. She rouged my face, made-up my lips, dressed me in silky panties and cuffed me to the bed. Then she pulled out the razor. I couldn't believe it. She had to use a hanky to gag me as she used the razor to shave my legs, doing it nice and slow till I was sore all over. Then she applied oils to soothe my skin, and that made me realise how sensuous and feminine my legs looked. We made love all night, while I was still chained to the bed. After that there was no turning back.'

'Classic reinforcement,' Mistress Shirer commented, turning to Kasia who nodded sagely.

'The cuffs,' Kasia said, 'did she need them again?'

Jaki looked embarrassed. 'No,' she confessed guiltily. 'Once I'd had my legs shaved, and under my arms too, I began to enjoy being a girl more and more. And she began to enjoy having me as a girlfriend, one that would do as she was told too. That's when the stealing began. She liked to test me, to see how far I would go. Stealing things was one of the tests. Stealing expensive lingerie from shops, or flirting with male shop assistants while she stole things. If I resisted she'd hurt me – slap me or pinch me. Sometimes she'd throw me out into the street. She liked to live right on the edge. Like she'd like to expose my body to complete strangers, or she'd threaten to sell me to groups of men so they'd fuck me. All sorts of weird shit.'

'Which turned you on, no doubt,' Mistress Shirer surmised.

Jaki nodded. It was a made-up story, but the telling of it was turning her on, exciting her the way her wildest fantasies always did.

'What happened between you?' Kasia asked, exchanging significant glances with Mistress Shirer.

'She kicked me out eventually,' Jaki said, the imagined emotion choking her up. 'By then I was her slave, devoted to her utterly and completely. She had been into the Mistress trip in a big way, and flaunted her dominance as often as she could. Her friends thought it was wild, and she played on that, making me do the most outrageous things to show everybody how much of a hold she had over me. But it was all show, after a while she grew bored with having a slave, and then when she met Pearl it was the beginning of the end.'

'The lesbian fantasy?' Mistress Shirer guessed.

'That's right. Pearl was a bored little rich girl living off her family's money. We met her at a party where she'd been boasting to everyone about how wild she was. My Mistress proved that she was even more wild, she had me pouting at her feet all night, kissing her heels deliriously, until, at the height of the party, she dragged me to the centre of the room, stripped me down to my knickers and had me use my mouth on her. She climaxed repeatedly, getting off on the exposure as much as anything, climaxing to cheers and applause. That night Pearl came home with us, captivated by what she had seen and obviously madly in love with my Mistress. A week later I was out and Pearl was the slave, and being paraded and humiliated just as I had been.'

'So why are you here?' Kasia asked directly. Her tone was less harsh than it had been, and Jaki hoped it meant that the story had been believed.

'Because I tried to steal my way back into her affections,' she confessed.

There was silence for a moment, and then Mistress Shirer rose from behind the desk. 'This changes things quite radically,' she explained. 'The induction period is usually set aside so that the new arrival can adjust to the Institute. For many the changes required are too massive to be made in one fell swoop, they have to be broken in slowly and trained. It seems to me that you have been partially trained, and that you are ready to accept in full the rigours of our treatment. Kasia?'

'I concur,' Kasia said, sitting back behind the desk vacated by Mistress Shirer.

'In that case we will expect complete submission. Any sign of defiance or disobedience will be severely punished. For your own sake,' Mistress Shirer warned, her face deadly serious and her eyes sparkling with dark power, 'do not transgress. You are dismissed.'

'Thank you, Mistress,' Jaki whispered, her breath fluttering excitedly.

'Thank Mistress properly,' Kasia directed, pointing to Mistress Shirer's steel-tipped high heels.

Jaki sank to her knees, her eyes fixed on the shining patent leather, on the heels that she had worshipped before. Her lips tingled with anticipation as she crawled forward to kiss Mistress's feet.

It was almost a relief when the door creaked open and Tina heard the shuffle of feet in the darkness. She had been expecting the nocturnal visit of the Sisterhood for some days, looking forward to it with a mixture of dread and excitement. She had been afraid that her single act of theft would be discovered, and that the punishment for it would mark her skin for days, and remain imprinted in her memory long after the marks had disappeared. Each time someone came into the office she was certain that they would check the records and find the disparity between what had been confiscated and what remained locked away.

But with the fear of capture there had been the excitement and the relief that she finally had something to deliver to the young women who called themselves the Sisterhood. She had been afraid of their sorority of punishment, but that fear was nothing to the thrill of anticipation when she imagined the rewards they would offer for her compliance.

'Well, bitch? What have you got for us?' the familiar voice of the leader of the group demanded. It was a voice accustomed to command, and it struck a chord that resonated with Tina's excitement.

'Yes, I managed to get what you wanted,' Tina reported, sitting up in bed and trying to discern the outlines of the young women before her. She had wanted to emphasise the risks she had taken, the efforts the task had required, but something told her that such pleas would cut no ice with the Sisterhood.

'How much?'

The question threw Tina, who had expected at least some gratitude. 'Enough not to raise too many suspicions,' she responded sharply.

'The mask,' the leader of the group snapped, and her minions pounced before Tina had a chance to react. There was a moment of blind panic, when her mouth and nose were covered and she could hardly breathe, and then she was free. The leather mask cased her skin, covering her face and eyes completely. She touched herself, fingers pressing over the unfamiliar leather face, the thick leather mediating her touch. That it felt good was no real surprise, she remembered how it had felt oddly reassuring the first time it had been put on her, and that feeling surfaced once more.

'Where have you put it?' a voice asked, sounding close enough to touch.

'I hid it behind my books,' Tina explained, her lips pressing against the hard lower edge of the mask.

'She's telling the truth,' a voice reported a few moments later.

‘There’s not much here though,’ another voice added.

‘That’s all I could get,’ Tina explained. ‘You don’t know how many chances I took. You think it’s easy?’

‘Shut up,’ the leader told her. ‘As a first payment this’ll do,’ she continued. ‘Next time you’ll do better.’

‘Next time?’ Tina cried.

‘Next time. Think of this as your subscription to an exclusive little club,’ the voice was cold and mocking.

‘Let me join properly then,’ Tina snapped back, angry that her efforts had produced nothing but mockery and ingratitude. ‘Let me join the Sisterhood.’

The laughter was even more mocking, a cutting edge to it that was cruel and insufferable. Tina’s tears were of anger and disappointment, the moisture that rained from her eyes pouring against the inside of the cool leather mask.

‘You don’t join the Sisterhood,’ the leader explained contemptuously, ‘you’re born to it. Haven’t you learnt anything from this place? You’re either a slut or a queen, and you’re just a little bitch who does as she’s told.’

‘But . . . but you promised,’ Tina cried, turning her head this way and that in an effort to see through the blindness across her face.

‘Oh yes, your reward for being a good little girl.’

A snap of the fingers and Tina was being grabbed and turned over, her cries muffled by a hand over the mouth. She was powerless and vulnerable, unable even to see through the darkness of the mask. Rough hands tore at her clothes, pinched her skin, slapped her roughly, scratched as she struggled. In moments she was naked and on her belly. She was faceless, and the heat of the struggle had become the heat of desire, all of it hidden behind the impassive leather face that was hers.

‘What are you doing?’ she begged, realising that, with the Sisterhood, reward and punishment were the same thing, and that it had been stupid to believe otherwise.

‘Shut her up,’ the leader ordered.

‘No . . . please . . .’ Tina cried, and tried to struggle. Her mouth was forced open and something warm and soft stuffed between her teeth. She breathed harshly, the heady scent of pussy filling her lungs. Her mouth had been gagged with her own panties, which had been torn off earlier, and the bouquet of her body filtered every breath.

Completely powerless, totally vulnerable, she gave in to the feeling of submission, losing all energy to resist. Her hands were held down, but there was no need. She had simply ceased to have a will of her own. She was now under the control of the Sisterhood, in the power of women she had never even seen.

She was pulled up at the waist and a pillow pressed underneath her, forcing her bottom up and slightly open. A hand stroked her inner thigh, the way a person might stroke an obedient animal. Another hand parted her bottom cheeks, and she heard murmured comments, appreciative whispers about her body.

'Bitch is creaming it,' another voice reported, dipping a finger into Tina's wetness.

'We're going to play a little game,' the leader whispered, her hot breath touching Tina's mouth and lips. 'You have to guess how many of us there are in the room. Get it wrong and we take you, get it right and you get to sleep like a good little girl tonight. See, it's easy. Just a number.'

Tina tried to speak through the gag, but the muffled sounds of complaint were nothing. She twisted round, hoping to be allowed to speak but her face was slapped and she was forced down again.

The laughter was silenced by a sigh from the leader of the group. 'Too bad,' she commiserated, 'but that was the wrong answer. The answer's five, not whatever it was that you said.'

'You need to speak clearer,' one of the Sisters laughed, and slapped Tina hard on the backside.

'You know what that means don't you?' the leader continued. 'No? Let me show you.'

Tina was pressed down hard, her face pushed flat against the mattress of her bed. Two fingers were applying a cold, oily substance to her backside, sliding the slippery lubricant up and down the anal cleft before pressing in against her arsehole. She winced at the violation, tensed up but she was already greased and the fingers slid in and out of her brown anal ring without a problem. There was pain, sharp but defined, and pleasure that made her sigh through the clammy dampness of her pantie gag.

She was grabbed by the waist and pulled up, lifting her rear side and opening her even more. She sagged, too weak to resist, the desire surging through her with all the force of adrenaline fear. Something cold and hard touched her. It was long and smooth with a curved tip that pressed against her anal hole. A cry of triumphant from around her, and Tina felt the dildo being forced into her hole. She squealed and cried, but nothing came through the gag except the same muffled sounds, which merged with the sounds of her pleasure.

In her mind she could picture it all: gagged and masked, held down, anus greased and open, being fucked by a female wearing a dildo around the waist. She could feel the girl thrusting into her, feel the thighs astride her own, feel the coolness of the artificial cock forced lovingly into her anal passage. Each stroke, each thrust, made her feel dizzy with pleasure, a pleasure darker than any she had known. Sodomised by another female, she climaxed as soon as a finger was touched to her clit.

'The hot bitch is really creaming it,' one of the voices reported, amazed and delighted by the fact.

The thrusts were faster and more powerful, and then there was a cry and it stopped, the body above her collapsed forward, and Tina felt warm sweaty breasts against her back. The woman had climaxed, and her orgasm had triggered an avalanche of pleasure that echoed through Tina's mind and body.

'Number two,' a voice whispered.

'Only three more to go,' another chorused.

Tina climaxed suddenly, the wet dildo plunged deep inside her rear hole again. Five women. She was going to be sodomised ritually by five young women, who were to use her for their pleasure until they were sated and then they would leave, casting her aside without a thought. And she would not even know who they were.

Chapter Eleven

The surface of the water reflected patterns of light on the enamelled surface of the bath, the waves of light crossing back and forth across the surface, moving with the slow rhythm of Nicola's breathing. The hot water soothed and relaxed, and the patterns of light that danced across the clear surface were hypnotically beautiful. Her body glistened with jewels of water, pink skin beaded with droplets that cascaded when she moved. Her nipples, soft and pink, bobbed below the surface of the water, breasts rising and falling as she lay as still as she could.

With eyes closed she imagined that she was far away, floating in the warmth of an ocean under the heat of a bright sun. She imagined that the water flowed with the rise and fall of the tides and not with her breathing, the water cooling her body from the harshness of the afternoon sun. Soon she would float back to the beach, letting herself drift along with the waves, until she too was washed ashore. There she would let relax on the golden sand, exposing her nakedness to the sun and enjoying the heat as it dried her skin. She would close her eyes, the sun would be bright orange beneath her eyelids, her lips tangy from the salty water. A dark shadow would cross her path, blocking out the bright sunshine for a moment.

He would be tall, muscular, dark hair bleached by the sun, bronzed body glistening with a thin layer of sweat. Dressed only in cut down jeans, his eyes would be fixed on her nakedness. They would exchange no words, instead their eyes would meet and the shared desire would be communicated with a single glance. In moments he would be beside her, his lips on hers, hands reaching for her hardening nipples.

'What are you thinking about?' Tiffany asked, her voice breaking the fantasy that had enveloped Nicola with a warmth that was entirely physical.

'Nothing,' she lied, her face colouring slightly. Her nipples had hardened, and the heat kindled in her cunny was beginning to spread sexily as the fantasy had deepened.

Lazily, Tiffany trailed her hand in the warm water, watched warily by Nicola. 'There's no need to lie,' Tiffany said, without rancour.

'I wasn't thinking about anything, really,' Nicola said, trying not to sound too defensive. She watched the ripples caused by Tiffany's fingers, felt the slight disturbance of the water surge across her breasts, tremors of warmth across her nipples.

'Are you really my baby?' Tiffany asked, twisting her head round to look doubtfully into Nicola's blue eyes.

'You know I am,' Nicola responded intensely, taking Tiffany's fingers and kissing them, her tongue lapping at the droplets of water that poured from Tiffany's hand. She was Tiffany's and it meant more to her than anything else.

'How much do you love me?' Tiffany asked, as though she did not believe, as if there were any doubt at all as to Nicola's professed loyalty.

'As much as I can,' Nicola assured her. She knew that there was to be a test. There was always a test, inevitably, invariably, as though her love was designed to be tested at every opportunity.

'Show me.'

'How? What must I do for you, Tiff? What must I do to show you how much you mean to me?'

Tiffany smiled, satisfied that Nicola was keeping to the script they had evolved together. 'Do you love me enough to fuck every girl in the building?'

'You know I do,' Nicola said, without a shadow of doubt in her mind.

'Do you love me enough to let me beat you with the riding crop?'

'Yes, you know that,' Nicola affirmed. She had borne the marks of that test for days, and shown off the black and blue bruises with pride.

'Do you love me enough to be sold to someone else?'

Nicola swallowed drily. 'Will I still get to see you?' she asked, in a voice so small and weak that Tiffany smiled.

'I won't sell you,' Tiffany promised, smiling happily. She trailed her hand through the water again, making the water rock back and forth, shifting Nicola bodily as the water crashed and splashed at each end of the bath.

Nicola relaxed. She felt safe, and secretly happy that Tiffany loved her enough not to sell her. She would have submitted to anything, any test no matter how painful or how humiliating so long as Tiffany would take her back at the end.

'Enough,' Tiffany declared, 'you've had a long soak, we'd better get you back to your room before we get into trouble.'

Nicola accepted without complaint. She knew how much of a risk it was to be out of her room at night, and how much of a risk it was for Tiffany to be with her too. If they were caught it would be instant retribution, and the two of them would wear the strap marks for a week, especially if Kasia was the one handing out the punishment.

She stood up quickly letting the water pour from her body, enjoying the warm rivulets running down her chest and between her breasts, loving the feel of the water rushing down between her thighs. Even better she loved the way Tiffany was watching, her dark eyes proud that her best girl was so beautiful, certain that her possession was cherished by so many other girls.

'Do you enjoy showing yourself off like this?' Tiffany asked casually, placing a hand on Nicola's breast, cupping the warm flesh and letting the water dribble down from the peaked nipple.

Nicola smiled, pushed her chest out, wanting to show herself off, and to excite Tiffany enough for them to make love. 'Yes, you know I do,' she admitted softly, taking Tiffany's other hand and placing it against her breasts also.

For a few moments Tiffany caressed her softly, massaging the breasts playfully and flicking her fingers across the swollen nipples. Her dark eyes were brimming with excitement, her gaze fixed on Nicola's expression of delight. She released one breast and ran her hand down Nicola's front, from the glistening valley between the breasts, over the flat smoothness of her belly to stop at the bush of brown curls that fringed Nicola's pussy. She rested her hand there, luxuriating in the wet curls of hair, cupping Nicola's sex in her palm.

'I'd like to see you more,' Tiffany said, lowering her voice to a husky whisper. She squeezed on Nicola's right nipple whilst her other hand ran back and forth through the light brown curls of pubic hair.

'What do you mean?' Nicola sighed, the pressure on her nipple turning slowly to pain, a pain that she adored because it came from Tiffany.

'How much do you love me?'

'Lots. I love you lots,' Nicola repeated vehemently, opening her eyes and staring at Tiffany.

'Then prove it, make yourself completely naked for me. Shave your pussy for me.'

Nicola hesitated only for a split second. 'If that's what you want,' she said, taking Tiffany's hand from her breast and kissing it lovingly. Losing her pussy hair was nothing to losing Tiffany. She had no doubts in her mind which was the greater loss.

'Do you mean it?' Tiffany asked coyly, the look in her eyes anything but coy.

'Let me do it,' Nicola insisted, 'I'll show you now.'

'Wait here,' Tiffany ordered, and then skipped up to her feet and left the room.

Nicola sat back in the bath, the clear water had started to cool but it didn't matter. Her heart was racing, the excitement rushing through with all the fears and misgivings that should have been her first reaction. Would it hurt? She hoped not, but it was something she had never done before, something she had never even contemplated. Would it be sexy even? If Tiffany desired it then it had to be sexy, because Tiffany knew about such things, she was the supreme arbiter of sexy things. No other girl in the Institute had such a clear understanding of it. But then Tiffany had the history to show it. The girl who had fucked her sister knew more about the forbidden delights of sexuality than anyone else.

'Stand up,' Tiffany ordered, returning with a small toiletries bag in her hand. She unzipped the floral patterned bag and carefully removed the contents to the side of the bath. Nicola stood up, her nipples puckering up from the cold, her skin crawling with goose-bumps. She watched silently as Tiffany set out the razor, a bar of scented soap, some baby oil, and finally an old fashioned shaving brush. The doubts were flooding in, crowding one on the other, surging in a great wave of panic that had Nicola's heart pounding.

'Out,' Tiffany snapped, tapping the edge of the bath with the razor.

Nicola inhaled sharply and stepped out of the bath, raining water all over the floor and forming puddles around her feet. She sat on the edge of the bath as directed, holding on to the edge nervously. A forced smile could not quite disguise her anxieties, but Tiffany ignored it any way.

'Open your legs wide,' Tiffany instructed, slapping Nicola's knees wide apart. She knelt down so that she could look directly at Nicola's pussy cleft.

The shaving brush lathered quickly on the perfumed soap, the creamy foam scented with the bouquet of wild flowers. The cream was soft and smooth but the horrible old brush felt rough against Nicola's skin, the thick hairs scratched the sensitive folds of her pussy. She watched, silently fascinated as her pussy was soaped and lathered, from her mons right over the pussy lips and down under the crotch. The silver strip of the razor glinted, the sharp edge catching the light as Tiffany moved it closer.

'Be careful,' Nicola cautioned, gripping the edge of the bath with all her strength. The razor cut cleanly through the blanket of foam, cutting away the whiteness to reveal soft pink flesh underneath. Tiffany pulled the razor over the mons twice, and the foam fell away with the wispy hairs caught in the white cream. A few more deft movements and most of the hair was gone, she concentrated hard, carefully working the pussy lips to rid them of any hair, and then lower still.

'Now bend over,' Tiffany said, her voice brooking no dissension.

'But we're finished!' Nicola exclaimed, looking down at her hairless pussy, flecked with soapy foam.

'No, not yet.'

Nicola stood up, turned around and then knelt over the edge of the bath, bending low so that her nipples grazed the surface of the water. She felt another stab of fear as Tiffany began to lather up again, rubbing the shaving brush against the soap to produce another reservoir of foam to play with. She caught her breath when the brush was applied again, under her sex, between the bottom cheeks, across the arsehole and then over the arse-cheeks. Her rear was coated with a thin layer of foam and then the razor was tapped clean and used again. Nicola was cleaned between the bottom cheeks, the razor swathing through the foam, under the sex, and then across the firm bottom cheeks where the silky down of the skin was cleaned away completely.

When it was over she immersed herself in the water, the slight sting a sign of just how clean her skin had been shaved. She stood up and looked at Tiffany, who smiled back happily. Looking down at herself, Nicola was surprised to see how different she looked. Her sex was exposed fully, naked in a way that it had never been before. She touched her backside and realised that there too she was clean, that not even the natural down of her body clothed her.

'Let me help you,' Tiffany offered, taking Nicola's hand and helping her out of the bath.

They kissed quickly, and then Tiffany handed Nicola a heavy towel to dry herself with. She packed away the shaving materials, washing them out in the bath water before pulling the plug to let it drain away.

'Well?' Nicola asked, waiting to hear Tiffany's words of approval. She hoped it had been worth it, because already she felt vulnerable, it had occurred to her that next time she was punished a Mistress might notice the change, and that it might prompt too many embarrassing questions.

'You're mine, aren't you baby?' Tiffany asked, in her usual off-hand manner.

'You know that.'

'When that pussy of yours is wet, I'm going to show them all,' Tiffany laughed. 'I want them to see just how sexy you are, and to see just how much you're mine.'

'I'm wet now,' Nicola admitted quietly. She touched herself, her fingers sliding against smooth flesh and down into the cleft of her pussy, touching the moisture with the very tip of her finger. She shivered with excitement and pleasure.

'Show me how wet you are,' Tiffany challenged, her voice low and sensual.

Nicola pressed her fingers into her quim, stroked her pussy and dabbed her fingers into her elixir. Slowly she slid her fingers deep into her sex, frigging herself with the fingers of one hand and using the fingers of her other hand to touch her joy-bud. She inhaled and exhaled heavily, frigging herself hard and teasing her clit at the same time, lost in the build-up of pleasure that fought away all the fears that had grown earlier. The feel of her bare pussy was a tantalising experience, the clean flesh a constant reminder of how exposed and open she was. She climaxed crying out Tiffany's name, the sweetest song her lips could sing.

'Good, now I want to see you spread your pussy juice over your hairless cunt,' Tiffany ordered brusquely. 'Smear it against yourself, and then I'm going to take you to my room and rub my pussy all over you.'

Nicola sighed. Her mind was filled with images of being fucked by Tiffany, the tight black curls of her sex rubbing against the hairless flesh of her own.

The first session of the morning was given over to a discussion group, to which Jaki contributed little. She still felt nervous and unsure of her place, and it was easier to sit and listen to the rest of the group than to say the wrong thing altogether. It wasn't that the discussion was not interesting, nor that it was not informed and intelligent, but rather she did not have the strong opinions or feelings that the others seemed to have. Instead she had taken the seat beside Andrea, who was the nearest thing she had to a friend, and listened to the discussion on the various strategies open to sexual minorities in a hostile environment.

The way the discussion took place was as interesting as the topic, for although a Mistress was involved she gave equal weight to other points of view and did not attempt to impose her own view, while managing to retain the sense of authority that was natural to her. It struck Jaki as an odd experience, to listen to an argument involving a Mistress who held back without lessening any of her dominant power. There was nothing false about her, she did not need to prove anything, the aura of sexual power was as natural to her as her long reddish hair and greyish blue eyes.

When the discussion fizzled out, dissolving into a long thoughtful silence, the Mistress ordered the group across to the library, so that materials could be collected for further discussion or for use in an essay. Two prefects were summoned to accompany the Mistress and the group, which consisted of six feminised males, to the library building.

'I want work from you all, including you, Jaki,' the Mistress warned.

'Yes, Mistress,' Jaki responded quickly, startled that she had been picked out by name.

They were led to the library by the Mistress, with the two prefects lagging a step or two behind the group. Jaki stayed close to Andrea, looking to her for guidance more than anything else. Mistress Kasia had spoken of rules, and Mistress Shirer of harsh punishments, and Jaki wanted to ensure that she did not unwittingly fall foul of one of these mysterious rules. The picture of Paula being harshly chastised by Pattie and then the two of them set for public display was both exciting and frightening.

Once inside the library the group dispersed, going off in ones or twos to look for books, magazines or journals which could be used to bolster or demolish an argument. It was Jaki's first time in the library, and she was quietly impressed by the extent of the collection, and the modern building in which the thousands of books were housed. Row upon row of books, neatly categorised and stacked, covered every conceivable subject, from the downright practical to the out-right obscure.

'You look lost,' Mistress noted, her sharp voice making Jaki jump again.

'Yes, Mistress,' she explained, 'I don't even know where to start.'

'Andrea, I want you to help Jaki get acquainted with the library,' Mistress ordered directly. 'Start with the index and the computer system and then help her find something she can use.'

'Yes, Mistress,' Andrea agreed, her tone completely respectful, despite the happy smile that lit up her face.

'I don't like people who don't contribute,' Mistress told Jaki. 'Next time we have a discussion you'll lead it, so be prepared.'

'Yes, Mistress, I'll be ready,' Jaki promised, her heart sinking at the thought. She hardly knew anything, and her views were hazy and imprecise compared to the forthright views that had been expressed by some of the other girls.

'Come on,' Andrea said, taking Jaki's hand and leading her away, 'I'll show you how the computer thing works. I know you're no good at computers but this is one thing you've got to learn.'

'I'll do my best,' Jaki agreed readily, realising that she and Andrea were speaking for Mistress's benefit. Together they crossed the lobby to a row of cubicles, two chairs and a computer monitor in each one. Only one of the cubicles was occupied, and for the first time Jaki saw that the massive library was almost deserted. Apart from her little group the only other people present were the prefects who had accompanied them and a small number of other prefects who worked there.

'What you looking at?' Andrea asked, pushing Jaki into a chair in front of the monitor and keyboard.

'This place – it's empty.'

'Of course it is,' Andrea explained impatiently. 'You don't think they'd let the male and female dorms mix, do you? It's our turn this morning, the rest of the week this is used by the female dorm.

'But we're supervised, why shouldn't we be allowed to mix?'

Andrea looked at Jaki strangely. 'You didn't really just ask that, did you? Get real. No matter how much they supervise us things would still happen. Think of it. They'd practically rip our clothes off to get their hands on us. These are women who are caged up, remember, caged up and horny.'

Jaki nodded. It made perfect sense to separate the sexes, and she could see now why it was such a problem keeping them apart. The atmosphere was already heavily sexual, the air tingling with an electric intensity. Allowing males and females to mix freely would have made for an explosive mixture.

'What did Kasia want you for yesterday?' Andrea asked, switching subject neatly.

'She wanted to show me off to Mistress Shirer, and they wanted to ask me some questions.'

'Oh?'

'About what I did before arriving here, that sort of thing,' Jaki explained. She turned and faced the computer monitor, the cursor blinking for input.

'Type something, pretend to do some work,' Andrea suggested, looking warily over her shoulder at the prefects by the loans desk.

Jaki quickly scanned the monitor and typed in a title of a book, her fingers flying over the keys quickly. She stopped suddenly, remembering that she was not supposed to know about computers and text retrieval systems. Andrea showed no signs of having noticed anything untoward. She leaned closer to listen conspiratorially to Jaki's story, but Jaki had nothing more to say.

'What did they say?' Andrea asked impatiently, a touch annoyed by Jaki's reticence.

'They warned me to be good, said that I'd be in big trouble if I ever did anything wrong.'

'Do what wrong?'

Jaki shrugged. 'Nothing in particular,' she said, slowly picking out individual keys on the keyboard in front of her. She was beginning to feel uncomfortable, there was something pensive about Andrea and it worried her.

'Write something down,' Andrea urged, pointing to the pile of scrap by the side of the monitor and the pen attached to the table with a length of wire.

Jaki did as she was told, scribbling down the title of the book, even though it was a title chosen at random and nothing to do with the project they were supposed to be working on. 'Did something happen after I left yesterday?' she asked, wondering if her departure had made any difference to the rest of the class.

'No, you saw Pattie and Paul punish each other. After you went they were left standing at the front, bums on display to the rest of us. Stupid cows, they knew they'd get caught.'

'Maybe they wanted to be punished,' Jaki suggested.

Andrea smiled. 'You're new still, you don't understand how all this works. Sure they got a buzz out of being punished, but that doesn't mean they did it on purpose. Punishment is punishment, it bloody hurts and it's humiliating. Gettting down on your knees to kiss the feet of your Mistress, or running an errand, or doing something for *her*, that's pleasure.'

'You're right,' Jaki agreed wistfully.

'What did you do before the Institute? I mean it took me ages to settle down, you seem dead comfortable being a girl.'

'That's what Mistress Kasia wanted to know too. I was dressing up before I came here. I had a Mistress too, so all of this is doesn't shock me. It surprises me that a place like this could exist, but what it actually does isn't a shock. Do you see what I mean?'

'Sure I do,' Andrea smiled. 'We better do some work. Look at feminism, anarchism, something like that, find out where it is we should be looking at least.'

Jaki keyed in the words and handed the pen and paper to Andrea to write down the results. Behind them both some of the other girls in their class were quietly discussing the books they had selected with the Mistress. A prefect was stamping out books for someone else, the thud of the date stamp an incongruous throwback to the days before technology had transformed libraries.

With a list of numbers and titles to hand, Andrea and Jaki went in search of books. It was still Andrea's game and, despite Mistress's instructions, Jaki was loath to get involved. She liked things to be visceral, immediate, sensual, and political discussions and deep meditations on life and identity were things she had always avoided. Her decisions had been made, she had found her own path and felt no need to pursue the difficult questions any more. Andrea and the others were not in such a fortunate position, and she could well imagine the shock they had experienced on arrival at the Institute.

The books they were looking for were in a secluded corner of the library, a row of shelves forming a small alcove. Andrea smiled at last, relaxed now that they were no longer in line of sight of a prefect or a Mistress.

'Here, have this,' she said, reaching under her skirt and pulling out a small bottle of bright scarlet nail varnish.

'Where did you get it from?' Jaki asked excitedly, taking the small bottle in her hands as though it were something precious.

'Never mind that,' Andrea said, lowering her voice, 'just keep it hidden. And for God's sake, if you get caught with it don't you dare say where you got it. OK?'

'I won't,' Jaki assured her earnestly.

'They'll really punish you for it. You know that, don't you? We're not talking about a few spanks on the backside. If you're too scared to take the risk . . .' She reached out to take the bottle back.

'No! I'll take the risks,' Jaki said, holding the small bottle tightly in hand.

'Good. I'm doing this as a friend. You've got no idea how valuable that little bit of nail gloss is.'

'I appreciate it, I really do,' Jaki said. She felt an urge to kiss Andrea, to reach out and touch her, to press their lips together lovingly.

'We'd better get going,' Andrea said quickly. She grabbed a handful of books and walked out of the alcove, before Jaki had had time to act on her impulse. Jaki carefully tucked the small bottle in her panties and then followed, wondering how Andrea would have reacted if they had kissed.

The librarian stamped out the books, her attention focused on Jaki all the while. She was a fair-haired young woman, slightly plump, her manner not quite as cool and impersonal as many of the other prefects. When Jaki smiled to her she even deigned to smile in return, though it was a smile that disappeared when she saw that another of the prefects was watching. The correct demeanour was cool and off-hand, slightly arrogant to emphasise the power difference between girls like Jaki and themselves.

The rest of the group had assembled by the exit, watched over by the two escorting prefects, and the Mistress was waiting impatiently for Jaki and Andrea. The books had been divided equally between the two of them, and Jaki copied Andrea in holding them forward to show that they had indeed been working and not gossiping idly.

'I'll expect a good report from you, Jaki,' the Mistress said, pointing to the thick tomes that Jaki was holding.

'Yes, Mistress, I'll really work hard on it,' Jaki promised dutifully.

They headed out of the library in single file, each girl following the one in front, completely silent whilst in the presence of the Mistress and her helpers. One of the prefects was holding the door open and counting the girls as they went through. For some reason Jaki lagged behind and was the last to go, following Andrea as before.

'You, stop,' the prefect ordered suddenly. She put out her hand and stopped Jaki following the others out into the corridor.

'What is it?' the Mistress demanded, looking first at Jaki and then at the prefect, regarding both of them with equal strictness.

'I think she's hiding something,' the prefect explained. 'I noticed that she isn't walking properly.'

'Lift your skirt up,' the Mistress ordered. Her voice was harsh and accusing. She seemed to know instinctively that the prefect was telling the truth.

Things had happened too quickly and there was no choice but to do as commanded. With shaking hands Jaki lifted the front of her skirt, to reveal, tucked in the tight lace of her underwear, the small bottle that had been given to her earlier. She looked down at herself, the bulge of her cock caught delicately in the lacy material, and beside it the bulge of the bottle of nail varnish. She did not wait for an order, guiltily she took the bottle out and handed it to the prefect, the glass warmed by contact with her skin.

'Need I ask where you got this?' Mistress began, her features set in solid ice.

'I found it on the floor,' Jaki lied unconvincingly.

'Call Andrea back in,' Mistress ordered the prefect, and then looked back at Jaki. 'Did she give it to you?'

'No, Mistress, I found it. Andrea didn't even see it,' Jaki claimed, looking away from Mistress's searching eyes. She felt fear, both of the punishment which was inevitable, but also fear that she would betray her friend. The swirl in her belly made her feel sick and dizzy, dragging her down in a spiral of apprehension.

'Do you know anything about this?' Mistress demanded when Andrea was brought back into the library.

'No, Mistress, I've never seen that before,' Andrea affirmed, her eyes widening tearfully.

'The truth, girl!'

'I am telling the truth, Mistress,' Andrea repeated desperately. 'I don't know anything about it.'

'Jaki, is this true?'

'Yes, Mistress,' Jaki replied miserably, 'I found it and didn't want to share it so I hid it. She's never even seen it before.'

'You're both lying. When we get back to the class I'm going to make an example of you both,' Mistress promised.

'Yes, Mistress,' Jaki and Andrea both responded automatically.

The walk back to the classroom was like walking on hot coals, the anticipation and dread psyching Jaki to greater and greater levels of agitation and disquiet. Her mind was in turmoil, driven by conflicting desires and needs. To wilfully disobey a Mistress was not in her nature, but by the same token nor was it in her nature to betray a trust so openly given as Andrea's had been. She wished more than anything that Andrea had not given her the nail varnish, or that she had really found it on the floor and so could tell the truth without hurting anyone. The fact that she was going to endure the punishment in the cause of Mistress Shirer was the only light in the darkness, igniting a small flame of martyred pride deep in her soul.

A hushed silence fell over the rest of the group as they filed back into the class, one by one taking their seats to wait for the exhibition to begin in earnest. There was no mistaking the excitement though, the exchanged glances and duplicitous smiles of the audience cutting directly through the forced silence. Andrea waited by the front of the room, her face pale, hands fidgeting nervously. Their eyes met, and Jaki saw the imploring look from her friend, she smiled back to reassure her that everything would be all right, despite the fact that they both knew it wasn't.

'Well? You've both had time to think about it,' Mistress stated coldly.

'I found the bottle on the floor, under the shelves where I was looking for a book,' Jaki said, knowing that her story was growing less and less believable.

'Andrea?'

'I don't know, Mistress, I didn't know about it until I was called back,' she reaffirmed, with only a little more conviction than Jaki.

'I am very disappointed in you, Jaki,' Mistress declared,

shaking her head sadly. 'You're new, and I would have hoped more sensible. Perhaps you haven't understood what punishment really means yet. As for you, Andrea, you've been punished enough to know better. Where did you get the cosmetics?'

Andrea inhaled sharply, her face paler and her eyes darting nervously. 'I don't know what you mean, Mistress. If Jaki says she found it on the floor then I believe her. Maybe it was dropped by one of the librarians?'

'Enough! I don't want to hear another word of this rubbish. Andrea, bend over across that chair.' Mistress pointed to one of the stiff-backed chairs near the front of the classroom. 'I think the cane needs to be reacquainted with your backside, girl.'

Jaki watched, secretly excited but openly afraid, her hands were trembling and beads of perspiration were forming under her arms. She wished that it had been her turn first, because the dreadful anticipation would have been over, the not knowing would have been swept away in that rush of sensation that tore everything else away.

Andrea walked to the chair and stopped to look back sadly at Mistress, hoping, the way that Jaki did too, that there would be a last minute reprieve. There wasn't. There never was but the hope was always there, flickering weakly but never going out. She lined her feet up with the chair and then bent over the back of it, supporting herself by sliding her hands down the chair legs as far as she could go. Her body was forced into position, locked into place across the back of the chair, her legs painfully taut, her skirt riding up slightly. A prefect quickly lifted the back of the skirt to expose Andrea's backside, clothed in a white g-string that was pulled tight into her rounded bottom cheeks. She looked good, Jaki thought admiringly, a body perfectly formed for physical correction.

The cane was long and supple, a thin yellowing strip of bamboo that swished lazily as Mistress held it. Andrea looked distraught, recognising that the wicked cane would bite mercilessly with even the gentlest of strokes.

'Watch this carefully, Jaki,' Mistress instructed, smiling

as she flicked the cane through the air, 'I want you to imagine how much this is going to hurt you. Perhaps you'll change your mind in a few moments.'

The instruction was superfluous, Jaki's mind was full of memories of being caned. She knew just how much the pain would connect with her consciousness. The first stroke whistled and snapped down quickly, a flick of the wrist was all it took, and Andrea whimpered painfully. It left a neat red stripe across the buttocks, a redness that could be seen even through the thin white strip of the g-string. Another quick flick of the wrist, another stroke, harder and louder, a thick line drawn on to pale white flesh. Another and another, the strokes falling at random, a pause and then a snap, a longer pause and then another snap. Andrea was groaning and crying out as her flesh grew pink and then a deeper shade of red, the muscle tone carrying vivid imprints of the swishing cane.

It ended as suddenly as it had begun, a final snap of the cane and it was over. Andrea remained locked in place, her body exposed deliciously, painful hindquarters latticed with cane marks. The white g-string was tight against her flesh, contrasting with the redness of her skin, as if to emphasise the degree of pain that she had received.

Jaki swallowed but there was nothing left, her throat was completely dry. From where she stood she could see that Andrea's punishment had had a direct physical response, the front of the white g-string was stretched with Andrea's lovely big prick. Jaki's own cock was equally hard, her desires flamed by the sight of her friend being expertly caned by the Mistress.

'Remain there,' Mistress ordered as Andrea began to straighten up. 'Now, Jaki, tell me the truth. Andrea's punishment is nothing compared to what you will receive if you do not cooperate.'

'There's nothing to say, Mistress,' Jaki whispered, her face red with emotion, feeling more self-concious than she had ever felt before. All eyes were upon her, every greedy eye waiting to enjoy the punishment she had selected for herself. They all knew that she was lying. The nail varnish had come from Andrea – there was no other sensible explanation.

'I am disappointed in you,' Mistress said sadly. 'Andrea will remain in place, the rest of you have work to do. Jaki, I want you to follow me.'

Jaki was speechless. She had resigned herself to a public thrashing with the cane, picturing herself in Andrea's place across the chair. She followed Mistress automatically, not fully understanding what had happened. Andrea too seemed confused, for, as Jaki walked towards the door, their eyes met in mutual incomprehension.

Chapter Twelve

The long walk from the classroom to Kasia's office gave Jaki even more time to think and brood over what was to come. A simple caning was obviously not enough, even though it would have been an ordeal of humiliation and pain to be thrashed in front of so many people. The mere idea of it had made her face flush red with shame, knowing how much vicarious pleasure her audience would have received, watching her prone figure bent over and exposed, her arse-cheeks traced with red by the cane. But that was not enough. It had sufficed for Andrea but something much worse was obviously in store for her.

She almost had to run to keep up with the purposeful strides of the young Mistress, whose imperious demeanour meant that Jaki did not even dare to ask a question. If not the cane then what? The possibilities were too frightening not to contemplate in detail: a tawse, a strap, a long tailed whip, a cat o'nine tails . . . Each instrument left a different mark on the body, each had its unique touch that made a body scream and cry with red-hot sensation. How much could Jaki take? Despite her years of training she was still sensitive to pain, she did not relish it at all. That pain turned to pleasure was a baffling accident, and each time she was punished it was a rediscovery, every touch of an implement a test of her resolve.

Mistress Shirer and Kasia had agreed on the 'full rigours' for her, and Jaki had not had the heart to ask what that might mean. Would they force her to tell the truth? The idea was horrific, because Jaki knew she would hold out for a long while, and that she would only break down under the strictest of terrors. The Institute was a secret realm, freed from the rules and regulations that governed the rest of the world. The sheer dangerousness of the situation, the massive potential for wrong, hit Jaki forcefully, waking her to the innate risks of an enterprise such as the Institute. No wonder Mistress Shirer was worried about what was going on. By its very nature the Institute was an abuse waiting to happen.

The sobering thoughts could go no further. Mistress went straight in to see Kasia and Jaki was left waiting at the door. She did not feel well, the fear was taking its toll, her head was spinning and she felt empty, drained of emotion and energy. The delicious tingling of anticipation that she had felt earlier had been displaced with a sick horror of the situation that she had found herself in. For a moment she considered telling the whole truth, not just about Andrea but about her reason for being at the Institute and the truth of her relationship with Mistress Shirer.

Mistress opened the door and grabbed Jaki and pulled her in. It was a shock to be treated so roughly, her shirt had been pulled from her skirt, her skin scratched raw on her chest. The anger in the room was intense, an open sore that pulsed violently. It was frighteningly real, without the ritualised gloss that mediated the exchange of power between Mistress and servant.

'You have nothing to say,' Kasia said, a question with its own answer. Her eyes were icy cold, and everything they touched felt that chill too.

'Andrea has been beaten and left on display,' the other Mistress reported.

'You had better return to your class now,' Kasia decided. 'Andrea is a problem that is known to us, but here we have a chance to do something before it becomes such a problem.'

The Mistress nodded and left, not sparing even a glance towards Jaki, who was looking down at the ground and trying to figure out what her next step should be. The door closed and she was alone with Kasia, who was dressed as usual in starched white, a uniform that was part medical and part penal.

'Andrea gave you this,' Kasia declared, slamming down the tiny bottle of pink nail varnish on the desk. 'I know that already. She has been punished for giving it to you. What interests me is how she came about this item, this is information that you can give to me.'

'But Mistress,' Jaki cried, 'I don't know that. I don't know anything about that.'

'Then you admit that Andrea sold you this?'

'I swear to you Mistress,' Jaki said earnestly, 'she did not sell it to me. I swear that is true.'

'You are lying,' Kasia told her brutally. She stepped forward and slapped Jaki hard, across the face with enough power to twist Jaki's head round. 'Andrea is a problem. I do not intend to let you turn out the same way. I believe in taking stern measures at the earliest opportunity. By the end of the day you will regret crossing me, you will wish that you had never been born.'

'No . . . That's wrong . . . You can't . . .'

Another hard slap across the face silenced Jaki's protests. Kasia grabbed her under the arm and marched her to the door, shaking her violently every step of the way. Jaki was pulled and pushed out into the corridor, a look of horror marking her face. A Mistress should have had no need for such histrionics or such violence, but a voice in the back of Jaki's mind told her not to resist, because Kasia was a woman who had lost control.

'Strip! Now!'

Jaki undressed hurriedly, dropping her skirt and her panties to the floor, pulling her shirt over her head and letting that drop into the same tidy bundle of clothes. She kicked off her shoes and was naked, completely, standing nervously in the cold corridor, prey to the eyes of anyone who walked through. A prefect arrived, carrying a black leather bag, like a doctor's case, which she handed to Kasia. The look on the girl's face was frightened. She too was afraid of Kasia's temper.

'Arms behind your back, a hand to each elbow. Do it!'

Jaki turned her back to Kasia and obeyed, sliding her arms together to hold each elbow with the opposing hand.

She was pulled back sharply and then straps were passed round her arms, pulled tightly together and then buckled up. It felt as though at least six pairs of straps were applied, the leather biting into Jaki's flesh.

'Now, legs apart, further.'

Ankle cuffs were applied, stiff leather lined with suede, a padlock on each cuff. A steel bar was then locked between the cuffs, forcing the legs far apart and restricting movement completely. Jaki felt spaced out, watching the proceedings without fear or panic, as though it were happening to somebody else. A thin length of nylon rope was looped around each upper arm and then tied together behind her back, forcing her bound arms back and her chest forward. Kasia was working methodically, checking every strap and knot as she went along, her attention devoted entirely to Jaki's bondage.

A leather collar was applied to Jaki's neck, a constricting band that was thankfully symbolic only and not connected to the other bindings. More rope was used to connect Jaki's arms and her ankles, the pressure arching her back slightly more, pressing her chest forward even more.

'You will have much to think about over the next few hours,' Kasia remarked, her voice clipped and controlled, despite the white heat of anger that was driving her.

The prefect looked surreptitiously at Jaki, her eyes were filled with sympathy but there was nothing that she could do or say. A sharp look from Kasia was enough to stop even that. The girl was impassive once more, her attention on the task at hand. She reached out the black case and pulled out a pair of chrome plated steel pincers, like metal claws that were snapped shut. Kasia grabbed them and smiled, holding them up to the light so that Jaki could get a better look.

'You are cold,' she said, touching the steel to Jaki's icy flesh.

'Yes, Mistress, it's freezing here,' Jaki replied softly, her voice faltering but hoping that she would still be able to win some mercy back.

'Warm her up,' Kasia ordered the prefect. 'Her nipples need to be kissed.'

The prefect looked at Kasia doubtfully but obeyed nevertheless. She put the bag down on the floor and stepped forward. Her hands were warm on Jaki's skin, their touch soft and delicate, holding Jaki by the waist to draw her nearer. As she bent her head, her warm breath touched Jaki's skin, the moist breath a sensual embrace. Her lips were soft, expressive, sensuous. Very gently she kissed Jaki on the chest, her lips grazing against the firmly muscled flesh. She moved with a lover's skill and timing, tasting Jaki's body with her mouth, her lips and tongue leaving a trail of sensation across Jaki's flesh.

Jaki sighed, caught her breath, the girl was circling the left nipple, teasing the masculine point as though it were as sensitive as a woman's. She licked it over and over, pressing it flat with her tongue, forcing the point to erection. She tugged at it with lips, catching it and crushing the erectile bud between the softness of her rosy lips. A bite that made Jaki moan, not hard but enough to send shivers of pleasure pulsing down Jaki's spine. A loving kiss and then the prefect moved to the right nipple. It was already puckered, the crenellated flesh ready to be sucked and licked. She moved exquisitely, her hot little mouth making Jaki squirm and writhe with pleasure.

'Enough!' Kasia decided abruptly, pushing the girl away from Jaki.

Jaki sighed, her breath deep and uneven. It had been an unexpectedly intense pleasure, her nipples budding and sensitive under the mouth of the girl. Somehow the pleasure had been heightened by the feeling of being bound, unable to react or resist, her body held in perfect stasis for the young woman to use as desired. Jaki's cock bulged, sticking out from her bound body, a beacon of her pleasure that could not be hidden. She could see that the prefect had been affected, the desire readable in the girl's eyes and in her longing look at Jaki's erect cock.

Kasia stroked the erect nipples, pulling on them until they were painfully red, sticking out like sharp points of flesh. There was something delightfully feminine about Jaki's erect nipples, and that too made her shudder with pleasure. She tried to move but realised that her balance was precarious, and that her strong binds and tethers would not allow her freedom at all.

'You will not orgasm,' Kasia stated, slapping Jaki's face again.

'Yes, Mistress,' Jaki responded, knowing that her thick cock was dribbling a silvery tear of juice. She was bent backwards, her chest forward, arms bound, and her cock poked out obscenely, openly aroused despite the severity of her captivity.

Kasia ceased playing with Jaki's nipples, which were ringed with red marks, the tips pink and sensitive. She fiddled with the steel pincers for a second and then placed the first over one of Jaki's nipples, she tweaked the nipple sharply until Jaki cried out and then snapped the clamp down tightly. It took but a second for the other nipple to be similarly clamped. She stepped back to admire her creation: Jaki bound tightly in place, with metal crab's claws sticking out from her chest. The pain was intense: it felt as though every sensation were amplified. The breeze in the corridor felt like a gale as the air passed over the squashed nipples, as though each nerve ending had been exposed. Every tremor of flesh rippled and echoed through Jaki's body, from the slight straining against the straps that bound her arms, to the unsteady breath that she gasped for.

'We have not finished yet,' Kasia told Jaki with a sly smile. 'There is much for you to think about, you have hours ahead of you, and I do not wish you to be distracted.'

She snapped her fingers and the prefect jumped to attention, handing her the last object contained in the black case. Kasia unrolled the package carefully, a black rubber panel that unfolded into an elongated oval shape. It took a second before the purpose was clear, but by then it was too late. The rubber hood was forced over Jaki's head, pulled down sharply and cutting everything off.

For a moment Jaki felt nothing but fear, and then she breathed again. The world was black, but she could breathe through her mouth and that gave her the air to calm the panic. The tight-fitting mask covered her head and face, right down under her chin. She could see nothing and feel nothing except the rubber moulded to her face. Vaguely, she could hear some sounds, but a hissing filled her ears, and the mask began to expand around her, pressing against her nose and eyes and mouth.

The sound stopped and there was nothing, only black silence through which she could hear and feel nothing. Her breath was ragged but free, a result of fear and excitement and not constriction. The punishment was about to begin, she realised, forcing herself to calm down. It was not going to be a beating, nor a thrashing or a ritual humiliation. She was to be left standing in the corridor, bound tightly, on display, with no sense of sight, hearing or smell. But she could feel all right. There was a sharp jarring on her nipples that felt like an explosion of pleasure. A door had slammed somewhere, and the vibrations had passed through the building to resonant lightly on her crushed nipples. In darkness, her sensory faculties removed from her control, she had been reduced to nothing but a heaving mass of sensation. Less than a person, and yet she could feel her cock straining upwards, waves of ecstasy pulsing as her body made itself known to her.

With nothing to focus on, Jaki turned inwards, unconsciously at first, concentrating on the effort to remain still, to balance, to adjust to her restraints. But as time shifted, elongated until it was meaningless, her focus changed also. Her body transformed itself, became something that was part of her and yet separate, as though it were an entity which was independent of her mind and spirit. There was no pain, only the tightness of being bound, and with that a feeling of security, of safety. Her body spoke to her, the cool surface of her skin impinging directly on consciousness, so that the breeze along the corridor, the vibrations from the floor, the movement of the sunlight on her body, all were passed unfiltered to her mind. For the first time her eyes did not interpret the world, she did not listen and transform sound into what she imagined it to be. Instead the pure, naked sensations touched her.

Time stopped, and her mind soared with exhilaration. She felt free, outside of herself, having access to a place that she had only previously glimpsed. It was a place that she could not describe, a place were words held no currency and which was freed of their constraints.

A finger touched her body, lightly bouncing the steel clamp on her breast, and it rippled and echoed endlessly, strobing blissfully round and round. It felt unreal, a pleasure that sighed on her body, like the resonance of a bell that never died away. There was no escaping such sensations, and neither did she want to escape such pleasure. Her body was bound and masked, forced into place and vulnerable to every touch and caress, yet that was not what she felt. Another touch, it could have been a second later or an hour later, another caress on her nipples, merging imperceptibly with the first. Hot breath touched her shoulder, and it seemed to ignite on her skin, as though fire had been breathed on her.

She did not want to escape or return to normality, her spirit roamed in a place that was limitless and beautiful, a place hidden from everyday view. A trigger of sensations was breathed on to her body, a hot tongue making contact with her skin. Every impression was intensified, it felt as though she were being caressed by a thousand tongues, as though her whole being was being licked sensuously. Her cock was being sucked, and it felt that her whole body had been engulfed. Nothing could compare with such bliss, her whole being screamed and cried pleasure, it surged through her being, from the base of the spine to explode in a thousand stars of energy.

It surged and ran, waves of pleasure that were wordless and powerful. No words. No thoughts. No identity. Just pleasure. Like an orgasm that did not stop, like that slow dive into oblivion that never ends. A dragon entered her body, climbing into her between her bottom cheeks, opening her, growing inside her until it was part of her.

Overloaded with pleasure, her body quivered as she was touched and licked and fingered and kissed. Without time there was no beginning or end. Without time no sensation was separate from any other, the continuum of energy knew no bounds. It was a climax that did not centre on her prick, there was no centre, as though her entire body was glowing with orgasm, every pore and every cell united in ecstasy.

'You're here now,' Jaki heard a voice say. Very slowly she opened her eyes, and saw, with a sense of deep confusion and pure disappointment, that she was back in her own room. Back in the four walls that were home, unbound but now unfree. It did not make sense.

'Can you speak?' the voice asked. Jaki turned towards the voice, trying to readjust to the world which now seemed dull and lifeless. Why had it ended? Why?

'Are you feeling better now?'

How could being back on the ground be construed as better? It was Nurse speaking, her voice crisp and clear, the concern fighting through the authority that was rightly hers. 'I'm not sure,' Jaki said, surprised by the sound of her own voice. 'How long was I . . . out?'

'Five hours in all. No wonder you look so disoriented. How do you feel?'

Jaki sighed. Five hours meant nothing. She had seen something that was so valuable that it nullified everything else. 'I felt strange,' was all she could think of saying after a long pause.

'How did you do it?' Nurse asked, her face breaking into a sly smile.

'Do what?'

'You didn't climax. No matter what was done to you. As I understand it several of the prefects went down on you, another frigging you in the arse and others played with your nipples and cock. You resisted. No orgasm despite all that attention and all those attempts.'

'Did I?' Jaki asked, though she sounded confused more than anything.

'Yes, you did. But don't worry, Nurse will take care of you now.'

There was a pause before Jaki remembered what to

say.'Yes, Nurse,' she responded, feeling her way back to reality.

'You can tell me now, where did you get the nail varnish from?'

It was a meaningless question, and somehow Jaki had forgotten the cause of her bondage ordeal. 'I can't tell you that, Nurse,' she replied softly.

'But Kasia wants to know.'

'I'm sorry, Nurse, but I can't tell you.'

Nurse smiled. 'Of course you can't, I know that. You're a good girl, Jaki, Nurse understands that. Which is why Nurse will look after you, make sure you're safe and well. Would you like that?'

Jaki suddenly realised that something was wrong. She was alone in her room, naked and lying on the bed, her nipples hard erect points. The mask, now deflated, and the bondage equipment were on the floor beside the bed. Her prick was beginning to fill, the glans oozing sticky fluid all over her belly. Nurse was standing beside the bed, gloved hands on hips, her smile one of stern approval. Her uniform was augmented by elbow length black rubber gloves and thigh length rubber stockings that contrasted with the short white skirt. The additions to her uniform augmented the look she had perfected, an object of desire that was primary and sexual yet utterly captivating and powerful.

'Well?' she urged, pursing her red lips tightly. Her eyes bore into Jaki, stripping away at the confusion that had formed.

'Yes, Nurse. Please look after me,' Jaki whispered in a small voice that trembled with fear of refusal and rejection.

Nurse reached down and touched Jaki's face, the gloved fingers smooth on Jaki's mouth and lips. Instinctively, Jaki kissed Nurse's fingers, flicking her tongue out and lapping at the fingers clothed in latex rubber. She opened her mouth and sucked deeply, rolling her tongue over and over Nurse's fingers, lapping like a pet dog licking its master's hand.

'Good girl, good girl,' Nurse said softly, her voice warm and soothing, a perfect salve for wounds that could not be seen. With her other hand she began to stroke Jaki's sore nipples, soothing ointment on to the punished buds that were red and raw.

'Oh, that hurts,' Jaki complained, her cock straining hard as the greased fingers rubbed feeling into her nipples. It hurt, but it was good, tendrils of pure feeling pulsing through her erect teats that glistened seductively. Nurse's gloved fingers were shiny smooth as the creamy ointment coated the black rubber, so that Jaki's flesh and Nurse's glove seemed part of the same whole.

'I know it hurts, darling,' Nurse whispered, bending down so that Jaki could look up towards her, 'but I like it to hurt you.'

Nurse's top few buttons were undone, and the swell of her breasts drew Jaki's eyes magnetically, the uniform opening slightly to give a glimpse of heaven. 'Then hurt me,' Jaki sighed, half-closing her eyes as the pleasure passed through her, an echo of that other world she had visited earlier.

'Good girl, good girl,' Nurse intoned, working both her hands over Jaki's chest and then using one hand to tease Jaki's erect penis. 'Nurse wants to look after baby, but baby's got to be good.'

Jaki moaned deliriously, Nurse had squeezed more ointment and was applying it tantalisingly to Jaki's cock. The fire in the pit of her belly was intense and she knew that only a few more strokes and she'd shoot the come that she had held back all day. 'I'll be good,' she promised, clutching at the bed helplessly as Nurse teased and caressed.

'You'll do as Nurse tells you?'

'Anything . . . anything . . .'

'Baby will be mine? Just mine and no one else's?'

'Yes, Nurse, I'll do whatever you want.'

Nurse kissed Jaki on the mouth, sucking at her breath whilst forcing her tongue invasively. She was taking possession, seizing what was hers and Jaki gave herself willingly. Her mind was reeling with pleasure, her cock twitching on the verge but not quite going over the edge.

'Nurse wants her girl to play,' she whispered between

hot, lingering kisses. She was teasing Jaki's nipples again, keeping up the tension and the excitement without finishing it.

It was agony for Jaki, and she wished it to go on endlessly. 'I'll play, Nurse, any game you want me . . . I'm yours . . . Yours . . .' she managed to sigh.

'Nurse wants baby's prick,' she said, touching her gloved fingers to Jaki's quivering erection, 'and baby's mouth,' she traced Jaki's lips with her fingertip.

Nurse stood up, allowing Jaki a chance to get a good look at her, from the tips of her heeled shoes, to the black rubber stockings, to the crisp white uniform open at the chest, to the moulded elbow length gloves and the frilly cap that sat on her head. Without saying a word she turned and climbed on to the bed, over Jaki's head and then squatted low, heels on either side of Jaki's face.

Jaki gazed disbelievingly as Nurse lowered herself, the short skirt forming a shroud, the shiny heels keeping her head in place. The rubber stockings were flawlessly perfect, the line of Nurse's long legs emphasised by the shiny tightness, the flesh bulging against the constricted latex tops. She was naked under her skirt, her pussy lips slightly open and exuding a musky heat that was pure aphrodisiac. Her rounded bottom cheeks were raised only inches above Jaki's hungry mouth, the anal crack deep and inviting, the roseate mouth of her behind a delicacy to be savoured.

Nurse squatted lower until Jaki's lips made contact with her flesh. Instinctively Jaki began to kiss and suck, her lips eager to explore the contours of Nurse's body. Deliriously she kissed the top of the thighs, the soft flesh of the arse-cheeks, caressing Nurse's full pussy lips, touching her tongue against the puckered anal hole. The kisses became more urgent, hotter, deeper, her tongue brought into play. Soon she was licking, pressing her tongue between Nurse's pussy lips, tasting the honey that poured forth, using her tongue to stroke lovingly the depths of Nurse's sex. She tickled Nurse's anal hole excitedly, pressing the tip of the tongue against the tight opening, and then working her tongue around the rim, round and round while Nurse pressed herself lower.

Jaki had no thought for herself, all she wanted to do was to serve, to give Nurse as much pleasure as humanly possible. Feverishly she sought Nurse's pussy bud, wanting to suck it into her mouth and tease it between her lips. Her own pleasure was peripheral, and yet whenever she heard Nurse sigh her own excitement grew in proportion, an echo of the pleasure she was giving.

Nurse climaxed suddenly, arching her back and tensing her body as waves of orgasm shook through her. Her pussy was soaked with honey, sucked gratefully into Jaki's mouth. Jaki did not stop, she sucked more urgently, now gently biting Nurse at the top of the thighs and then going back to tease her swollen clitty.

Jaki sighed when her cock was stroked, fingers wrapping round the firm fleshy rod and caressing it tightly. The desire swelled up again, making her cock even harder, flexing powerfully against the strong grasp around it. She sighed, exhaling deeply between Nurse's sticky thighs. A tongue caressed her cock, licking it from the base to the glans and down again, a long slow play that felt like heaven. For a moment there was confusion as Jaki realised that it could not be Nurse's mouth, because Nurse was sitting upright over Jaki's face.

'Don't stop, I want to fill your mouth with my pussy juice,' Nurse said, noting the hesitation in the play of Jaki's tongue.

Jaki's will was to obey, and she resumed her task, sucking greedily the droplets of juice that matted Nurse's pussy hair. Her cock was being mouthed greedily, sucked deep and hard, but by whom she had no idea. In moments Nurse shuddered to climax again, her cries rasping through her throat as she orgasmed.

'Now my other hole,' Nurse ordered, 'suck me there.'

Jaki lapped sex nectar on to her tongue and then touched it to Nurse's tight rear hole. She wet it sensuously, swirling her tongue round and round the smallest hole, gratified to know that it was to be hers too. When Nurse moaned she stopped and began to push her tongue into the hole, pushing against the warm tightness that seemed to resist. She stopped for a moment, and then pushed her tongue hard, pressing through the resistance and into the hole. At the same time she felt something against her cock, the same resistance, the same tightness, and then that too stopped.

Nurse's moan was echoed by another voice, soft and female, as Jaki understood what was happening. She had pushed her tongue into Nurse's back hole at the same time that her cock had been forced into another woman's anal hole. Now she was butt-fucking one woman, whilst simultaneously rimming another. An image filled her mind, her body was being used to give pleasure to two women at the same time, used to pleasure their anal holes and to drive them to climax.

In moments all three bodies were writhing, moving together with frenzied passion. Jaki was thrusting her pelvis upwards, forcing her cock into the tight anal passage of the woman riding her, at the same time as she lashed her tongue against Nurse's anal bud. She was consumed with pleasure, deliriously happy to be serving two women at the same time. Nurse climaxed repeatedly, digging her heels down and pinching Jaki's nipples forcefully. Another cry filled the air and the second woman collapsed forward as her orgasm took her. At last Jaki climaxed too, jetting waves of come deep into the unseen woman, spurting wads of juice that had been building up all day.

Nurse climbed off, and Jaki fell back, thoroughly sated, her body aglow with the afterheat of orgasm. She hardly had the energy to look at the second woman sprawled on the bed, a prefect judging by her clothes scattered along the floor.

'Have I been a good girl?' Jaki asked, her voice a hoarse whisper that barely came out.

Nurse leaned forward and wiped Jaki's brow with her gloved fingers. 'Yes darling, you've been a good little girl,' she murmured softly, touching her voluptuously red lips to Jaki's skin.

Jaki sighed. That was all she had hoped for, all she could ever hope for.

'Has she passed?' Nurse asked the other girl quietly.

'Yes, she's passed this and the other test,' the girl replied softly, retreating towards the door, scooping up her clothes as she went. 'Have her ready tomorrow night.'

'Don't worry,' Nurse assured her, 'she'll be ready.'

Jaki was hardly aware of the words, she felt exhausted but pleased. At the moment of orgasm she had glimpsed again the strange inner domain to which she had journeyed earlier – and she understood then that orgasm was a window on to that place, a place in the deepest part of her soul.

Rebecca listened at the door but was unable to make out anything from the slight murmur of voices. What words she did catch made her feel paranoid: slave, punishment, Mistress. They were like key-words that stuck in her mind, each one branching out with connotations and implications of which she was only dimly aware. They were talking about her and she felt a chill in the pit of her stomach.

She had only caught a glimpse of Simone's visitor, but one glimpse of those sharp green eyes was enough. The woman was obviously of the same stamp as Simone; austere, commanding, in control. Rebecca had always liked powerful women, but she had rationalised that as part of her feminism, taking pride in women that were strong role models, examples of what women could be like. Only now she was aware that there was more to it, and that she was getting turned on by these same women, turned on by the thought of submitting to them.

No, that was wrong, she told herself, but her self-denial lacked conviction. Was there anything wrong in being turned on by powerful women? Why did she feel so uncomfortable with herself, why could she not accept the pleasure that submission was giving to her? It only took the thought of submitting to Simone to make her wet her knickers. But it was wrong, women had to be strong, they had to be equal.

She leaned closer to the door, her curiosity getting the better of her good manners. If they were discussing her then she had a right to know, she wanted to hear for herself all the gory details.

'I'll be seeing Jaki tomorrow morning,' Simone was saying. 'I'll have a proper session with her on my own.'

'Is that wise?' the other woman asked. 'Won't it cause problems?'

'No, don't worry, Harriet, I can handle her easily enough. Besides,' Simone added, 'Jaki is my number one priority. I owe it to her . . .'

The world seemed to spin round. Rebecca gasped, felt a surge of emotions that fought for coherence. Simone had someone else. Jaki. Simone didn't care about her, she could be handled. Jaki was the number one priority.

'You bitch!' Rebecca screamed, pushing the door open and rushing into the room.

'Rebecca!' Simone cried, looking stunned.

'I can be handled, can I? I'm just the stupid little cow who thought she meant something to you!'

'Simone, who is this girl?' the other woman asked, looking just as shocked as Simone.

'You keep out of this, you fucking bitch,' Rebecca screamed hysterically. 'I'm out of here Simone, I'm out of here for good.'

'Listen here . . .' Simone began to say.

'Out of here!' Rebecca screamed and then turned and ran, fighting her way through bitter tears.

The whole world had collapsed and the hurt was like a gaping wound, pouring with emotion that could not be staunched.

Chapter Thirteen

Kasia glared at Jaki angrily, the venom of the previous day as virulent as it had been before. Jaki looked away rather than risk Kasia's ire again, she felt no respect for her, only intimidation of the coarsest and most brutal kind. When the door slammed Jaki visibly relaxed, feeling safer in the presence of Mistress Shirer than in Kasia's.

Mistress Shirer, seated behind Kasia's desk, regarded Jaki for a moment and then spoke. 'I understand you were punished yesterday,' she said, rather calmly.

'Yes Mistress, I was,' Jaki said softly. 'Did Kasia tell you how or why?'

'Mistress Kasia.'

Jaki shook her head. 'She's no Mistress,' she said quietly, surprised at the disquiet she felt. The feeling of bitterness was new to her, she had always been accustomed to trusting everyone and accepting her rôle without question.

'You tell me,' Mistress Shirer said, 'how and why?'

'The why is easy. I was given some make-up and I would not reveal where I had got it from.'

'And the how?'

'I was bound, arms together, ankles apart, masked with an inflatable mask and left to stand for several hours in the corridor.'

'How did that feel?' Mistress asked.

The question was a surprise. 'Very weird,' Jaki admitted. 'I felt as though I was floating. Like in a dream only it wasn't a dream. It felt special, fantastic really, but weird . . .'

'That happens sometimes when a punishment session is very severe,' Mistress explained, 'or the submissive is receptive enough. The physical cause is an endorphin rush, the brain producing natural opiates that cause a very powerful high. Spiritually, some people experience it as an altered state of consciousness, others see it as an out of body experience. Were you OK afterwards?'

'It took some time before I felt all right, but I'm sorry, Mistress, that kind of severe punishment is way too much for the offence.'

Mistress Shirer accepted the remark without comment, her dark eyes intense and fixed on Jaki's. Finally she nodded slightly, recognising that Jaki's concern was well placed. 'I'm afraid that Kasia's overreaction was an indication that she is out of her depth here,' she said, very quietly but without hesitation. 'It's a matter that I am aware of. Now, Jaki, is there anything more you'd like to tell me?'

Jaki shook her head. 'I haven't found out anything yet,' she reported. Mistress had agreed with her, and the thought pleased her immensely because it meant that her opinion counted for something in Mistress's eyes.

'Nothing?' Mistress asked, her disappointment coming through clearly.

Jaki hesitated, then shook her head. There was nothing. Andrea had made vague hints about knowing the right people, but that was hardly earth-shattering news. 'I'll have to keep trying until I have something to report,' she sighed.

'Is that what you want?' Mistress asked, raising her eyebrows quizzically.

Jaki's face coloured slightly. 'Yes,' she whispered, surprised at herself for feeling ashamed. The Institute was strange and exotic, an ordeal to endure and enjoy. She thought of Nurse and the desire flashed through her, making her cock stiffen quickly under her skirt. It struck her then that as soon as she had found out what was going on she was going to have to leave, and in so doing lose Nurse.

Mistress detected the hesitation and the look of guilt. 'Are you sure that you're telling me everything?'

'Yes, Mistress,' Jaki assured her quickly.

'Have you noticed anything untoward? Do you have any clues at all as to what's going on?'

'Only that Kasia doesn't belong here,' Jaki asserted.

'You've told me that already,' Mistress pointed out. 'Is there anything else?'

'Nothing, Mistress,' Jaki said, slightly chastened.

'Do nothing to provoke Kasia.'

'Me?' Jaki demanded, raising her voice.

'Don't forget yourself, girl,' Mistress warned. 'One more word and I'll have you taken out into the courtyard and thrashed with the riding crop. You are here for one reason and one reason alone, keep that in mind. Kasia is still a Mistress. You'll do as she commands, whatever she commands. She had recommended that you be kcpt in isolation for the next seven days. I have persuaded her that this is too harsh for a new arrival. You'll be kept in isolation today and tomorrow, then you can rejoin the rest of your group. I expect you to behave yourself, my girl, and I suspect that the rigorous punishment inflicted so far has been a good thing so far as our plans are concerned. At the very least any suspicions about you would have been allayed. I expect to see you again in two days, after you've rejoined your group. Until that time keep in mind what your Mistress has brought you here for.'

'Yes, Mistress,' Jaki agreed, disappointed to hear that she was to be taken out of circulation for a couple of days.

'Good. You may thank your Mistress before you go.'

Jaki smiled and knelt down, her disappointment evaporating. She crawled along the floor and began to kiss Mistress's high heeled shoes, running her tongue up and down the curved heel, her lips pressed close against the patent leather. When Mistress reached down and stroked her, Jaki shivered with pleasure, her cock throbbing in the tightness of her lace knickers.

Isolation meant being confined to one's room, without uniform and with the punishment glass removed. It meant having no one to talk to, nothing to read and nothing to do. It was the absence of contact that was the punishment, because in the unrestrained atmosphere of the Institute to be alone was to be out of the game. The cane or the strap would have been preferable, public humiliation better – even the masked bondage had been better than being alone.

Without the mirror or her clothes Jaki had hovered on the borderline of her sensual personalities, part J.K. and part Jaki. For a while she had fantasised about Nurse, day-dreaming ingenious punishments that were outrageously cruel and deliciously sexy. She had longed to submit completely before her, giving herself completely to Nurse in return for nothing more than attention. It would have been bliss to have been scolded, or smacked, or just cuddled by the strictly uniformed Mistress.

Again and again the idea returned to Jaki that Nurse should have been running the male dorm of the Institute, not Kasia. Would Mistress Shirer have accepted such an idea? Jaki did not know. All she knew was that both of them were in agreement as to Kasia's unsuitability. A true Mistress did not have to rely on physical punishments alone, she commanded by virtue of herself, the power was within and not without. Kasia lacked the inner strength and confidence that marked out a Mistress as a creature to be worshipped, a Goddess that deserved abject surrender from her love slaves.

Jaki managed to fall asleep early in the evening, drifting off as she lay naked in bed, wrapped in the warmth of the duvet. In her dreams she sought the realm that Mistress had talked about, the altered state of consciousness that had been Jaki's reward for accepting her punishment. She sought a way in, looking for the key that would open the door to it. In her dream she could find no way in, and then the realisation dawned that the only way in was to submit completely. It was a realm guarded well, and only extreme pleasure-pain would get her there.

'What?' Jaki asked, struggling through the fog of her dreams.

'Wake up, it's time for you,' a voice whispered in the darkness.

For a moment Jaki was confused, caught in the no-man's-land between dream and reality, then the frigid temperature of her room convinced her that the dream was over. 'Ready for what?' she asked, trying to focus her eyes on the dark shapes all around her.

'For your service,' the voice replied.

There was something cold and hard in the voice, an icy tremor that struck a chord. Jaki swallowed hard. She knew instinctively that she was about to find out what was going on at the Institute and it frightened her. 'What is it? What do you want?' Jaki asked, hoping that the fear would not be communicated in her voice.

'Listen, bitch, you've been tested and we know you're ready. Tonight you learn what it is to serve us.'

'Who sent you? Is it Kasia?'

The laughter seemed to spring out through the darkness, coming at Jaki from all sides and united in contemptuous amusement. 'That stupid cow's got no idea,' one of the figures explained, 'she thinks she's running this place when we're the power here. We're the Sisterhood, and we expect you to earn your keep.'

'You passed the test that Andrea set you up for, and you did well with Nurse last night, which means you're ready now.'

Jaki hardly had time to make a reply, she was grabbed roughly on both sides and hauled out of bed. She could see the girls holding her, two of them, both prefects and used to being obeyed. Vainly she tried to cover up her nakedness, but her hands were slapped away.

'Good, you're naked. It saves us the trouble of stripping you,' one of her captors gloated.

'Now, girl, we want you to submit for real. Hands and knees time, like the little bitch that you really are. What do we want now? What are you going to do for us?'

'This isn't right!' Jaki squealed, forced down on to hands and knees against her will.

'Don't talk crap, girl! This is our domain now, we make the rules,' one of them said, her voice a cold sneer. 'We want absolute obedience, total and abject surrender from our slaves. We know you like the strap. Do you really want to test how much you like it?'

'No,' another disagreed, 'the strap's too good for her She needs to be fucked good and hard . . .'

'. . . And then made to suck her taste off . . .'

'. . . No, she needs to be watered by each of us in turn . . .'

The taunts echoed around the room, lewd and obscene, louder and louder until Jaki felt dizzy and out of control. She crept forward slowly, almost crashing to the floor in the darkness, seeking out the leader of the group. Her eyes had begun to adjust, and she could vaguely make out the slender figure in front of her. Without prompting, with the taunts still ringing in her ears, she inched forward, her face almost flat against the icy floor, and touched her lips to the girl's heeled shoes. She licked long and slow, cleaning the cool leather with her tongue, lapping at it again and again until the voices had been silenced. She began to lose herself in the sensuality of foot worship, paying homage to the young woman whose shapely feet were held tightly in the black stiletto shoes.

'Good, that's very good,' the girl remarked, lifting her foot and pressing the sharp heel down on to Jaki's bare back. 'I like you, bitch, I think you're going to become one of my best girls.'

Jaki continued to lick clean the shoes, this time running her tongue along the back of the heel, tracing the ridge of leather that touched the warmth of bare skin. Her excitement was growing, and she felt glad that the darkness hid her cock as it stiffened to erection.

'Here, bitch,' another girl called, patting her thighs as though she were calling a pet puppy to attention.

'It's all right: you do her too,' the first woman agreed, removing her heel from Jaki's back.

'That's right, bitch, only this time it's not shoes you're going to be licking,' the other girl laughed coarsely.

Jaki scuttled across the floor towards her, excited by the thought that her abject surrender was being witnessed by the rest of the young women in the room. Light flared in the darkness, casting a flickering orange light, and the match was used to light a candle. In the soft light Jaki could see that there were four women in her room, and as she had surmised they were all prefects. The woman who had called her was waiting, and in her eagerness she had hitched up her skirt and was showing white knickers pulled tightly into her pussy.

'Suck good or she'll really wet you,' one of the others remarked, to laughter from her friends.

Crawling forward, Jaki tentatively touched her lips to the girl's thigh, breathing the natural perfume of desire on her skin. She nuzzled her face into the panties, breathing deeply the scent of sex and teasing her tongue under the tight band of the panties. The girl stroked Jaki's face and then pulled her panties from her body, giving Jaki access.

'She's good,' one of the other prefect's exclaimed, enjoying the view.

Jaki licked up and down the girl's pussy, roughly across the labia and then teasing deeper. She could taste the girl's sex juices, and she pressed her tongue into the warmth to suck it all out. It tasted divine, and Jaki shivered with pleasure, certain that she was pleasuring the girl with her tongue. The girl began to frig her sex-button as Jaki concentrated on sucking deep into the pussy, penetrating into the wet heat with her tongue. She was sucking and biting feverishly, her own excitement fired by the moans of delight from the girl.

The girl pushed Jaki's face tightly between her legs as she climaxed ecstatically, waves of nectar filling Jaki's mouth. She was panting when she released Jaki, but the smile told the full story, a smile of purest pleasure.

'Now, bitch,' the first girl said, her voice breaking the momentary silence. 'It's time you swore the oath of loyalty to the Sisterhood.'

'Please, Mistress,' Jaki said softly, 'I don't understand what's happening. What is the Sisterhood?'

The prefect sighed impatiently. 'Kasia's no fucking good. She treats this place like a freak show. Look at her. You know she's not a natural Dominant. The only person in this dorm with any natural power's Nurse, but she has to do as Kasia says. Can you believe that? Nurse could walk all over her. We're dedicated to running this place properly. We *understand.* So, when it's dark the dark powers take over. Understand now?'

'I think so,' Jaki replied softly.

'We know that the best way to train you is to put you in servitude. You need this, you need to be taught that your place is at a woman's heel, grovelling on the floor like the bitch-fuck that you are. See?'

'Yes. You're doing this for me?'

'We're doing it for all of us. Now, you have to swear the oath.'

Jaki crawled to the centre of the room and stopped. She was surrounded on all sides by the four prefects, looking down at her imperiously, arrogant and disdainful. She felt small and insignificant, a worthless creature prostrated before such potent and attractive women. It was her natural place, naked and vulnerable and abject and servile.

'Swear to the Goddess that you will serve her completely,' they intoned solemnly.

'I swear to the Goddess that I'll serve completely.'

'Swear to the Goddess that you will worship her form for ever and always.'

'I swear.'

'Swear to the Goddess that you will obey without question and without reward.'

'I swear.'

'Then by the power of the Goddess we take you as ours.'

Jaki looked down at herself, at the streams of golden liquid that poured over her body. She was being bathed, her body drenched in the waters that the four girls pissed on to her. It had been unexpected but effective, baptised and anointed by the natural rain that rippled over her skin and ran down her body, splashing into her hair, on to her face, over her cock. It was a ceremony so deeply affecting that her normal reactions were stilled. She felt no revulsion, no disgust, but only excitement and gratitude. The four girls stepped back and looked at her, body glistening and sitting in a pool of yellow liquid.

'Now you belong to the Sisterhood, slave,' the leader of the group announced solemnly.

Jaki was led through the dark corridors of the Institute to the shower where two of the prefects watched as she washed herself. Even after scrubbing her skin with soap she was still aware that her body had been scented by the four girls, a scent that marked an animal ownership of her. She did not bother trying to hide her thick cock, achingly hard as it had been during the strange ceremony.

The four young women had evidently believed every word of what they were saying, Jaki was certain. She understood the sentiments exactly. They had been right. Kasia was no good for the Institute. They were right too about Nurse. Jaki only wished that it had been Nurse who had led the ceremony. She tried hard not to imagine sitting under Nurse and being bathed in her rain. The image of it was intoxicatingly powerful and she was afraid that she'd come if she thought about it.

'Finished?' the prefects asked, restlessly.

They switched off the shower and handed Jaki a thick towel to dry herself with. It was cold and she was shivering. The building seemed deserted and no other prefects had been encountered along the way, which was enough to convince Jaki that the girl's claims about the power of the Sisterhood were true. Neither was the place running with scores of girls, which meant that some semblance of order was still in place. Where were the staff?

'Now you earn your keep,' one of the prefects said, smiling meaningfully.

Jaki was led down several flights of steps, moving quickly in and out of the shadows like a thief. She was taken down into the basement, where two prefects handed her over to the girl who had led the ceremony earlier.

'Mistress?' Jaki ventured to ask, nervously.

'You call me Sister, that's all,' came the reply.

Jaki nodded. It made sense not to give names, identification would be so much more difficult that way. Already she was wondering how to break the news to Mistress Shirer; it would not be easy.

'Right, in there,' the girl ordered, opening the door to a small dark room.

Jaki peered into the blackness nervously. It was more of a cupboard than a room, and the complete lack of light frightened her. She tried to hold back, but the girl pushed her into the darkness – shoving hard and slamming the door after her. A torch shone out of the blackness, binding Jaki completely.

'Listen,' the voice behind the torch began, 'you get in there and stay quiet until you're collected. Keep your mouth shut, otherwise you'll be gagged next time. Now, in!'

Jaki regarded the open laundry basket nervously. The large wicker box was stuffed half full with clothes, and the girl holding the torch was holding the lid open too. With no other option but to obey, Jaki climbed into the basket. The lid clamped down after her, and then she heard the heavy click of a lock shutting tightly.

In the darkness again, Jaki waited, comforted slightly by the heavenly scent of perfumed lingerie and underclothes that she was sitting on. The basket shuddered and began to rock gently as it was pushed along, and her in it. A castor squeaked, a muffled sound that barely made it through the walls of the basket and the insulation of the clothes. It only took a few minutes for the journey to end, the basket stopped moving as suddenly as it had started.

Thankfully when the lid opened it was to light and not more gloomy darkness. Jaki sat up and peered over the top of the basket.

'Out you get, and keep that pretty little mouth of yours zipped,' a new girl hissed.

Jaki nodded to show assent and then climbed out. She was suddenly aware of her nakedness, of her cock that oozed sticky wetness against her thighs and of her nipples puckering up from the cold.

'Welcome to heaven,' the girl, a petite blonde with an angelic smile, whispered.

'Where am I?' Jaki asked.

'In the female dorm, of course. Now, follow me and keep silent. If we get caught then it's the end for all of us.'

Jaki followed, out of a tiny cupboard similar to the one in the male dorm, into a darkened corridor. Each corridor and flight of stairs was negotiated carefully, pausing at every stage to see if the coast was clear. If the Sisterhood held absolute sway in the male dorm then their hold in the female dorm was less secure, that was for sure.

'In there,' the blonde said, pointing to a door at the top of the last flight of steps. 'Hope you enjoy it.'

'Enjoy it?' Jaki asked, glancing up at the door.

'Hurry up,' the girl whispered, pinching Jaki's nipple playfully.

Jaki edged along the wall and climbed the steps, wishing that she could remain with the blonde. She stopped at the door and looked back the way she had come, but the place was deserted, the walls and the stairs lost in the shadows.

'You took your time!'

Jaki paused to take in her surrondings: a small room like her own, with a bed and a chest of drawers – the bed an absolute mess. There were two women in the room, one dark skinned and angry, the other half naked and sitting on the floor.

'Well?' the angry one demanded. She was beautiful, brown sugar skin, long frizzy hair that reached down over her shoulders, full sensuous lips and eyes that could kill.

Jaki began to stutter an excuse, her eyes drawn to the other woman, who was curled up around the feet of her angry friend. Her thighs were bare, and her skin was tanned a soft rouge near her bottom. 'There was a ceremony,' Jaki finally managed to say, tearing her eyes away from the freshly spanked girl to the one who had obviously inflicted the punishment.

'That shit,' she snorted contemptuously.

'It was beautiful,' Jaki whispered quietly.

'Tiffany invented it,' the spanked girl said, her weak voice filled with pride, the sort of pride that only a slave can have in her Mistress. Jaki smiled at her, and the girl's face flushed pink with shame and delight. The two of them were submissives, and they recognised each other at once – spiritual sisters in this if nothing else.

'It's still crap,' Tiffany declared, 'even if it's good crap. A lot of the troops believe it, and it keeps sluts like you two happy. Especially the snivelling little queens in the male dorm.'

'You mean you don't believe in it?' Jaki asked, feeling hurt by the contempt in spite of herself. It had seemed a beautiful ceremony, sexual and sensual, and it had struck a chord because it reflected her obeisance to Mistress, not just any Mistress but an ideal Goddess that transcended everything.

'Of course I don't believe in it,' Tiffany laughed. 'Why, not even Nicola believes in it, do you?'

'No, Mistress,' the girl replied obediently, looking up lovingly into her Mistress's eyes with nothing but pride and affection. Jaki could see the marks of a recent punishment. Nicola was not quite sitting on the cold floor, as though her backside were too tender, and the top of her thighs and buttocks were patterned with finger marks.

'Enough of all that,' Tiffany decided, 'now it's time that you learn what servitude to the Sisterhood really means.'

Jaki stepped back, shaking her head. 'I don't like this, I don't like this at all.'

Tiffany laughed, the delight shining in her eyes. 'That makes it all the better then. I can see that you're going to be the dirtiest, sluttiest bitch I own.'

'You can't make me do anything I don't want to,' Jaki protested, backing up against the door.

'But that's the point. You do want to do it. I'm going to work you hard, I promise you that. I'll have you sexing half the female dorm every night, sucking pussy like it's going out of fashion. And that tight arsehole of yours is going to take some frigging I can tell you that too. It's going to earn me a fortune.'

'No . . . no . . .' Jaki whispered, stuck against the wall as Tiffany advanced towards her, heels snapping hard with every step.

'And this,' Tiffany reached out and stroked Jaki's stiff prick, 'is going to screwed down to the bone. Just think, slut, what a good bitch you'll be, fucking for money and handing it all to me.'

Jaki's heart was pounding with horror, but with the revulsion and the disgust there was a powerful feeling of excitement. She was fascinated by the plan that Tiffany had outlined, appalled and excited because she understood that she was ready for it. Another barrier had been breached, another limit left far behind. It seemed to Jaki that there was nothing she would not do.

Tiffany grabbed Jaki's hair and pulled her back across the room, Jaki running along on tiptoes to lessen the pain. She felt weak and powerless to resist, her mind spinning with feverish excitement. She was pushed down on to the floor, down beside Nicola who watched open mouthed.

'What do you like the best? The cane or the crop I wonder?' Tiffany asked, smiling as Jaki turned away from the question. 'I guess that means I try it out for myself. Everyone tells me that you took all that Kasia could give you, but that doesn't surprise me in the least.'

'Don't try to resist,' Nicola whispered under her breath, 'it'll only make things worse for both of us.'

Tiffany walked to the chest of drawers where her instruments of punishment had been laid out earlier. It took only a moment for her to make a decision – the riding crop tipped with a small ring of stiff leather. She turned and smiled, confident in the power of command. For the first time Jaki noticed that Tiffany was wearing leather: a short black skirt and bustier top, ankle-length boots and a leather band fitted tightly on her left arm. She held the riding crop in her right hand and beat the tip of it softly into her left palm, the gentle smacking sound beating out the rhythm of her steps as she crossed the room.

'In position, both of you,' she ordered, her voice cold and unemotional, as though she enjoyed no pleasure in her command.

Nicola moved first, sitting up on all fours and then looking up expectantly at Tiffany. Jaki was rewarded with a better look at Nicola's punished hindquarters, her skin tanned red and pink, the imprint of fingers still etched on her bottom. Her flesh was completely bare, the full lips of her pussy bare and hairless, revealing all and hiding nothing.

The crop whistled down and caught Jaki on the upper arm, biting hard and making her cry out loudly. She had been transfixed by Nicola, excited by the unnatural nakedness of her sex and by the sight of her freshly spanked backside. The first bite of the crop was enough. She too got into position, side by side with Nicola. She was aware that the two of them were being displayed perfectly, long legs slightly parted, bottoms pressed upwards and backs arched. They were vulnerable and willing, open to examination and ready to be punished or violated as their cruel Mistress saw fit.

'You both remain silent,' Tiffany warned when they heard a scrabbling at the door.

'Yes, Mistress,' they said in unison.

The door opened a few inches and somebody else slipped into the room. A young woman, still dressed in the standard Institute uniform. Her eyes swept across the room and fixed on the two slaves, her face breaking into a lecherous smile.

'Well, Tina, how do they look?' Tiffany asked, looking down at the cowering figures at her feet.

'Wow! Two of them, this is better than I imagined.'

'Good, so what have you got for me?'

Tina handed over a small package, a nervous look in her eyes. Tiffany opened the plastic bag and rifled through the contents, which clinked together as she did so. 'Where'd you get all this make-up and jewellery?' she asked in amazement.

'Well,' Tina explained conspiratorially, 'I've got my sources. If this works out between us I'm sure we can trade again.'

'Yes, I'm sure too. Now, which one do you want? Nicola or Jaki?'

Tina's eyes lit up. She started to say something and then stopped. She tilted her head to one side and stared openly at Jaki's behind. 'She's a man,' she whispered, astonished by the discovery.

'Ever thought about a career in biology?' Tiffany asked cuttingly. 'Look, darling, it seems to me that you need some help to choose.'

'Help?'

Tiffany reached down and stroked Jaki's backside, smoothing her palm back and forth over the rounded contours of buttocks and thighs. With the tip of the riding crop she touched Nicola's bottom, tracking the suede tip of the crop playfully up and down the anal crack. Jaki couldn't help herself; she felt degraded by the proprietorial touch and yet she arched her back and forced her rump higher. She wanted to look good, to draw the admiration and attraction of Tina. She tried not to look at Nicola, whose face was next to hers, aware that in some way the two of them were in competition.

'Try them. You wouldn't want to make an uninformed choice, would you?'

Tina's touch was hesitant and nervous, but Jaki relished it anyway. She lifted herself shamelessly, parting her thighs a little more so that her bottom was even more round, the arse-cheeks slightly more open. Tina stroked the thigh and then the bottom cheeks, and then, gaining in confidence, she gently squeezed Jaki's erect cock.

'Feels good,' Tina remarked, exchanging a smile with Tiffany.

'But Nicola's snatch feels good too,' Tiffany replied suggestively.

Jaki felt disappointed when Tina turned her attention to Nicola. Jaki watched jealously as Tina caressed and stroked Nicola's hairless pussy, the smooth fleshy lips parted to reveal moist pink flesh within, an enticing glimpse of heaven. Nicola closed her eyes and sighed, unable to hide the pleasure she received from being handled, and shamed by the way she too was flaunting herself, moving sinuously as Tina caressed her.

'It's an impossible choice,' Tina sighed delightedly. She placed herself behind the two slaves and was touching them both, holding them confidently, relishing the feeling of ownership as they contorted themselves to attract her attention.

'How tight is Jaki's hole?' Tiffany asked, as though pointing out an important factor in Tina's decision.

'What will I use to . . . ?'

'I've thought of that,' Tiffany assured her. She went back to the chest of drawers and returned with two pairs of shiny plastic pants, each of them with solid black penis attachments poking out. 'They're both in need of a good hard fuck. One each.'

'Wow! You've thought of everything,' Tina marvelled. 'In that case I'd better decide quickly.'

Jaki caught her breath but did not cry out when she was violated. Tina's finger entered roughly, forced unexpectedly deep between Jaki's arse-cheeks. In and out several times, the pain of penetration lessening slowly as she forced herself to relax. Nicola was not so restrained and she screamed when Tina inserted a finger into her anal hole. For a few moments Tina enjoyed herself, anally frigging the two slaves as she tried to decide which of them to sodomise.

'Nicola shouldn't have screamed,' Tiffany said ominously. 'I think she deserves to be chastised for that. Would you want to do it?'

Tina nodded eagerly. 'Before I decide which one I want I think I'll have to thrash them both. Would that be all right?'

'No problem. Here, use this. Do them both at the same time.'

Tina accepted the offer, taking the riding crop and testing it through the air a few times. Tiffany walked round and knelt down in front of her two slaves, smiling to them encouragingly, her beautiful eyes so soft and loving and without a trace of the cruelty that was naturally a part of her. She cupped her large breasts, lifting them proudly and offering the nipples to her two eager slaves. Jaki and Nicola both inched forward and began to kiss and suck Tiffany's breasts, their mouths closing around the chocolate coloured nipples and sucking tenderly.

Jaki was in rapture, suckling from Tiffany's breast, her tongue lashing the hardening nipple excitedly. She arched her back in preparation, her skin tingling with anticipation. She didn't care, let the pain wash through her, she was on hands and knees worshipping a Mistress. Tiffany's skin tasted beautiful, and her nipples felt divinely sensitive . . .

The cutting pain was intense, the swish of the crop a loud whistle that touched flesh with a sharp snap. The pain was made bearable only by Tiffany's presence. Jaki did not want to disappoint, she sucked harder, not hesitating or stopping in any way. She heard the whistle of the crop and this time it fell hard on Nicola, who winced visibly. Again and again the riding crop was lashed down, sometimes on Nicola and sometimes on Jaki, without pattern or rhythm, but all that counted was serving Tiffany, sucking on her nipples to bring her to the peak of pleasure.

'I want Nicola,' Tina announced at last, after Tiffany had climaxed.

'Good. In the arse or in the cunt?' Tiffany asked callously, brushing a hand through Nicola's hair as she said it.

'I want to really enjoy that shaved pussy,' Tina admitted.

Tiffany stood up, took off her skirt and slipped on the shiny black pants, the tight material glossy against her demerara skin, the dildo protruding proudly from her body. She looked perfect, long thighs leading up to the shiny black plastic cock, her breasts held up by the stiff leather bustier, the reddened nipples poking out over the edge. She walked on high heels that did nothing to her balance, her poise was powerful and feminine, controlled and ferocious.

She bent over and touched Jaki's behind, tracing the thick red lines etched by the riding crop. Jaki ached in silence, aroused by the pain and by the fact of her complete obedience. There was nothing else in her mind, all that mattered was that she serve. Tiffany wet her fingers and then pressed her fingertips to Jaki's rear hole, wetting the tender skin before pressing the head of the plastic cock against it.

'We must do this again,' Tina whispered as she pressed the dildo into Nicola's compliant flesh. She was holding Nicola tightly by the waist and moving her pelvis in and out, in a rough, unsteady rhythm. Nicola's eyes were closed and she was making soft, wordless mewing sounds.

Her body was swaying back and forth, her breasts moving sharply as she was fucked harder and harder.

'It depends if you can pay,' Tiffany gasped, beginning to find her own rhythm as she sodomised Jaki.

Jaki closed her eyes too, enjoying the pleasure of being fucked by a woman. She loved the feel of Tiffany's sharp nails in her skin, she loved the feel of the hard cock sliding in and out of her tight arsehole, of being on hands and knees on the floor and being fucked like an animal. Tiffany was slamming hard, her belly slapping into Jaki's rear, slapping against the stripes of pain left by the crop.

'Oh . . . Jesus . . .' Nicola whispered.

Jaki opened her eyes and turned to her, their lips met and melted into a kiss. They sucked at each other, exploring each other's mouth deliriously as they were forced to the edge of orgasm. Tina was crying out, grunting animal sounds as she felt the pleasure grow in intensity. Tiffany's body was bathed with jewels of perspiration that trickled down her smooth skin.

Tina climaxed first, screaming a torrent of obscenities as she peaked. She fell forward over Nicola, embracing her and kissing her hotly on the shoulder and neck. Jaki climaxed next, shooting thick spurts of semen from her cock as she was relentlessly fucked in the arse. It was release and more, her final submission before the Goddess. Tiffany and Nicola seemed to climax at the same time, their bodies separate but linked permanently by the spiritual bond that existed between the two.

'You'd better go,' Tiffany whispered a few moments later, sitting on the edge of the bed, drenched in perspiration, her dark skin blushing pink with the glow of orgasm.

Tina looked dazed. She merely nodded and proceeded to dress herself. 'When can I do this again?' she asked, her voice weak but full of yearning.

'Depends. You know what it costs,' Tiffany said lazily, motioning for her two slaves to crawl towards her.

'I'll see you soon, don't worry,' Tina said. She looked wistfully at the two slaves, gratefully kissing Tiffany's feet, then left.

'Stupid cow,' Tiffany whispered, to herself more than to Jaki or Nicola, 'she's been keeping stuff back from the Sisterhood. I guessed that she had, now I've got the evidence and she's going to have to pay dearly for breaking my rules.'

Jaki kissed Tiffany's heels, filled with dread and awe. Tiffany was a Mistress but cruel and devious, an obverse to Kasia, who was merely cruel and stupid. It was all so very complicated, and the passing of the hours was making her feel very tired. She would have to return to her room soon, smuggled back into the male dorm using the laundry basket. She did not want to leave. The silence and loneliness of her room held nothing but a fitful time while she struggled with the dilemmas that had presented themselves. It was so much easier to kiss Mistress's heels and to submit without question.

Chapter Fourteen

It has been the most difficult night of Jaki's life, a long sleepless, fruitless night of doubts and anxieties. She had been returned to her room a few hours before dawn, retracing the tortuous route that connected the male and female dormitories. The laundry basket had carried her back, in silent darkness, and then she had been met and escorted back to her room. That had been the easy part. She had not needed to think about things, all that was required was that she obey in silence.

Once back in the safety of her bed she had hoped that her exhaustion would lead straight to sleep. It was a vain hope. She was dog tired but her mind was filled with thoughts and ideas that led anywhere but to sleep. She had lain awake until after dawn, thoughts chasing thoughts as she struggled to find a clean solution to all the problems she had uncovered.

There was no doubt in her mind that she had stumbled on the key to the problems at the Institute. Nor was there any doubt that she had enough information to go back to Mistress Shirer immediately. But reporting all did not resolve the problems. It was the resolution that worried her. Some things she was clear about: Kasia's incompetence, the route between the male and female dorm, Tiffany's corrupt plans. Other things were not so clear: how much did Nurse know of what went on, and what were the motives of the young women involved in the Sisterhood?

The main worry that she had, and the main reason why she had not come to any conclusion, was that things looked bad for Nurse. And under no circumstances did

Jaki want to cause Nurse any trouble. Instead she felt a bond of loyalty that she would have felt to any true Mistress. That was the worst part of it, she now had a choice and it was an impossible one to make. Who should she choose, Mistress Shirer or Nurse?

Jaki had forgotten that she was still under curfew, the second day of her isolation started with the breaking of the dawn. She felt as though she carried the weight of the world on her shoulders, a weight that she could hardly support. Why had she been selected? For the first time she wished that she was back home, serving Harriet both as Jaki and as J.K., the two parts of her self devoted to a Mistress that she loved and who loved her in return.

Breakfast was signalled by a knock on the door, and when she opened it a tray had been left outside. She took it in and picked at the cereal, her appetite reflecting the dark depression that was slowly overtaking her. The day stretched ahead interminably, a day in isolation where she would have no company but her thoughts. It almost made her want to weep.

She dressed because there was nothing else to do, and then lay on the bed and closed her eyes. She wished for sleep, but the more she thought about it the more it receded. A headache developed and added to her frustration and depression. Never had she felt so low. Even when she was being severely corrected she felt better. To be a slave did not mean neglect, her reward was attention, and now that it had been denied she felt denuded of the dignity that was hers by right.

How was Andrea? Jaki had been paid for her services, a stick of bright pink lipstick pushed into her hand after she had been dismissed by Tiffany. That was it, her pay, the reward for allowing her body to be used. For a moment she had felt pleasure, excited by the humiliation of being paid for sex, and then she felt happy, looking forward to applying the lipstick to her lips and sharing it with Andrea. The Institute was dowdy. She liked to look her best, to be pretty and flirtatious and happy, but the regime would not allow such frivolities. She had looked forward to making-up her lips, pouting in the mirror and then showing herself off to everybody. It would have been worth the punishment to enjoy even a moment's attention.

The futile musings were unexpectedly interrupted, and when Jaki looked up and saw Nurse her heart raced with excitement. Nurse was in her normal uniform, but even without the rubber stockings she looked powerfully erotic.

'Hello baby,' she smiled, walking across to Jaki's bed, 'how are you feeling this morning?'

'Can I be honest with you, Nurse?' Jaki whispered, her heart pounding as she contemplated her next move.

'Of course you can,' Nurse replied soothingly, 'you're Nurse's best girl, you can tell me everything.'

Jaki closed her eyes and relished the feel of Nurse's fingers on her body. Nurse was stroking Jaki's inner thigh, rubbing up and down teasingly, heightening Jaki's arousal. 'Something happened to me last night,' Jaki whispered, finishing with a sigh when her skirt was lifted to reveal her thick cock cased in pretty pink lace.

'Tell me all about it,' Nurse said softly, coaxing whilst at the same time touching Jaki's excited body.

'At night I was taken from here and . . . and . . . forced to serve others.'

'Did you enjoy it?' Nurse asked, smiling softly, her full lips pursed slightly.

Jaki looked up into Nurse's eyes and felt herself teetering on the edge of complete submission. She would have done anything then, no matter how terrible or degrading, she would have sunk to any depths to prove her devotion. 'Yes,' she croaked, 'I enjoyed it.'

'That's all right then, isn't it? Nurse will look after you, Nurse will make sure nothing bad happens to her girls.'

'But the Sisterhood?'

'They loved you, they bathed you in their waters, they did it for you, Jaki for you.' Nurse's voice was low and persuasive. She was stroking Jaki's cock as she spoke, working up and down the veined rod with a lingering touch that caused butterflies of sensation to spasm through Jaki's body.

Jaki fought through the pleasure, doing her best not to let go, not to let the pleasure wash through her. The agony was excruciating. How easy it would have been to just give in, to accept what Nurse was saying without question. Easy, but there was something inside her which would not allow it. 'Why did they sell me?' she managed to ask.

'They didn't sell you, baby. You have to serve, Jaki, you belong to us now, you have no other aim in life but to serve us.'

'But Tiffany did sell me, she sold me and then gave me some lipstick as my share,' Jaki complained.

Nurse shook her head. 'Oh, baby,' she purred, 'you've got it all wrong. Nurse would never let one of her girls be treated like that. The lipstick was a reward for being a good girl, because that's what we want, lots of good, obedient girls to do as they're told.'

Jaki's response was taken from her. Nurse swooped down and seized her mouth, locking their lips together in a passionate kiss that had Jaki reeling. She sucked at Jaki's breath, sucking away her resolve at the same time. When Nurse released her, Jaki was dazed, dizzy with pleasure.

'Turn over now,' Nurse ordered briskly.

'Yes, Nurse,' Jaki said, turning over on to her belly. She lifted her backside slightly higher, wanting to show herself off as best as she could. It was delightful to have Nurse there, so soothing and sympathetic, sensual and direct.

'That's a good girl. Nurse just wants to see that her best girl is feeling fine.'

Jaki's bottom cheeks were parted, the tight brown orifice displayed. Jaki lifted herself higher, her cock brushed against the soft cover on the bed. Every time she was called Nurse's best girl her cock quivered, the words going to the heart of her secret desires, igniting flames of passion that could not be doused.

Nurse rubbed a finger up and down Jaki's anal crack, pressing hard against the rear hole and under the ball sac. She rubbed two fingers up and down, again and again, massaging the space between Jaki's smooth-skinned bottom cheeks, and making Jaki moan softly. 'You're dry,' she remarked softly, and presented the two fingers she had been using to Jaki's lips.

Jaki understood, she licked the fingers eagerly, tasting herself as she lubricated them with her spit. Nurse pushed her fingers into Jaki's mouth, and Jaki accepted that too, sucking forcefully on the two fingers, her mouth filled with the taste of her own behind. She lapped her tongue round and round Nurse's long, elegant fingers, wetting them completely.

Without a word Nurse resumed her ministrations, pressing her wet fingers between Jaki's bottom cheeks, now raised higher, and concentrating on the anal hole that was so temptingly offered. 'Open yourself for Nurse,' came the order, issued with strict formality.

The response was instantaneous, Jaki reached back and pulled her arse-cheeks apart, opening herself completely and stretching her round arsehole so that it was ready. Her face was buried in her pillow, her skirt pulled up in an untidy bundle around her waist, her fingers gripping her bottom flesh tightly.

Nurse's fingers pressed against the tight sheath of muscle. There was a moment of resistance and then it slipped deep into Jaki's anal passage. A flicker of a smile appeared on Nurse's face as she began to slowly frig Jaki's behind, twisting her finger round as it went in and out slowly. Jaki closed her eyes, letting the pleasure flood through her, waves of sensation building up as she was penetrated repeatedly, finger-fucked in the arsehole by Nurse.

Jaki moaned, deliriously. Nurse was using two fingers now, pressing them into the tight ring of muscle. She could feel the rectal muscles rippling and gripping on the two hard fingers that entered her, the two fingers joined together and forcing her arsehole apart. She was being penetrated, opened forcefully with every thrust. Nurse used her other hand to hold Jaki's heavy ball sac, cupping the cool sac in her palm, holding tightly and causing just the right degree of fear and discomfort. Jaki was controlled, there was nothing she could do but hold herself open, shamelessly, to Nurse's handling.

'How would you like Nurse to fuck you? Would you like me to strap a dildo on to myself and make love to your tight little pussy?' Nurse teased, her smile of amusement tinged with disdain. 'Or would you like Andrea to fuck you? Would you like her to use her cock on you? She'd love to fuck you girl to girl, her cock would fill your arsehole nice and tight.'

Jaki cried out, unable to hold back. She collapsed forward, releasing her grip on her behind as Nurse's fingers pushed in as deep as they could go. Her cock spurted thick pools of semen into Nurse's waiting hand, filling it with warm wads of creamy juice.

'Good girl,' Nurse whispered, showing Jaki the waves of come that she had collected.

Jaki started to sit up but a stern look from Nurse stopped her. She felt weak, her rear hole was sore and her body was shaky from the strength of orgasm.

'Open yourself, Nurse hasn't given you permission to move yet,' Nurse continued, her voice severe and unyielding.

Shaking the fuzziness from her head, Jaki resumed her position: face down and arms reaching behind to hold her bottom cheeks apart. She had no idea of what was to follow, but an order was an order and that was enough.

'You look fit enough for service again tonight,' Nurse informed her. 'You're a good girl, Jaki, and you need to do as the Sisterhood command. Tonight you're going to be used again, in whatever way is required of you. But don't worry,' she finished. 'Nurse will always check you the next day, to see if you're OK. We love you, Jaki, that's why we have to do this to you.'

Jaki was only barely listening. She held herself open, her anus still tingling after the hard frigging that had been inflicted. She winced at the first touch, surprised by the unexpected wetness that was applied. It took a second before she realised what was going on, and by then Nurse had almost finished. Jaki felt desire surge through her again, as she felt her warm come oozing from her rear hole, where Nurse had spread it back into Jaki's body.

* * *

It was wrong. And, no matter how Jaki tried to rationalise it, it would not stop being wrong. The most painful part of it was that she still felt a thrill of desire every time she thought about Nurse, or Andrea, or Tiffany. The pleasure of submission, the revelling in degradation and humiliation had never been as intense, but that did not alter the facts.

Mistress Shirer listened in stony silence as Jaki outlined all that had happened to her, from the moment of her arrival to the moment where Nurse had spread Jaki's own come into her arsehole. Jaki had not tried to hide the facts, and that included the fact that she worshipped Nurse, and that she would have gladly submitted completely to the Sisterhood if it had not been for the niggling voice of conscience in the back of her head.

The moral dilemma had been an agony of doubt, but in the end Jaki had listened to her conscience. Right was more important than her own pleasure and, though she hated herself for what she was doing, it had to be done. The Sisterhood, led by Tiffany and Nurse, were exploiting people, selling bodies for profit, turning sexual slavery into financial slavery. The fact that it accorded with some of the deepest fantasies of the victims did not alter the fact that it was morally wrong.

'I have some news also,' Mistress Shirer announced when Jaki had finished. She was seated in Kasia's chair, in the cramped office which somehow now seemed less imposing than it had done before.

'Kasia's gone,' Jaki whispered, certain that her guess was correct. There seemed to be an almost tangible feeling of relief, as though a malign presence in the building had been exorcised.

'She resigned this morning,' Mistress Shirer confirmed. 'She was never really happy here. The Institute was something that she failed to understand. There was never any passion in her soul, the Institute was never part of her imagination.'

'What about Nurse?' Jaki asked. Her face was red. She felt embarrassed to be admitting her love for the uniformed Mistress, especially after what Nurse had been doing. But, even with her flaws, Nurse was a Mistress worthy of pure devotion.

'I'll be honest with you, Jaki, I don't know what to do yet.'

'Will she get into a lot of trouble?'

Mistress Shirer stood up and walked to the front of the desk. She was wearing a short black leather skirt, with black stockings and stiletto heels. She looked tired, the strain finally showing through. Jaki was filled with sympathy and wanted to do nothing more than fall to her knees and kiss Mistress's feet, to offer herself as some form of consolation.

'Nurse has identified a real need here. She and the Sisterhood have inspired a depth of loyalty that I and the other staff were unable to crack. What she did was wrong, and I understand how difficult it must have been for you to tell me about it, but it's not all bad. The shame of it is that in other circumstances she would have made the perfect head of the male dorm, especially now that Kasia is out of the way.'

'Do you think she might still be put in charge?' Jaki asked hopefully.

Mistress Shirer shook her head sadly. 'Too many errors of judgement for that to happen. On the other hand I don't think her time, or her influence, here is over. We have a lot to learn from Nurse, good and bad.'

Jaki nodded. Mistress Shirer was so right, and she was grateful to her for being so wise and level headed about things. The fear that Nurse might get into terrible trouble had been like a nagging headache that she couldn't get rid of. Now at least some of the worst fears were laid to rest.

'It's time for us to go home now,' Mistress said softly, her voice like sweet sugar. She opened her arms and Jaki went to her, accepting her warm loving embrace with gratitude. Mistress's arms were around her, holding her warm and tight, so that Jaki could rest her head on Mistress's chest and feel the heart beating with excitement.

Mistress and Jaki kissed, and the bond between Mistress and slave was complete. Desire and excitement, trust and belief, an intensity of emotion that had survived everything.

Jaki was beautiful. Dressed in her shiny PVC maid's uniform, short fluffy skirt and high-collared top, a pretty white apron around her waist and a thick white ribbon in her hair, she felt undeniably sexy. The shiny black high heels, with tight straps around the ankles and a silver strip along the outside length of the heel, were matched by seamed stockings that emphasised the curve of her limbs. She wore lacy panties and matching suspenders, which could be seen whenever she moved, the short skirt fluffed up with petticoats that swirled with every step. Her left thigh was ringed with a pretty pink garter belt, a frilly band that accentuated the effect of sheer black stockings on her white thighs.

She was standing in a corner, waiting expectantly for Mistress Shirer and Harriet to call her over. Not for the first time she threw a pose, head back, lips pursed and sexy, eyes half closed. Her lips were etched in brilliant scarlet, her eyes darkened by mascara that fluttered on her eyelashes, eyebrows picked out in pencil to frame her pretty eyes. When she was a maid she was dressed to serve, and dressed to display herself, and dressed for punishment – it was the ideal outfit and she knew that it fitted to perfection.

Mistress Shirer snapped her fingers, not bothering to even look towards Jaki, and continued her conversation with Harriet. Both were dressed up and waiting for the car that would take all three of them to a late evening soirée somewhere in London. Mistress Shirer was dressed very simply in a tight-fitting black rubber dress, a garment that was moulded seductively to her body. That she wore nothing underneath was obvious, her breasts were displayed in glistening detail, the full roundness supported by the constricting rubber, her nipples causing protrusions against the shiny surface. Her rounded belly and the firmness of her backside contoured effortlessly by the slinky material.

Jaki marched over towards them, stamping her heels hard on the ground for extra effect, delighting in the sound and in the way her skirts fluttered up and down. She loved the way flashes of bare thigh could be seen under the flowing petticoats and dark shiny PVC. Harriet held up her glass and Jaki refilled it with chilled champagne, the dark green bottle wrapped in a crisp white napkin. Harriet barely acknowledged Jaki's presence, and neither did Mistress Shirer who waited for her glass to be filled and then turned her back to Jaki again.

It didn't matter that she was barely noticed, that her presence was taken for granted. To serve was all. Jaki stood to attention again, adopting a pose that displayed her as a pretty ornament to be commanded at will. Harriet was wearing a tight black and red jumpsuit of shimmering plastic, which ran from her calf-length boots to the low cut top which revealed her ample breasts bulging against the red trim on black. Apart from the display of cleavage, only her hands were not cased in the skin tight material, which extended up to a high collar around her neck and down to cuffs at the end of her sleeves.

The car had been arranged to whisk the three of them away for an intimate party in one of the grand houses in the West End of London. Jaki could hardly wait. The glamorous surroundings, opulent and decadent, were a world away from the bleak surroundings of the Institute. The party had not been arranged as a reward but that was how Jaki decided to see it, a reward for pulling through the most difficult time in her life. It was over and she felt stronger for it. She had made the right decision but it had been painful. Now she was looking forward excitedly to the party, her imagination filled with the delicious anticipation of the entrance the three of them would make. With Mistress Shirer and Harriet in the lead all eyes would be upon them, and she would trail in their wake, their beautiful slave-maid, desirably sexy in her uniform.

The door opened suddenly, startling Jaki who stared open mouthed at the spiky haired young woman standing defiantly in the doorway.

'Please, Simone, don't say anything,' she said, breathlessly, 'just hear me out. That's all I ask.'

Mistress looked at her for a moment, and then she nodded curtly. Jaki turned from Mistress, whose hair was almost glossy black, and whose dark skin was complemented by the shimmering blackness of her outfit, to the slight, nervous-looking girl at the door.

'I've done a lot of thinking while I've been gone,' she began, running her fingers through the spikes of her blonde hair, 'and I think I understand now. I'm sorry for going off the handle like that, really I'm sorry. But the thing is Simone, this is so heavy for me. I've never been into anything like this before. Do you see that? It's not easy for me, and I know what a cow I've been to you and I'm sorry. It's about power and things, and freedom and choice and being a woman and . . . and I'm rambling but do you see what I mean?'

Mistress looked at her stonily, revealing nothing of her thoughts and feelings, a picture of stern, erotic authority. Harriet too looked at the blonde icily, though Jaki was certain that at least Harriet knew who the blonde was.

'I'll go if you want me to,' the blonde said quietly, her eyes filling with the look of defeat. 'It's not your fault,' she whispered. 'Everything we did turned me on, but turned me on more powerfully and more completely than anything I'd ever done before. It frightened me, especially as you seemed to know more about what I felt than I did. You still frighten me, Simone, because I want you more than ever. Want isn't even the right word. I *need* you.'

'You've had your chance before, Rebecca. We've discussed this more than once,' Mistress Shirer pointed out. She sipped from her champagne as the blonde considered this, her dark eyes fixed on Rebecca and waiting for a reaction.

'I know, and I'm sorry for what happened last time. But I've had time to think things through now. I know it's hard to believe but I've matured, really I have. Take me back, Simone, and I'll do anything you want me to.'

'There's nothing wrong with having questions,' Mistress said, 'in fact not having questions is by far the greater wrong. On the other hand you seem too impetuous, too distrustful for this.'

'No, not any more,' Rebecca insisted. 'I see it now. This is my life, my body, my freedom. What greater proof of that freedom than to give it willingly to someone else. It's the ultimate affirmation of my autonomy. I become free when I give myself to you.' She was breathing hard, but her manner was earnest and fervent, she believed every word of what she was saying. Jaki caught Harriet's eye and nodded. She understood what the young woman was saying and it made perfect sense to her.

'And when I punish you?' Mistress Shirer asked, a half-smile forming on her glossy lips.

'Then I'll love you for punishing me,' she avowed.

'And if I give you to someone else?'

'Then I'll do my best to make you proud enough to take me back.'

'If I make love with someone else?'

'Then I'll serve the both of you,' Rebecca promised, a note of pleading in her voice.

'Jaki,' Mistress snapped her fingers, 'bring me the cane.'

Jaki moved quickly, her heart racing. The new girl was to be tested and she wondered what form the test would take. Already she liked Rebecca. There was something very earnest about her, painfully honest in a way that would add to the intensity of sensations that she would feel. Jaki could remember every inch of Mistress Shirer's home, every room was filled with a thousand memories, all of them beautiful and erotic.

The long supple cane was curved into a handle at one end, and Jaki had taken the liberty of placing it on the silver platter that had held the bottle of iced champagne. She crossed the room solemnly, part of a ritual that still affected her deeply. Her heels counted out the steps, and she was aware of Rebecca's eyes, fixed on the image of the servile French maid carrying the chosen instrument of correction.

'Well, Rebecca, it's time to see if you really are ready to accept the position of slave,' Mistress Shirer announced, picking up the cane from the platter.

'I am, Mistress,' Rebecca said, breathing deeply. She

swallowed hard and walked further into the centre of the room. She was wearing a shapeless skirt that reached down to her knees and a baggy top that defined nothing of her body. Only her eyes sparkled with excitement. She had not even dared to colour her lips and eyes.

'Good,' Mistress smiled, 'that's how you'll address me in the future. If I accept you as my slave then I'll expect nothing less than total surrender. Now, drop the skirt and bend over.'

Harriet smiled approvingly and Jaki was taken by surprise when the skirt went down and revealed that Rebecca was naked underneath. Her limbs were long and smooth, and combined with the floppy sweatshirt to make her look young and vulnerable.

'Are you wet?' Harriet asked her.

Rebecca's reply was to touch a finger into herself and draw out the glistening wetness. She showed it to all three of them, her face blazing red with embarrassment as she did so, but there was no denying her arousal.

'Bend over now, legs apart and then hold on to your ankles,' Mistress instructed, giving her glass of champagne to Jaki and walking over to Rebecca. The cane she balanced in the crook of her arm, letting it swing casually as she stroked and caressed Rebecca's prostrated form. She too pressed her fingers between Rebecca's cunny lips, playing in the sticky ooze of juices in her sex. Rebecca closed her eyes and let out a long, low moan of pleasure.

'Harriet, one for you I think,' Mistress suggested, a wicked smile lighting up her face. Her eyes glittered like dark jewels of excitement and her face lost the stone-cold austerity that could reduce the toughest slave to tears.

'I'm honoured, Simone, thank you,' Harriet said, accepting the honour graciously. She took the cane and moved to a position behind Rebecca.

'Be good,' Mistress Shirer counselled, 'make your Mistress proud.'

'I will Mistress, I will,' Rebecca sighed, her eager voice filled with hope. She looked up and her eyes met with Jaki's for a moment they gazed at each other and then Jaki smiled.

The first stroke whistled through the air and broke hard across Rebecca's parted bottom cheeks. She winced, gripped her ankles harder and remained in position. The curves of her rear side carried one thin red stripe, and Jaki knew from experience how it had to hurt. Harriet waited for a moment, twisting her head as she studied Rebecca's prone position and then let loose with another harsh strike. The cane hissed through the air and then snapped to, almost doubling over as it made contact with Rebecca's tender flesh.

'What do you think?' Mistress Shirer asked Harriet, as though discussing the performance of an actor on stage.

Harriet nodded. She raised the cane high and swung it down again, this time cutting Rebecca at the very top of the thighs, the cane striking across the bulging pussy lips at the same time. Rebecca moaned but did not otherwise react, her eyes were closed and she was biting her lips. Jaki could see that the three lines were neatly paralleled, imprinted as red streaks against paler skin.

'Jaki,' Mistress Shirer said softly, 'I want her to pleasure you as she receives her punishment.'

Jaki stepped forward at once, lifting the front of her uniform eagerly. She released her cock from the layers of frills and the tight-fitting panties, holding it out as a prize for Rebecca. She had been on heat all evening, her cock permanently hard and flexing against the lacy material of her frilly knickers.

Rebecca kissed the base of Jaki's cock, reverently worshipping the thick, veined rod with her lips. She kissed and kissed, working her way up the underside, her mouth sucking feverishly. Each time the cane was snapped down her breath came a little faster and she sucked a little more greedily. At last she was swirling her tongue around the glans, licking it tenderly before opening her lips and taking it in.

Jaki was standing with legs apart, sighing softly as Rebecca feasted on hard cock. The uneven rhythm of the cane did not cease. Harriet was working Rebecca's body methodically, inflicting the right degree of pain so that it was always pleasure. Jaki held on as much as she could, delighted by the image of herself in full maid's uniform being sucked deliciously by another slave girl, in front of their Mistresses. Rebecca *was* a slave, there was no doubt about it. Jaki identified with her, imagining that their positions were reversed and becoming even more excited by the vision.

'It's OK, Jaki,' Mistress Shirer whispered, 'you can come in her mouth.'

Jaki gasped as Mistress Shirer touched her from behind, stroking a rubber-clad hand over Jaki's stockings to caress the bare flesh at the top of the thighs. Rebecca's mouth and tongue were causing delicious spasms of feeling, electrifying pulses of sexual energy driving through her body. She felt dizzy, her senses overloaded with passion. Her eyes were filled with the image of Rebecca being caned and herself being sucked, her body responded to the maddening rush of fellation and being stroked between the bottom cheeks, her ears responded to the rhythm of correction beaten out by Harriet. She could breathe the scent of rubber and perfume all around her.

Jaki screamed and reached out, afraid that she'd fall. Her cock pumped hot juice deep into Rebecca's mouth, every drop of it eagerly sucked down and swallowed. She could feel her arsehole gripping tightly against Mistress Shirer's invasive finger, pressed deep into her behind.

Moments later Jaki realised that Rebecca had climaxed too, but that she had continued to suck on Jaki's cock until it was over. Now Rebecca was allowed to stand, her backside a mesh of stripes on her pert arse-cheeks, her skin coloured a hundred shades of red and pink.

'Our car is here,' Mistress Shirer announced.

'Do you want to stay here?' Harriet asked Simone, and then looking meaningfully at the dazed figure of Rebecca.

Mistress Shirer paused and then broke into a smile. 'No,' she decided, 'I think we can take two slaves with us. Jaki, a collar for Rebecca, who starts her training tonight.'

Rebecca sighed, her breath uneven and ragged. She pulled off her top and was totally naked, her nipples erect and uckable evidence of her desire. Without prompting she fell o her knees and crawled towards Mistress Shirer, her upple bottom cheeks displaying to perfection the marks of ner correction. She kissed Mistress's heels, a reverent, grateful action that brought smiles to everyone else in the room.

Jaki smiled too, filled with an intense emotion that made her tremble with excitement. Her own journey was far from finished, and for Rebecca it had only just begun.

NEW BOOKS

Coming up from Nexus, Sapphire and Black Lace

Discipline of the Private House by Esme Ombreux
January 2000 £5.99 ISBN: 0 352 33459 2
Jem Darke, Mistress of the secretive organisation known as the Private House, is bored – and rashly accepts a challenge to submit to the harsh disciplinary regime at the Chateau, where the Chatelaine and her depraved minions will delight in administering torments and humiliations designed to make Jem abandon the wager and relinquish her supreme authority.

The Order by Nadine Somers
January 2000 £5.99 ISBN: 0 352 33460 6
The Comtessa di Diablo is head of the Order, an organisation devoted to Mádrofh, demonic Mistress of Lust. Tamara Knight and Max Creed are agents for Omega, a secret government body charged with investigating the occult. As they enter the twilight world of depraved practices and unspeakable rituals, the race is on to prevent the onset of the Final Chaos, the return of Mádrofh and the ushering in of a slave society over which the Comtessa and her debauched acolytes will reign supreme.

A Matter of Possession by G.C. Scott
January 2000 £5.99 ISBN: 0 352 33468 1
Under normal circumstances, no woman as stunning as Barbara Hilson would have trouble finding a man. But Barbara's requirements are far from the normal. She needs someone who will take complete control; someone who will impose himself so strongly upon her that her will dissolves into his. Fortunately, if she can't find a man to give her what she wants, Barbara has other options: an extensive collection of bondage equipment, an imagination that knows no bounds, and, in Sarah, an obliging and very debauched friend.

The Bond by Lindsay Gordon
February 2000 £5.99 ISBN: 0 352 33480 0
Hank and Missy are not the same as the rest of us. They're on a ride that never ends, together forever, joined as much by their increasingly perverse sexual tastes as by their need to satisfy their special needs. But they're not alone on their journey. The Preacher's after Hank, and he'll do anything to Missy to get him. The long-awaited third novel by the author of *Rites of Obedience* and *The Submission Gallery*.

The Slave Auction by Lisette Ashton
February 2000 £5.99 ISBN: 0 352 33481 9
Austere, masterful and ruthless, dominatrix Frankie has learnt to enjoy her new life as mistress of the castle. Her days are a paradise of endless punishments and her nights are filled with cruel retribution. But with the return of her arch-enemy McGivern, Frankie's haven is about to be shattered. He is organising a slave auction in which lives will be altered forever, and his ultimate plan is to regain control of the castle. As the dominatrix becomes the dominated, Frankie is left wondering whether things will ever be the same again.

The Pleasure Principle by Maria del Rey
February 2000 £5.99 ISBN: 0 352 33482 7
Sex is deviant. Disgusting. Depraved. Sex is banned. And yet despite the law, and the Moral Guardians who police it, a sexual underworld exists which recognises no rule but that of desire. Into this dark world of the flesh enters Detective Rey Coover, a man who must struggle with his own instincts to uncover the truth about those who recognise no limits. Erotica, science fiction and crime collide in one of Maria del Rey's most imaginative and explicit novels. A Nexus Classic.

A new imprint of lesbian fiction

Getaway by Suzanne Blaylock
October 1999 Price £6.99 ISBN: 0 352 33443 6
Brilliantly talented Polly Sayers had made two big life shifts concurrently. She's had her first affair with a woman, and she's also stolen the code of an important new piece of software and made her break, doing a runner all the way to a seemingly peaceful coastal community. But things aren't as tranquil as they appear in the haven, as Polly becomes immersed in an insular group of mysterious but very attractive women.

No Angel by Marian Malone
November 1999 £6.99 ISBN 0 352 33462 2
Sally longs to test her limits and sample forbidden pleasures, yet she's frightened by the depth of her yearnings. Her journey of self-discovery begins in the fetish clubs of Brighton and ultimately leads to an encounter with an enigmatic female stranger. And now that she's tasted freedom, there's no way she's going back.

Doctor's Orders by Deanna Ashford
January 2000 £5.99 ISBN: 0 352 33453 3
When Dr Helen Dawson loses her job at a state-run hospital, she is delighted to be offered a position at a private clinic. The staff at the clinic do far more than simply care for the medical needs of their clients, though – they also cater for their sexual needs. Helen soon discovers that this isn't the only secret – there are other, far darker occurrences.

Shameless by Stella Black
January 2000 £5.99 ISBN: 0 352 33467 3
When Stella Black decides to take a holiday in Arizona she doesn't bargain on having to deal with such a dark and weird crowd: Jim, the master who likes his SM hard; Mel, the professional dominatrix with a background in sleazy movies; Rick, the gun-toting cowboy with cold blue eyes; and his psychotic sidekick Bernie. They're not the safest individuals, but that's not what Stella wants. That's not what she's come for.

Cruel Enchantment by Janine Ashbless
February 2000 £5.99 ISBN: 0 352 33483 5
Here are eleven tales of temptation and desire, of longing and fear and consummation; tales which will carry you to other times and other worlds. Worlds of the imagination where you will encounter men and monsters, women and gods. Worlds in which hermits are visited by succubi and angels; in which dragons steal maidens to sate special hungers; in which deadly duels of magic are fought on the battlefield of the naked body and even the dead do not like to sleep alone.

Tongue in Cheek by Tabitha Flyte
February 2000 £5.99 ISBN: 0 352 33484 3
When Sally's relationship ends everything seems to go wrong for her – she can't meet a new man, she's having a bad time at work and she can't seem to make anything work at all. That is, until she starts hanging out around the local sixth-form college, where she finds the boys more than happy to help out – in every way.

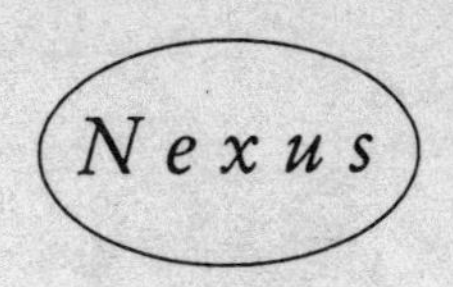

NEXUS BACKLIST

All books are priced £5.99 unless another price is given. If a date is supplied, the book in question will not be available until that month in 1999.

CONTEMPORARY EROTICA

THE ACADEMY	Arabella Knight	
AMANDA IN THE PRIVATE HOUSE	Esme Ombreux	
BAD PENNY	Penny Birch	
THE BLACK MASQUE	Lisette Ashton	
THE BLACK WIDOW	Lisette Ashton	
BOUND TO OBEY	Amanda Ware	
BRAT	Penny Birch	
DANCE OF SUBMISSION	Lisette Ashton	Nov
DARK DELIGHTS	Maria del Rey	
DARK DESIRES	Maria del Rey	
DARLINE DOMINANT	Tania d'Alanis	
DISCIPLES OF SHAME	Stephanie Calvin	
THE DISCIPLINE OF NURSE RIDING	Yolanda Celbridge	
DISPLAYS OF INNOCENTS	Lucy Golden	
EMMA'S SECRET DOMINATION	Hilary James	
EXPOSING LOUISA	Jean Aveline	
FAIRGROUND ATTRACTIONS	Lisette Ashton	
GISELLE	Jean Aveline	Oct
HEART OF DESIRE	Maria del Rey	
HOUSE RULES	G.C. Scott	Oct
IN FOR A PENNY	Penny Birch	Nov
JULIE AT THE REFORMATORY	Angela Elgar	
LINGERING LESSONS	Sarah Veitch	

THE MISTRESS OF STERNWOOD GRANGE	Arabella Knight		
ONE WEEK IN THE PRIVATE HOUSE	Esme Ombreux		
THE PALACE OF EROS	Delver Maddingley		
PENNY IN HARNESS	Penny Birch		
THE PLEASURE CHAMBER	Brigitte Markham		
THE RELUCTANT VIRGIN	Kendal Grahame		
RITES OF OBEDIENCE	Lindsay Gordon		
RUE MARQUIS DE SADE	Morgana Baron		
'S' – A JOURNEY INTO SERVITUDE	Philippa Masters		
SANDRA'S NEW SCHOOL	Yolanda Celbridge		Dec
THE SCHOOLING OF STELLA	Yolanda Celbridge		
THE SUBMISSION OF STELLA	Yolanda Celbridge		
THE SUBMISSION GALLERY	Lindsay Gordon		
SUSIE IN SERVITUDE	Arabella Knight		
TAKING PAINS TO PLEASE	Arabella Knight		
A TASTE OF AMBER	Penny Birch		
THE TEST	Nadine Somers		
THE TRAINING OF FALLEN ANGELS	Kendal Grahame		
VIRGINIA'S QUEST	Katrina Young	£4.99	

ANCIENT & FANTASY SETTINGS

THE CASTLE OF MALDONA	Yolanda Celbridge		
THE FOREST OF BONDAGE	Aran Ashe		
NYMPHS OF DIONYSUS	Susan Tinoff	£4.99	
TIGER, TIGER	Aishling Morgan		Dec
THE WARRIOR QUEEN	Kendal Grahame		

EDWARDIAN, VICTORIAN & OLDER EROTICA

ANNIE	Evelyn Culber		
ANNIE AND THE COUNTESS	Evelyn Culber		
BEATRICE	Anonymous		
CONFESSIONS OF AN ENGLISH SLAVE	Yolanda Celbridge		Sep
THE CORRECTION OF AN ESSEX MAID	Yolanda Celbridge		

THE GOVERNESS AT ST AGATHA'S	Yolanda Celbridge		
THE MASTER OF CASTLELEIGH	Jacqueline Bellevois		Aug
PRIVATE MEMOIRS OF A KENTISH HEADMISTRESS	Yolanda Celbridge	£4.99	
THE RAKE	Aishling Morgan		Sep
THE TRAINING OF AN ENGLISH GENTLEMAN	Yolanda Celbridge		

SAMPLERS & COLLECTIONS

EROTICON 4	Various		
THE FIESTA LETTERS	ed. Chris Lloyd	£4.99	
NEW EROTICA 3			
NEW EROTICA 4	Various		
A DOZEN STROKES	Various		Aug

NEXUS CLASSICS

A new imprint dedicated to putting the finest works of erotic fiction back in print

THE IMAGE	Jean de Berg	
CHOOSING LOVERS FOR JUSTINE	Aran Ashe	
THE INSTITUTE	Maria del Rey	
AGONY AUNT	G. C. Scott	
THE HANDMAIDENS	Aran Ashe	
OBSESSION	Maria del Rey	
HIS MASTER'S VOICE	G.C. Scott	Aug
CITADEL OF SERVITUDE	Aran Ashe	Sep
BOUND TO SERVE	Amanda Ware	Oct
BOUND TO SUBMIT	Amanda Ware	Nov
SISTERHOOD OF THE INSTITUTE	Maria del Rey	Dec

- -

Please send me the books I have ticked above.

Name ....

Address ....

....

....

.... Post code.........................

Send to: **Cash Sales, Nexus Books, Thames Wharf Studios, Rainville Road, London W6 9HT**

US customers: for prices and details of how to order books for delivery by mail, call 1-800-805-1083.

Please enclose a cheque or postal order, made payable to **Nexus Books**, to the value of the books you have ordered plus postage and packing costs as follows:

UK and BFPO – £1.00 for the first book, 50p for the second book and 30p for each subsequent book to a maximum of £3.00;

Overseas (including Republic of Ireland) – £2.00 for the first book, £1.00 for the second book and 50p for each subsequent book.

We accept all major credit cards, including VISA, ACCESS/MASTERCARD, AMEX, DINERS CLUB, SWITCH, SOLO, and DELTA. Please write your card number and expiry date here:

....

Please allow up to 28 days for delivery.

Signature ....

- -